Second Chances

A.M. Mahler

Fox Chase Books, L.L.C.

Richmond, Virginia

Published by Fox Chase Books, L.L.C.

P.O. Box 5868

Midlothian, VA 23112

Second Chances/A.M. Mahler – 1st ed.

FOX CHASE BOOKS
L.L.C.

For my readers who have

stuck with me this far, you
motivate me to keep going.
Happy Holidays!

A Note from the Author

I've been so excited to write this book! While I was writing *The Perfect Game* and *Breaking Free*, ideas would pop into my head, and I had to scramble to get them down before they disappeared just as quickly as they'd come. Ethan was never supposed to be with Brooke. He was supposed to be with Eric's sister, Holly, who is a mystery writer and was being stalked. Eric was going to hire Ethan to protect her, and they were going to fall in love. Sounds good, right? Brooke didn't think so! She showed up on his farm in her fancy heeled boots and designer clothes, and Ethan fell flat on his face. They're from totally different worlds, but I couldn't resist seeing what happened when a farm boy and Marine got together with a former debutante.

Having said that, this book was difficult for me to write. I had to stop and come back to it a few times. It wasn't right, and it needed a lot more time than I originally anticipated. Writing is challenging, and publishing is terrifying. If something doesn't feel exactly right, it's best to let it go for a bit and come back to it with fresh eyes. This book deals with post-traumatic stress disorder, which comes in many forms. It is not just a condition that affects soldiers, and it hit a bit home for me.

I hope you enjoy spending Christmas in Grayson Falls! While you immerse yourself in Ethan and Brooke's story, I'll moving on to Eric and Natalie.

One

BROOKE LARRABE, OF the Boston Larrabes, pushed her shoulder into the solid wood door. It stayed stubbornly stuck. Of course, it would have to be replaced with something more up-to-date, preferably with glass in it so she could see who was standing on her stoop.

Speaking of which, the front stoop also needed to be redone. It was crumbling beneath her feet. Chunks of concrete littered the ground around the stone and slate stairs. She didn't think it was dangerous—at least the building inspector didn't seem to think so—but it was falling apart. She liked the rustic masonry popular among homes in the area, and so she hoped to find someone that could restore it or replace it in the same style.

She sighed as she tried the door again, slamming her shoulder so hard she felt sure it would bruise—or dislocate. Still, the old door didn't budge. She leaned against the wood and blew her chocolate-colored bangs out of her eyes. What good was owning a house if you couldn't even get yourself through the front door?

She could hear her parents' heavy sighs now, telling her she deserved nothing more for living below her class. A suitable home wouldn't need any work done to it. It would be pristine with state-of-the-art appliances and every luxury that could be thought of. It certainly wouldn't be a handyman special in Grayson Falls, New Hampshire, with a door she couldn't even open—a house that needed all new windows, electrical wiring, plumbing, a remodeled kitchen and bathroom—the latter of which there was only one—and insulation. And that didn't include any gifts they may find once walls started coming down.

Her parents wouldn't spend five minutes looking at this house. They would have looked right over it as they drove by. Of course, that was assuming they would even deign to set foot in Grayson Falls—her haven from the bourgeoisie she had grown up with and the life she once thought was essential to her existence. She didn't know who that girl was anymore. She left her behind the day of her accident.

A woman carting her children to school had spilled coffee on herself and the split second she looked down was all it took to rear end Brooke's Lexus with the woman's second-hand Toyota Camry. No one was hurt. The Lexus would need some body work. The Camry was toast.

As Brooke sat on the guardrail waiting for her butler to bring the Mercedes and to take her place and stay with the Lexus to the body garage, she overheard the woman in tears on the phone. Her husband was deployed, and she was on her own with the kids while working full-time. The Camry was their only car. Now, she didn't know how she would get anything done. His paycheck wasn't enough for them to live on alone, and without a car, she wouldn't be able to get to work.

Brooke watched as the woman tried to have her meltdown so the kids wouldn't notice. Shaky breaths and choked sobs came out between her words. Three kids were crying and climbing all over her. The woman finished one phone call to her mother, and the next was to her job to let them know she would be late. This woman was just in a car accident and was *still* planning on going to work! It was then that Brooke noticed the woman was wearing medical scrubs. She had a job that meant something. That woman *meant* something to people—to her job, to the person she was on the phone with first, to her kids, to her husband who trusted her to keep their life running smoothly.

Who did Brooke matter to? Her parents used her as a business asset, marrying her off to the son of the man who ran the company her father was merging with. Her husband wasn't faithful. On the morning of the accident, she just received confirmation he had slept with most of her friends. They didn't have any children.

So, who did she matter to?

That was the day she decided to change. And now, standing outside the small cabin in the Great North Woods that she bought with her own money, she knew she mattered to people. She mattered to her cousin, Sophie, and her aunt and uncle. She mattered to the friends she made here and the ones she reconnected with. Standing on her own two feet now, she bought the house for a song and knew she'd blow her savings on renovations.

Throwing her shoulder into the door again, Brooke huffed out a breath. Well, at least she could be assured that if she was ever on the inside of the door, she'd be safe. Nobody was getting through this sucker. It was like the damn thing was sealed with the Superglue some guy on TV was always trying to sell. Her shoulder was beginning to ache from constantly hitting the ancient entryway. Would nothing get through this beast?

When Brooke heard the sound of tires crunching on her gravel driveway, she figured her contractor had just arrived. She stopped fighting with the door, positive he'd be able to get them inside with ... some sort of complicated tool.

Turning toward the driveway, Brooke sucked in her breath when she saw who had just pulled up to the house.

Ethan Donahue carefully got out of the driver's seat then reached back into the truck cab, emerging again with a covered dish. His German Shepherd Bravo, stayed in the cab of the truck barking a greeting to her. As Ethan limped toward her steps, Brooke took the time to appreciate the man before her. The man who made her pulse speed up and her voice breathy. She never reacted to any other man the way she did to Ethan, and that included the time she was at boarding school and thought she was in love with the school's golden boy, Ryan Willis—who she would later learn was Ethan's brother.

"Housewarming present," Ethan said, holding up the foil covered dish. "Nat's special brownies."

Natalie was Ethan's roommate, and the whole town thought they were a couple—though they both denied it. Given the way Ethan looked at Brooke when he thought she couldn't see him, and his body language—his body turned towards her, eyes following her around the room—when he was around her, she didn't believe the rumors. She had come to know Ethan a little since she moved to town, and he definitely did not seem like the type of guy that cheated on a girlfriend.

"Usually when people call brownies special, it's because they're laced with weed."

Raising his eyebrows, Ethan looked down and studied the dish for a moment. Shaking his head, he looked back up, his stunning blue eyes boring into her. "No. I'm pretty sure she didn't do that." He looked back down at the aluminum foil covering the dish as if he could see right through it and into the brownies to confirm there was no marijuana baked into them. "No," he said again with more confidence. "She's a nurse. She wouldn't risk it."

"I was only joking." Brooke waved her mitten-covered hand. "I'm waiting on my contractor. I'd invite you in, but I can't seem to get the door open."

Handing her the dish, Ethan stepped by her to the door. Brooke moved around him on the small stoop. Their bodies brushing together. The electricity that shot through her like lightning was not a surprise. But if he was at all affected by their accidental touching, he didn't show it.

She wondered what he thought as he was taking in the rusted lock and handle. Was he wondering what a rich girl like her was doing with this run-down mess?

"Yeah, it's one of these bastards," he said. "They're finicky. Sometimes they take a little more finesse. They're ancient and don't want to work anymore."

Pulling on the door handle, he lifted up, turned the key, and the door swung open.

"No way." Brooke gaped. *For the love of Christmas, he made it look like it was so easy.* "How'd you know that?"

Ethan shrugged. "It's just a rusted out lock I've encountered before." He stood back so she could enter ahead of him.

The first room was a three-season porch with white tiled floors. Knotty pine paneling covered the bottom half of the wall, and old storm windows ran along the top. It was big enough to hold furniture and would make a nice entryway. She walked into the main part of the house with Ethan behind her.

The living room had a cathedral ceiling. More knotty pine ran floor to ceiling, and scuffed up pine blanketed the floors throughout the house. The boards complained underfoot as Ethan and Brooke walked through the house. The centerpiece was a beautiful beast of a stone fireplace leading all the way up to the roof. Somewhere along the line, someone had converted the chimney to accommodate a wood burning stove. Brooke looked forward to the warmth that it would bring. She wished she could light it now. Her breath came out in puffy white clouds as New England's November settled into her bones.

Looking up to the loft she planned to renovate into a small office, Brooke envisioned adding a dormer off the back to increase the space up there. At the moment, the ceiling ended at the peak of the house, and the room was an awkward triangle. She had thought about converting it to a guest room, but then realized she didn't have anyone who would visit her for an overnight stay.

Off the small living room was a bedroom. It wasn't very large, but it had a nice sized closet. She had bought a queen-sized bed online that would fit and had drawers underneath, lining the bottom for her clothes, so she wouldn't need a dresser. The musty commercial carpeting was pulling up on the edges. That would come out. The whole house would get new hardwood, wide-planked flooring.

She passed by the tiny bathroom. It wasn't even big enough for a bathtub. But that was no matter. She had everything she needed in there. And once the fiberglass shower was replaced with a tile one with multiple jets, what it was now would be a distant memory.

Moving into the next room, the kitchen had knotty pine cabinets, yellowing linoleum, a hung ceiling with water stains on the tiles, and appliances that belonged in a museum. She would enjoy watching this room transform. Another small bedroom stood off the kitchen. She thought she might make that a home gym, or take out the walls and expand the living room/dining area. She could turn it into the TV area, as there wasn't much room for one in the current living room.

But the *piece de resistance* was the other room situated off the kitchen—another three-season porch that ran the entire length of the house. The room had large windows that looked out over the lake that her property was set on. The views of the unmarred mountain across the lake with its changing leaves were killer, and the room would make a perfect studio.

Turning around, she smiled. Ethan was standing in the middle of the kitchen studying the house. Brooke put the brownies she was still holding on the countertop—a Formica deal with little boomerangs on it that had mostly likely been in the house since the 1960s.

"Well?" she asked. Holding her breath, she realized that Ethan's opinion of the house was crucial. What if he didn't see the potential she did? What if he only saw that rich girl draped in Dolce and Gabbana, gingerly walking through the mud of his farm in her Jimmy Choos?

"Your contractor has his work cut out for him," Ethan noted. Walking back into the living room, he studied the high ceilings. "Sky lights would be nice—give you a lot more light in here. It's got a lot of possibilities. It would be a fun project. Are you going to flip it?"

"I'm going to live here," Brooke replied.

"You are?" He asked, brows raised. Letting out a breath, Brooke deflated. So he did see her as the rich girl playing at small town life. She knew what people thought of her. They waited for the city girl to hightail it back to the land of country clubs and high-brow civilization once she was done with her little social experiment.

But that's not who she was anymore. She had been in Grayson Falls for just about a year now. She invested in Sophie's general store, and now it was *their* business. Brooke worked with Sophie to make improvements, and the store was thriving. They finally were able to convert the upstairs apartment to a space with comfy furniture and a place for local artisans and authors to sell their work on consignment.

Of course, that milestone for the store also rendered her homeless. For now, she was staying with Sophie and her fiancée Ryan—the same Ryan Brooke she had lusted over all through school. She was appreciative of them letting her stay with them while she saved her money for the house, but it was time to get back out on her own.

Her fingers itched to get back to work on her side passion—making beautiful quilts anonymously for the store to sell on consignment.

She promised the contractor an extra ten thousand dollars if she could be moved in within a month. That was definitely going to hurt her budget, but she could dip into the small inheritance she had from her grandmother. She had other plans for that, but she should be okay if she took a little out. Technically speaking, she had a substantial trust fund, and she was looking at a sizable settlement from her soon-to-be ex-husband. But she'd rather starve than touch any of that money.

Ethan stood before her, tall, well-muscled, short dark hair, chiseled jaw that was covered in a closely shorn beard. He wore a Henley over a thermal shirt, topped off by a thick flannel coat. His hands were shoved in his jeans' pockets, and he wore work boots. He was a man's man, rugged around the edges, but Brooke knew that rough exterior protected the most pure heart she had ever come across. There was nothing Ethan wouldn't do for someone he cared about.

"I know, crazy, right?" Brooke replied, looking around the room and trying not to let her embarrassment show. "You probably see me in some glitzy palace surrounded by marble and crystal. What's that girl doing here?" Looking down at her hands, she gave a small shrug. Butterflies grew in her stomach when she felt Ethan's finger under her chin to hook her gaze up to him.

"Buying a house, renovating, and moving in means you're planning to stay for a while," Ethan said. "Making a business investment is one thing. Putting down roots is something else entirely. I think you're going to do an amazing job with this place. And I'm glad you're planning on sticking around."

Brooke felt her face heat up, and she stepped away. Ethan's jaw clenched. She cursed herself. Did he see that as a rejection? She laid her hand on his forearm.

"Thanks," she said. "That means a lot." Smiling, he looked down at her lips and back up to her eyes. Electricity pulsed around them. So many times she fantasized about grabbing him by the back of the head and planting a hot kiss on him.

But the moment was broken by a knock on the door. Shoulders slumping, Brooke moved to let in the contractor with the horrible timing.

ETHAN WALKED THROUGH his brother's showroom with his Bravo at his side. Ryan's facility took up the second barn on their sister Jackie's property. From the outside, it looked like any other American barn. But on the inside was a multimillion-dollar engineering firm specializing in building stock cars. Standing inside, you would never know that the outside shell was a barn.

Heading for his brother's office, he walked right by Ryan's assistant, who never bothered to try and stop him anymore, and into Ryan's office. His brother was kicked back in his chair with his feet on his desk, throwing a rubber ball up against the wall and catching it again while he was on a conference call. He shared the same eye color as Ethan and the rest of their siblings, but where Ethan's hair was dark, Ryan, once a blonde, now had light brown hair.

Ethan sat in one of the visitor chairs in the office, and Bravo sat next to him on the floor. Ryan held up a finger indicating he'd be done in a minute. Two walls of Ryan's office were windows, so Ethan busied himself looking out onto the floor where Ryan's employees worked on the various cars Ryan currently had in production. One car was still only a metal frame; others had panels but weren't painted. One shiny, pristine, car sat up front as the prototype.

Ethan's leg began to bounce with nervous energy, so he got up and began to pace. His new dynamic response foot enabled him to move around with only the slightest of limps. However, the stump of his leg would often become sore still by the end of the day, depending on his level of activity. Bravo whined in response to his human's restlessness. Ryan watched Ethan with arched brows. Ethan was the laidback sibling—quieter than the others and introverted. It took time for him to get back to his old self after the accident—if he ever *could* be the same again. His dog helped a lot, but he could feel himself slipping now and wasn't sure what he could do to stave off the oncoming mood. He was growing increasingly irritable and depressed, not so bad, but he could notice the difference in his mood and reactions to things that happened around him.

Ryan hung up the phone and studied his brother. Staying quiet, he let Ethan work out what he wanted to talk to him about. Not really sure where to start, Ethan sat back down and dove in.

"I haven't been with a woman since my accident," he announced, cringing at himself. This wasn't an easy thing to admit, but if he couldn't talk to his family, who could he talk to?

Dropping his feet to the floor, Ryan leaned his elbows on the desk and stared at Ethan before popping up. He walked to the mini fridge and pulled two beers out, tossing one to Ethan. Sitting back down, Ryan propped his feet back up.

"My condolences," Ryan said, taking a pull of his beer.

Ethan groaned, and Bravo laid his snout on Ethan's leg. Absently, Ethan stroked behind the dog's ears. "Maybe I should head over to Zach's or Sebastian's," he said, referring to their younger and older brothers respectively.

"No, no!" Ryan waved his hands around. "I can do this. I guess I'm wondering, like, why are you telling me this? What's going on?" Ethan's pause gave Ryan just enough time to draw his own wrong conclusions. "Oh, I get it. Um, more than your leg was hurt? Do you not have, um, well, fully functioning parts?"

Ethan furrowed his brow. "Everything down there works just fine, dickhead. I should talk to Sebastian about this." Sebastian had been watching Ethan extra carefully since he moved to town, and while Ethan was appreciative of his brother's diligence, he hadn't been ready to let it all out just yet.

"No!" Ryan said. "Look at it from my point of view. What would you think if you were me? Stay there and tell me what the problem is. You and I are a team. I got your back. Just rip the band-aid off and spit it out. You haven't been with a woman since you lost the bottom half of your leg, I get it. I don't think that's too unusual."

Cocking his head to the side, Ethan studied his older brother. "You don't?"

"Not at all," Ryan said. "You told me yourself you had a long recovery and then physical therapy. Once you were on your feet again, so to speak, you moved here where you didn't know anyone. You split your time between this farm and Nat. The whole town thinks you're involved with her."

"And that really grosses me out," Ethan replied. Why the people of Grayson Falls were so obsessed with the status of his relationship with Natalie was totally beyond him. Why couldn't people just accept that he and Natalie were friends?

Of course, they weren't just friends, they were twins, but nobody seemed to pick up on the resemblance. Ethan supposed people were too blinded by his supposed romance with his sister to see that. Ethan and Natalie were rarely seen in public together when it was just the two of them. They usually only went out together in the big group with their siblings and spouses.

Of course, no one could know that Natalie was their sister, due to her status in the Witness Protection Program, but that was something they would never reveal.

Natalie had witnessed an assassination by a drug cartel when she was doing relief work in Mexico. She testified in court, and the drug kingpin was sent to jail. But now there was a price on her head. Natalie worked with the U.S. Marshalls' WITSEC program to be placed here in Grayson Falls to be near Jackie and Ryan, the siblings she had just discovered she had. Her intention was to never let them know who she was, but then Ethan, Sebastian, and Zach showed up. The obvious conclusions were drawn that Natalie was indeed their missing sister Sarah Currie. Rather than Natalie taking off for parts unknown and assuming a new identity, they had ensured her utmost safety, which included Ethan moving in with her with his former military working dog. For Natalie's own safety, they could never reveal or acknowledge her secret in public.

Ethan was closest to Natalie of all his siblings, with Ryan in a close second. He loved all his siblings, but those two seemed to understand him the most. And he couldn't talk about this with Natalie.

"What I'm saying is that it's not so strange that you haven't had sex since your accident," Ryan said. "Lately it seems like it's the furthest thing from your mind anyway."

And there it was, the big, fat elephant that always seemed to be in the room when he was with any of his siblings. The nightmares from Ethan's accident while deployed were back. He had been having them off and on for the past two months, but they had changed and began to take on different forms. Usually, he tried to send Bravo with Natalie when she went about her errands and to the hospital when she went to work, but the past couple of weeks, Ethan needed his trusty pet at his side.

Ethan was on patrol with his battalion in Iraq, working as a dog handler with the Marines. Bravo hadn't alerted in time to avoid the roadside bomb that went off. Ethan's Humvee went airborne. The driver and front passenger were ejected from the vehicle. But Ethan, Bravo, and the passenger in the back with them were wearing seatbelts and stayed inside as the Humvee rolled and rolled before finally coming to a stop on its roof.

When Ethan closed his eyes, he heard the screams of his dying brothers in arms still trapped in the Humvee. He heard the moans of his friend, Brian, in the back with him, as well as Bravo's whimpers. Ethan had punched out the window to pull himself and Bravo out, but with his injuries, he didn't have the strength to rescue his brothers. When help arrived, Ethan had to give Bravo the stand down command so the medics could get close enough to treat Ethan.

Taking a cleansing breath, Ethan stood up and walked away from Ryan's desk. He looked back out the windows over the floor below, watching over the operation that Ryan had built in New York and then relocated up to New Hampshire to be by their sister. From what Ethan understood, Ryan hadn't even wanted to move to New Hampshire, but family stuck together. Ryan couldn't stomach the thought of Jackie living up here by herself. Now, Jackie was married with a baby, and Ryan was engaged to be married in a few weeks at Christmas.

Ethan had found his place here in this small town with his new siblings. He and Bravo were healing here together. They thrived as Ethan brought the small farm on Jackie's property back to life. He had a purpose again, something to wake up each day for. There wasn't too much to do now with the winter months and snow on the ground, but he kept busy.

"I'm working through it," Ethan told his brother. "They're just nightmares—just dreams."

But their brother Sebastian, another physician that worked with Jackie at the Grayson Falls Hospital, thought it was more. His brother might not have been off the mark. Ethan had cut his hand pretty badly a few weeks ago on the broken window of the tractor cab, when he may or may not have put his hand through the glass during a blackout. And if he was blacking out, then things were getting worse not better.

Ryan's silence was deafening. The words not said bounced around Ethan's head like a pinball game. *Are you seeing a therapist? Have you considered medication? What if you black out when you're driving? Do you have any suicidal thoughts? Do you want to hurt yourself? Do you want to hurt others?*

"Okay, then," Ryan said. "Let's get back to the reason why you're here." Ethan raised his brows while he looked out onto the floor and workers below. One mechanic was pushing a large tool cart across the floor. Others were buried under hoods. One was welding a frame, and the sparks kept Ethan's attention. "I think it might be related to what we're not talking about. Have you thought of that?"

Duh, of course he had. Nightmares came and went. He could go up to six months without one, then they leaked back in like an oily ooze. It was bad enough Natalie knew about the nightmares. He couldn't face a woman he woke up after having a one. What if he accidentally hurt her during a nightmare, or worse, a waking blackout?

Ethan didn't want to kill himself. He never even considered it—not even when the pain from his injury was at its worst during therapy. He didn't want to hurt himself and most especially anyone else. That was his worst fear.

Sensing the change in him, Bravo walked over, sat down next to him, and leaned against the thigh of his good leg. Ethan imagined if Bravo could speak, he'd be saying, *"I'm here for you. We're here for each other. We'll get through this."* In response, Ethan reached down and scratched Bravo's head.

"Yes," Ethan admitted. "I have thought of it. Before the reason was simply because I was in so much pain and still healing. Then it was embarrassment over how a woman might react when I take off half my leg with my pants. Now, it's hurting her if I'm gripped in a nightmare. I couldn't live with myself if that happened. I've never hurt a woman, and I never want to—even if it's through no direct fault of my own."

"Well," Ryan said. "You don't have to spend the night with this theoretical woman. It's pretty common for people to have sex and go home."

"Then it would be something I never get past," Ethan said. "I don't want casual sex. I'm getting too old for that lifestyle. Plus, this is a small town. I don't exactly want to run through all the single ladies, you know?"

"Ethan," Ryan said slowly. "Is there a specific woman you have in mind? Is this an issue now because there's someone you're interested in?"

Breathing heavy, Ethan faced his brother and thought of his almost-kiss that morning with Brooke. "Yes, I think there is."

Two

I T WAS STILL dark when Brooke let herself into the Grayson Falls General Store and disengaged the alarm. Her previous self didn't even know five a.m. existed, but the new her—the business-woman, the person that cared about more than just herself—woke up at oh-dark-thirty to come to the store and make the pastries they sold to the morning commuters. Most of the work was done before she left each evening. She just had to finish them off and pop them in the oven. Then she started the coffee and powered up the latte ma-chine, before turning on the computers and the lights and doing her walk-through of the store.

It felt so damn good to have a purpose. This store was likely never going to make her and Sophie rich, but she could live comfortably. She had discovered she had a head for business—likely something she inherited from her father—and so she enrolled in online classes to finish her college degree.

Sophie had bought the General Store years before Brooke came to town, and she had made positive changes. The store was housed in an oversized farmhouse. The clapboard siding was painted white and the shutters black. Rocking chairs sat on the porch, and in warmer weather, people sat outside with their breakfast and coffee to read the paper.

When the house became a business, numerous additions had been put on to expand the retail space, and now the building was a series of rooms with different items for sale. What used to be a garage was now the hardware section. There was also a pet supply room, toy room, dry foods room, clothing room, health and beauty room, can-dy room, candle room, and the entire upstairs was dedicated to New

Hampshire artists, writers, and artisans. In the main area, there was a small café with a counter for pastries and coffee, two little café tables with chairs, and chalkboard menus. The counter also sold sandwiches for lunch.

Turning on the lights as she walked, Brooke began her morning walk-through. She made sure everything was in its place and no strange mishaps happened overnight. She noted items that were low on her tablet as she walked and used her keen design eye to study the displays, as she looked for any way to improve their presentation. Entering the clothing department, she smiled lightly. The latest couture they did not sell but rather items that were fit for harsh New England winters and milder summers—heavy sweatshirts and flannel shirts, fair isle sweaters and Irish fisherman sweaters, boots and heavy socks, parkas, scarves, hats, and gloves. There was no place in Grayson Falls for high fashion.

Of course, that didn't stop Brooke from dressing up for work every now and then, but in the winter, she dressed smartly and not sharply. She glanced down at her outfit for the day—black leggings, a long sleeved black thermal shirt, a gray knit waterfall sleeveless sweater that matched her gray knit hat that was still on her head. Her long chestnut hair was down, and she wore her favorite fuzzy boots. Practical, comfortable, yet still stylish. It may not be Dior and Gucci shoes, but she still managed to look polished.

Heading upstairs to the New Hampshire department, she turned on the lights on the staircase and upper level. Smiling at what they created, she walked around the floor. Everything was in tidy, welcoming sections. The lighting and shelving accentuated the handmade pieces—pottery, knitted blankets, carved wood animals. It was the best New Hampshire had to offer, and one day, Brooke wanted to expand this area as well. She wanted to make this store a destination—a must-see place to explore when you were in town to ski or a place to

Christmas shop on your way home from work after you got off the commuter train.

The last display was her favorite. It was where they showcased their products from Stitches from Sadie. There were handmade bed quilts, table runners, wall hangings, bags, Christmas stockings, and lap blankets. The items arrived at least quarterly from the mysterious Sadie, and payment was sent to a post office box in town.

Of course, while Sadie's identity was only known to two other people in town, Brooke knew who she really was because Brooke was Sadie. Growing up, Brooke and Sophie's grandmother taught her how to quilt, bake, make a decent dinner. Brooke's family money came from her father's side of the family. Her mother's family was middle class. Sophie and Brooke had very different upbringings, but their grandmother made sure that Brooke learned life lessons and skills. Brooke lived for those visits with her grandparents in Virginia. She missed sitting at their kitchen table while they showered her with love and attention—two things she often didn't get at home.

Running her fingers gently over the quilts, her heart swelled with pride in her craftsmanship. Her so-called "friends" in Boston would never believe she was a quilter. Now, they had no reason to know because Brooke didn't plan on ever contacting them again. She wouldn't say she had any close friends in Boston, but there were acquaintances she socialized and served with on various committees. The sting of betrayal when she discovered her husband's infidelity wasn't lessened because she wasn't close with the women he slept with.

Walking back downstairs, she mentally went through what projects she would be able to get through by Christmas. She currently had space set up at Piper Lewis's house. Piper was an artist and owned her own gallery in town. She was engaged to Ethan's brother, Zach, and figured out Sadie's real identity. When Brooke needed a place to work away from Sophie and Ryan, Piper had generously cleared out a corner of her studio for Brooke to set up in. Though Piper had encouraged Brooke to let Sophie in on her secret, Brooke wasn't ready yet, and Piper agreed to respect Brooke's wishes.

As the alarm on her watch went off, Brooke made her way back to the kitchen to take the pastries out of the oven. The smell of fresh-brewed coffee and baked goods was welcoming on this winter morning. A small storm had come through overnight, leaving a few inches of snow behind. After Brooke put the pastries in the display case, she would go out and shovel the walkway from the parking lot to the front steps.

She was happy in her little life in Grayson Falls. Her parents' disappointment, of course, reached her here. Her mother still called and tried to cajole her daughter home for various events, and her father called his "little princess" frequently when he traveled and usually forgot that Brooke wasn't living in Boston anymore, claiming Brooke was so busy he couldn't keep track, when really, he was just too busy to care.

The bell above the back door rang, and she her body tingled in anticipation. She knew without checking who it was. Ethan came by every morning for coffee and a bagel and to start the wood stove before heading off to the farm to take care of the animals and anything he was working on there. The familiar gait gave him away—one foot only a little heavier than the other as his prosthetic touched the ground in his boot. He walked with a slight limp, and she learned that cold days bothered his stump more. Not that he was the one to tell her that. She figured that out on her own—along with a few other things he would be shocked to discover she knew.

This morning though, someone else was shuffling in behind him. Curious, she craned her head to see who had intruded on the best part of her day.

Natalie was close behind him, tugging off her mittens and looking up at the chalkboard menu.

Brooke liked Natalie. She was sweet and didn't gossip or butt into problems that weren't her own. She typically had breakfast at the diner in the mornings with Zach and Sebastian, so this little deviation in routine was curious. Was it catty of her to hope that it wouldn't become habit? Brooke really did look forward to these quiet few morning minutes with Ethan each day. It was the whole reason why she told Sophie she would handle the early morning rush.

Ethan smiled at Brooke, and she nearly melted on the spot. Brooke's body reacted to Ethan in ways she never knew it could. She was breathless, with clammy palms and, she imagined, a dopey grin. She was hopelessly infatuated. The last man she had been infatuated with was Ryan Willis, and even he didn't instill these responses. When his eyes moved quickly to Natalie and back at Brooke, they looked almost apologetic.

"Good morning," he said.

"Good morning." She was lost in the way his smile lit up his face and actually reached his eyes, highlighting the laugh lines around them.

"Ethan said you started carrying a new kind of coffee that was most excellent, so I decided to give it a try today," Natalie said by way of greeting. Natalie frequently changed the color of her hair and the way she wore her makeup. She was an understated dresser, preppy, but nothing that would stand out. Other than the frequent changes to her hair and makeup, Natalie always appeared to be a pretty low-maintenance woman.

"It *is* delicious," Brook agreed, pulling out two ceramic mugs for them. She assumed Ethan would be eating here, as was his usual routine before taking another cup of coffee to go. "I'll join you in a cup. I haven't had mine yet."

Natalie's hair was brown today, and she had vibrant blue eyes, the same height and high cheekbones as Ethan. Brooke often wondered why they hid the fact that they were related from everyone one, but she never dared asked. She nearly died of curiosity every time she saw them together, but she wouldn't reveal the secret. Having secrets of her own, Brooke respected other people's privacy. But how had others not picked up on their similarities? Brooke figured them for cousins.

"Ethan also shoveled your walkways," Natalie said, waving at Ethan.

Touched, Brooke looked over at him. "You didn't have to do that. I was going to head out in a little bit."

"It's no trouble." Ethan shrugged his shoulders. That was Ethan. He quietly helped people without looking for any compliments or thanks. He did what needed to be done. It was one of the many reasons why people in Grayson Falls found him so endearing—one of the reasons why he was so beloved around town.

"Then breakfast is on me this morning," Brooke insisted. "One good turn deserves another."

"I won't say no to that." He shrugged out of his coat and draped it over a chair while Brooke poured the steaming morning nectar into three oversized mugs. The mugs were made by a local artisan and sold upstairs. They were a popular product as they were bigger than a regular mug, but not big enough to be the size of two. She brought the mugs to the counter by the register and retrieved Ethan's bagel. She liked that he took his coffee black like she did.

Ethan and Natalie sat down at one of the little café tables, and Brooke came around and leaned up against the counter, taking her first sip of the morning and savoring the warmth. The store was still chilly. She didn't usually raise the heat until about half an hour before opening. She still had time.

"Ethan said you're renovating a house," Natalie said, blowing on her coffee before taking a sip.

Brooke nodded. "It's not much, but it was darling. And it's on the lake, so I couldn't resist. It needs a complete overhaul, but the contractor said as long as the inspections are timely, it'll be done by Christmas. And I'll be able to spend the holiday in my first house that I bought entirely on my own."

"With the wedding coming up, you must be clamoring to get out of Ryan and Sophie's house," Natalie continued.

"The love birds are a bit much," Brooke agreed. "But it's been good for the wedding plans, too. With the wedding and reception at the ski resort, it's already decorated for Christmas, and the events lodge they have on site is so rustic and charming. It looks great with twinkle lights and evergreen bunting, so I can spend more time worrying about all the little details."

Brooke had planned Jackie and Danny McKenzie's wedding back in the spring. It was backyard farm chic and so fun to do. Sophie was so impressed, she "hired" Brooke to plan her Christmas wedding, and Zach and Piper asked her to plan their Fourth of July nuptials. That one was a little more challenging because they were getting married on the town baseball field and literally invited the entire town.

So, not only was Brooke a business owner and a quilter, but it also seemed she was now an amateur wedding planner—at least for her family and friends. She didn't think she wanted to get a wedding planning business going or anything so official as that. Her focus was the shop.

Shivering, Natalie brought her mug up to her face to warm her nose. Brooke was used to the morning temperature of the shop in the winter. It certainly wasn't cozy, but Ethan would start a fire in the wood stove before he left. Brooke always waited to turn up the heat until she knew how the stove was heating. Both Sophie and Brooke liked to save on expenses wherever they could. Sophie had taught Brooke how to be frugal—sometimes brutally so—but every penny pinched would help in her visions of expanding the store even more, assuming she got Sophie to agree. Brooke wanted to bring the store online. It had a webpage now, but not one you could order from. Brooke saw that as the next step.

Natalie downed the rest of her coffee and stood up. "Thanks so much, Brooke," she said as she rose and pulled her mittens on. "E, settle up for me. I've got to get to work. Have a great day, you two!" And she was out the door.

Ethan sighed and rolled his eyes. Brooke laughed. "Don't worry about it," she said. "It's on the house."

He picked up his mug and raised it to her. "How about you fix me up a to-go cup and I get the fire going? It's freezing in here this morning. If I don't warm up soon, I won't be able to walk."

He pushed himself up from the chair in one fluid movement and walked over to the wood stove that stood just to the other side of the café counter where you walked into the store. Brooke returned behind the counter to start making his coffee, eyeing him as he moved. He favored the injured leg only slightly. If you didn't know Ethan, you would never know he was missing the bottom part of his leg.

As he went in and out the side door, stacking wood inside for Brooke and Sophie to be able to continue to feed the fire throughout the day, Brooke kept her attention on slowly preparing his coffee. When he finally removed his jacket to begin building the fire, she set the steaming cup on the counter and stared down at the mug.

"Is that true?" she asked. "Does it really freeze?" She never talked with Ethan about his injury. She wasn't sure if it was a taboo subject with him or not. When she heard him chuckle, she assumed not.

"No," he said, piling wood into the stove. "But it is very sensitive in the cold months, and that makes it a little more difficult to move around. And it tends to ache more at the end the day. It probably would have been smarter for me to move to Florida with my parents."

Brooke knew Ethan was referring to his adoptive parents. Ethan, Ryan, Jackie, Sebastian, and Zach were all related through their biological mother, and none of them knew about each other growing up. They only met a few years ago, and eventually, Ethan, Zach, and Sebastian moved to Grayson Falls after Jackie and Ryan did. Beyond that, Brooke didn't really know the full story.

"Why didn't you?" she asked. "If you would be more comfortable there, what made you stay here?"

Ethan paused and looked into the fire. Brooke thought perhaps she had overstepped her boundaries. She was just about to tell him to never mind and busy herself with checking email when he answered.

"Well, the obvious reason is Jackie and Ryan were here, and we hit it off. When we met, I felt like I'd known them forever, you know? I just fit right in. I fit in at home with my parents, but Ryan and Jackie were blood relatives. I never had that before. We have physical features in common, mannerisms, things like that too. I love my parents. They provided well for me growing up, but this was a connection I could never quite get. Not to mention, I'm a farmer. I was raised on a farm, and Jackie's little farmette was screaming out to me. I enjoy that work."

"And the unobvious reason?" she asked.

Sighing, Ethan closed the fire doors and opened the vents on the stove all the way before standing up. "I've never told anyone before."

"Oh." Straightening up, Brooke waved her hand in dismissal. "I'm sorry for prying. Just ignore me."

"Baby," Ethan said, softly. "I couldn't ignore you if someone paid me a million dollars to do it." Brooke felt her face flush and slowly met his eyes. There was the attraction she knew he felt. Why did he fight it sometimes? "The unobvious reason is after serving in the desert, I want to be where it's cold. There's no good place to have a war, but the desert was hellish. I always promised myself while I was working with all the gear on, trying to keep Bravo and myself hydrated, out of the sun, and not overworked in the heat, that when I got out of the service, I'd go to a colder climate. After I met Jackie and Ryan, this town was everything I wanted. My parents understand. I visit them, but never for more than a few days at a time. I can't stand any longer than that."

Brooke blinked her eyes when she felt tears well up. Ethan did not want people's pity. She knew that well. But more importantly, he had just shared something with her that he had never told anyone else before.

"Did that make me sound pathetic?" he asked.

Shaking her head, Brooke pushed back her melancholy and said, "Not at all. Thank you for trusting me with that."

"Thank you for allowing me to do things for you that make me feel useful."

While she stood there, speechless, he grabbed his coat, coffee cup, and breakfast, smiled at her in his devastatingly charming way, and disappeared out the side door.

Ethan Donahue was a very complicated man.

Three

BUNDLED UP AGAINST the cold, Ethan walked to the barn doors to slide them closed. He was about to go out on a ride and wanted to trap the heat in the barn while he was gone. Ethan kept a big plaid pillow in the barn for Bravo to curl up on. He expected the dog to join him on his ride like Bravo usually did, but today it seemed as though his partner had other plans.

"Really?" Ethan asked, as he watched Bravo curl up on the pillow then look up at him with hopeful eyes. "It's not that cold out. You can lay around when you're dead." Bravo's ear twitched, but he showed no signs of moving. Once the dog put his head on his paws, Ethan knew the battle was lost. "Civilian life has made you soft. I'll let you off the hook this time, but only because of our promise. Back to work tomorrow."

Ethan closed the door to the barn door and walked toward the stall that held the gray thoroughbred he had recently acquired. Her name was Christmas Morning, and she was raised for racing. She was actually bred by a very reputable farm in Tennessee, but sold to less reputable owners. Christmas Morning was one of thirty horses seized in a raid after it was discovered the horses were injected with performance enhancing drugs, along with other illegal and inhumane treatment. The horse was put up for adoption, and Jackie helped him finance the money for the donation to bring her to New Hampshire. She deserved an easy life—just like Bravo.

Ethan had made a promise to his canine friend as he was lying on the street after the explosion and Bravo was draped across his chest in protection. He promised the pup that he would have him discharged and together, they'd lead a lazy life on a farm in Nebraska where Ethan was from. Of course, he didn't know at the time that his parents sold the farm due to financial constraints, so the Nebraska part didn't really pan out.

Neither did the lazy part, come to think of it. Farms weren't for the lazy. Ethan and Bravo literally worked every day. These farm animals depended on him for everything, so even if all they could do at the farm because of weather was feed and care for the animals, that's what they did. Ethan was at the farm every single day—minus the occasional short visits to his parents in Florida. Then his siblings would all pitch in based on their availability. But if Bravo wanted some time off, Ethan was going to give it to him.

Ethan wasn't the only one who walked away from the accident with demons. Bravo had his own form of PTSD. He often cried when he was separated from Ethan and startled more than normal at loud noises. Danny requested Bravo's services a few times during drug busts, but Ethan only sparingly allowed that just to keep Bravo's skills fresh. He wasn't sure why he did it, since he didn't believe police work would be a good fit for Bravo. The dog put in his time and earned his rest. Ethan was considering an offer from Danny to have him train police dogs, though, and Ethan was seriously considering it. He loved working with the dogs in the service, and he was definitely an animal lover.

When a car slid abruptly to a stop on the dirt road that led from Jackie's house to Ryan's, Ethan lifted his head. Brooke opened the door of her SUV and scrambled out. Her mouth went agape, with her eyes on the thoroughbred.

"Who is this magnificent creature?" she asked, raising her hand to stroke the horse.

"This is Christmas Morning," Ethan said. "She's a beauty. She just got here yesterday. I was just about to take her out and stretch her legs a bit, show her around."

"Christmas Morning," Brooke whispered, looking up at the horse. The awe and instant love in her eyes moved Ethan. If she ever looked at him like that, he'd be toast. "She's just gorgeous." Brooke ran her hand over the horse as she circled the animal and studied her closely. "Did she race?"

"She did," Ethan said, clearing his throat. The obvious appreciation in her eyes for the horse was doing strange things to him. What if she looked at him liked that? He'd be on his knees—and getting on his knees was no easy feat. "She got caught up in that High Winds Farm scandal."

Nodding her head, Brooke looked back into the horse's eyes. "I love her. Can I ride her?"

When she turned that hopeful look on him with the awe and the joy and the instant love, it hit him so hard, he nearly took a step back. What was it about this polished princess from Boston that he couldn't shake? They were opposites—certainly from opposite worlds. But she was the first woman that got to him since his accident.

"You're not dressed warm enough," he replied. When her face fell, Ethan cursed himself. Why was his immediate reaction to deny her? What was he scared of? "I'll wait if you want to get changed. I'll saddle Kodak."

Spinning on her heel, Brooke ran back to her car and tore down the dirt road towards Ryan and Sophie's. Ethan returned to the barn and walked toward Kodak's stall. Kodak was a white and black Appaloosa and another rescue. Ethan mainly took in rescues on the farm—the misfits, if you will, broken or damaged in some way or just too old to serve a purpose where they were. Kodak was malnourished and sick when he came to the farm, but he thrived now under Ethan's love and care.

Seeing his master, Bravo perked up his ears, but still made no move to get up. Ethan shook his head. That dog slayed him sometimes. Bravo had personality in spades with people he was comfortable around. Ethan had to be very careful with who he allowed near the dog. Military dogs were trained to work. They were trained to be suspicious of everyone and everything. Bravo did okay with Ethan, Natalie, and Emma, their friend Eric Davis's daughter. He was cautious around everyone else. Ethan had to pay special attention to Bravo's mood when he was out in public places with him. Kids wanted to pet him, and Ethan couldn't always let them. Parents around town began to tell their kids that Bravo was "working" and couldn't play when Ethan subtly shook his head at them. It was easier for kids to understand than "Bravo's just not in the mood today."

Brooke pulled back up as Ethan was leading Kodak out of the barn. And wouldn't you know it? Bravo jumped to his feet, wagging his tail. "Oh, sure," Ethan whispered to the dog. "When it's just me, you couldn't care less about going out, but now that there's a pretty girl coming along, you're game?"

As Bravo walked to her, Brooke cautiously held out her hand. She was used to his moods now and was checking to see how he was doing today. When Bravo pushed his nose into her palm, she scratched around his ears. "Hey there, handsome guy," she greeted the dog. "Ready for a bit of a run?"

They walked over to Christmas Morning, and Brooke gave the horse another appreciative stroke.

"She's known pain, but she's happy to be here." Brooke swung up into the saddle and Ethan stepped forward to adjust the straps for her feet.

"Are you the *Horse Whisperer* now? I think that job's been taken," he said.

"What animal wouldn't be happy to be here with you, Ethan?" she asked. He then gave the strap one last jerk before moving to the other side.

When he finished with her foot straps, he closed the barn doors and mounted Kodak. He was used to the twinge of pain that accompanied mounting a horse and almost didn't acknowledge it anymore. He tried not to be vain regarding his injury and wasn't always successful. It was what it was, and it wasn't going to change. The human body couldn't regrow a leg. What he found over the few short years since he'd first put the prosthetic on was that other people were uncomfortable around him when the prosthetic was showing. Not everyone, obviously, but there were those that avoided eye contact and shifted where they stood so they couldn't see the glaring reminder of the reality of war. He was the one with the injury, and yet *they* were uncomfortable.

There were many different kinds of prosthetics to choose from, and Ethan had what was called a dynamic response foot. It was designed for more active people. It was lightweight and had a higher shock absorption than his other prosthetic that was more for general movement around the house. He wondered if he could get the New England Maverick's logo put onto one. Maybe Zach could help him out with that. With his parents' help, he had bought two of them so he wouldn't have to be without if he had a problem with one of them.

No matter how comfortable this particular prosthesis was, his limb still ached at the end of the day. And the incision site was sensitive to bitter cold. He'd still take that any day over the heat, though.

"Take it nice and easy with her," Ethan instructed Brooke. Not that she needed his guidance. He knew she had been riding since she was a little girl in boarding school. He even knew from previous conversations that she had found solace with the horses when she missed being home. Ethan had never been one to fall victim to the "poor little rich girl" story, but the fact that she was sent to boarding school to be raised tugged at him. If Ethan ever had kids, he wouldn't let them leave his home until college. It didn't matter that he would never have enough money to pay for boarding school. Ethan was thankful every day that his parents had adopted him and he didn't have the kind of upbringing Natalie experienced.

Brooke reached down and stroked the neck of the horse as they plodded along. He noticed she was always touching Christmas Morning with a loving hand. Brooke was enamored with the thoroughbred. She felt that way about Kodak and his third horse, Kojo, as well. It wasn't unusual for him to come into the barn in the afternoon and find her caring for the horses—and other animals—once she was finished at the store for the day. And if he came in to find a horse missing, he never worried. He knew she was out on the trails he showed her. She knew where she could take them for easy walks or a fast, all out ride.

They plodded along through the snow at an easy pace for a trail ride. He watched how Christmas Morning moved, assessing her for any injuries or lingering issues from her earlier treatment. She seemed to be doing well. His eyes continued to drift up to the rider. Despite the cold, Brooke had her face tipped up to the sun and her eyes closed. She was a vision by any man's standards. The fact that she was a nice person and pleasant to be around was an added bonus.

Pleasant to be around? Are you looking for a chess partner, you dumbass?

"I was thinking," he began.

Turning in her saddle, Brooke gifted him with a brilliant smile, the force of which nearly knocked him off his horse. "I'd love to," she said, enthusiastically.

Ethan opened his mouth, closed it, opened it again, closed it. She'd love what? What did she think he was going to ask? Come to think about it, what *was* he going to ask? For the life of him, he couldn't remember now. He was too intrigued by what she might have thought he was going to say.

"Love to what?" He asked, dumbly. If he were a wittier guy, he would have said, "Great!" and let her wonder what he was going to say and put *her* on the spot instead of him now.

"I'd love to go over to Over the Hop with you after the ride," she said, so confidently, he nearly thought he actually asked her himself. "I'd love one of their big hot chocolates and a pretzel. Laurie loves you. If we call ahead, she'll reserve that cozy table by the fireplace."

The cozy table set away from everyone else by the fireplace that screamed, "We're on a date"? What had he just gotten himself into?

"Good ... that's ... yeah," he stuttered. *Good that's yeah? You're just slaying it, aren't you? Talk much?*

"I was trying to figure out how to ask you, but you took all the worry away," she said. His head was spinning. He was out of his league. Were they playing the same game? Was he even playing a game? If they were, she was pro level, and he was the floundering rookie. She looked pleased with herself. And she damned well should be, he thought. Because he couldn't even remember what he was going to say in the first place.

JUST AS BROOKE HOPED, Laurie reserved the table by the fireplace for them. Brooke hadn't told Laurie who she was bringing, so that would take her friend by surprise. Laurie Kennedy owned Over the Hop Brew Pub with her brother and cousin. They bought a floundering sketchy bar and gave it new purpose. It was now the most popular spot in town to hang out with friends and family.

The restaurant was decorated for Christmas with two trees and evergreen bunting all over the beams and fireplace mantle.

"It's not even Thanksgiving yet," Ethan grumbled as they sat down and Bravo crawled under the table out of the way.

"I love it!" Brooke gushed, plucking off her hat and mittens and setting them aside. "I love Christmas. Growing up, Sophie and I would spend the week between Christmas and New Years with our grandparents in Virginia. Sophie actually lived nearby, but she came and stayed with us anyway. We'd spend the week baking cookies, learning to cook, watching movies, and learning to sew. I didn't have any of that when I went home. We had servants for everything, and it was so impersonal. But that time with my grandparents was always so normal and full of laughter and love. I miss them now that they're gone."

Laurie came with a tray of water glasses and the beer each of them liked. She raised her brow at Brooke with a slight head nod toward Ethan's direction. Smiling, Brooke looked back at Ethan.

She played dirty to get him here. Given his befuddlement earlier, she was positive he wasn't going to ask her out. But she knew she wasn't reading him wrong. He was attracted to her, and for whatever reason, was holding himself back. By lighting a little spark under him, she hoped to push him along.

He was handsome, sure. Dark hair he kept short, stunning blue eyes he shared with his siblings, a beard he had recently let grow in, and a lean physique. But he was more than what he looked like. He was caring, a nurturer like his sister Jackie—an introvert to Brooke's extrovert. The town viewed him as a war hero, and she knew he didn't like that. Brooke had never had a relationship with a genuinely nice guy—someone who didn't want her for her money or connections. Her attraction to Ethan was immediate as soon as she met him. The fact that he was missing the bottom half of his leg was of no moment to her. That alone showed how much she had grown since she left her former life in Boston. There was a time when appearances were everything—winning over all the other girls was essential. Having Ryan Willis in school was the brass ring. She was so focused on making sure he was hers that she never even clued in that Sophie was in love with him.

She hated her former self—hated that she could be that wrapped up in herself at school that she didn't see Sophie's pain. Brooke was an entirely different person at their grandmother's growing up, not caring about any of the things she was obsessed with at school or home.

"Are you a Christmas fan?" Brooke asked Ethan.

Shaking his head, Ethan shrugged and sat back in his chair. "I guess. I mean, I'm not not a fan." He waved his hand around at the decorations. "I do think the Christmas season should start after Thanksgiving though."

Brooke looked around at all the festive decorations. They would start to decorate the store this weekend and put their Christmas stock out, so she was just as guilty for jumpstarting Christmas. "I think they're for the tourists going to the ski resort. It's going to get pretty busy in here soon. All the local businesses will want to take advantage of that."

"Yup," Ethan agreed. "So, they'll see less of me until after the holiday."

Frowning, Brooke leaned forward on her elbows. "Why would you go into hiding?"

After sipping his drink, he put the glass back down and looked out at the people in the restaurant. "Crowds aren't really my thing. They never have been. Growing up, I was an only child, and I lived on a farm. There were no other kids around except for school. And it was in a rural area, so there weren't that many kids there either. I like coming here before or after the rushes."

She could see that about him. Even when they gathered with his siblings, he talked, but not a lot. He was an observer and didn't speak for the sake of getting his two cents in during a conversation.

"It sounds like Megan is doing well," Brooke continued. Ethan's oldest brother Sebastian's girlfriend had a heart condition. She had been scheduled for surgery, but before it could be done, she had a heart attack at their book club meeting. Brooke remembered the fear and grief they all felt as they watched Jackie and Natalie give Megan CPR. Sebastian had completely lost it when he got to the meeting. Brooke never saw raw, debilitating grief like Sebastian showed. It made her realize how short life was.

Now, she was going after what she wanted. If Ethan didn't want her then that was a different story, but at least she would know she tried.

"She is," Ethan nodded. "She came through the surgery and is getting stronger every day. She should be leaving the hospital soon. Sebastian has been by her side the whole time. Jackie said he was a mess during the surgery. I couldn't imagine what he must have been feeling—the pain of the very real possibility of losing someone that central to your existence. I've lost people in my life—very close friends when I was overseas—and the loss hurt every time. But to be completely destroyed like that, I just can't imagine it."

"You will someday when you fall in love," she said. His gaze snapped up to hers, and for a fleeting second, there was fear in his eyes. "When you find the right person—the one person you know you can't live without."

Ethan went back to studying his beer, paused a minute then looked back up at her. "Did you think your husband was that person?"

Swallowing involuntarily, Brooke shifted in her chair. She wasn't expecting the statement to be turned around on her like that. Still, if she wanted to explore a relationship with him, she needed to be honest about her past, even if it painted her in a bad light. She didn't want there to be any surprises.

"No," she confessed, her eyes drifting to another couple settling in at the next table. "I never thought he could be the one. I always knew I was fulfilling a family obligation by marrying him. It was a business merger, and I was part of the package. I knew it wasn't going to be a grand love affair, but I thought I could at least be content and happy. I ended up miserable. Given the many extramarital affairs he had, I can only assume he was just as miserable. The difference is, I was faithful. I was willing to keep my wedding vows. If there wasn't love between us, there could have at least been respect and truth. If he told me he was going to pursue other women, I could have handled things differently."

"Would you have really wanted to be in an arrangement like that?" he asked, leaning forward on his elbows as someone squeezed behind him to get to the bar. "You wouldn't have lasted a month. You have too much fire to be wasted on someone that can't appreciate you and is too stupid not to realize what he has."

Blushing at his compliment, Brooke met his eyes. "The woman sitting at the table with you wouldn't have. She wouldn't have ever gotten married to the snake. But the girl I was saw prestige, standing at the country club, corporate fundraisers to be seen at, and endless shopping trips to Paris. That's what I was raised for, Ethan. It's what I was *bred* for—being the wife of an important man. Being a shop owner, buying a fourteen hundred square foot house to actually live in, driving a practical SUV instead of a zippy little Lexus or Aston Martin, I know it sounds crazy coming from the life I had, but it's fed my soul. That's something I rarely got to indulge in growing up."

Ethan reached out and squeezed her hand. "I told you once before, Grayson Falls is a pretty good place for second chances. People here don't have to forgive what they don't know. You could be anybody. But if the woman I see sitting across from me is the real you, I don't know about anyone else, but I like what I see."

Taken aback for a second by the intensity of his gaze and the conviction in his voice, she was at a brief loss for words. His hand felt electric on hers. The moment seemed to solidify in her mind. Echoes of the other voices swirled around her with the warmth coming from the fireplace in the festive setting. She sucked a breath in and in that moment, she knew she was going to fight like hell for this man.

"That's the nicest thing anyone's ever said about me."

"I doubt that." He sat back in his chair and picked up his beer, breaking the perfect moment was broken. The restaurant was beginning to fill up. The sounds of holiday music played around them and a waiter came by to stoke the fire.

"I think I'm a pretty good judge of what people have said to me," she said, lifting her chin up. "And that compliment has certainly meant the most out of any others I've gotten. It was genuine, and I am rarely given a genuine compliment. The compliments given to me are typically superficial."

Smiling, Ethan answered, "Well, I'll have to remember never to tell you how beautiful you are then."

Playing along, she said, "I would greatly appreciate it."

They shared a laugh, and she took a moment to appreciate how his eyes lit up when his smile reached them. Resting her chin in her hand, she realized she successfully got him out on a busy night, but with his dislike of crowds, she would have to get creative about what she could convince him to do during the holiday season. She liked him and wanted to see him, even if she had to keep tricking him.

Four

ETHAN WOKE UP in a cold sweat, panting and shaking. Rolling over in bed, he grabbed his anxiety medication and the water bottle he kept there, took a sip, and swallowed the pill. Swinging his legs over the side of the bed, he began taking deep breaths to try to slow his heart rate and breathing down. He was a professional at this now. Bravo crawled over to Ethan on his stomach and quietly laid his big head in Ethan's lap. Absently, Ethan began stroking his faithful pet as his system began to calm.

He looked over at the clock—four a.m. shined back at him in blood red. Sighing, he ran a hand down his face. He wouldn't fall back asleep now if he lay back down, so he reached over and grabbed his prosthetic to attach it. Usually, at the end of the day, Ethan took the prosthetic off and moved around the house on crutches, if he needed to move at all. Most mornings he did that as well. But he had negative energy to burn off this morning.

After hitting the bathroom, Ethan walked back to the kitchen door, let Bravo out, then hit "brew" on the coffeemaker. Natalie set it up each night before she turned in so neither of them had to think overly hard at making coffee in the morning. Ethan had lobbied for a coffeemaker with pods simplifying things even more, but Natalie liked freshly ground beans. She would be waking up soon herself. She was an early bird and ate breakfast most mornings at the diner with Zach and Sebastian. Given how early he was up today, Ethan considered joining them himself, but then that would mean he'd miss his morning with Brooke. Unless he went to the store after. Was that overkill?

Generally speaking, Ethan was also an early riser. Farm life started early to get the most out of the day, but even he was prone to hit snooze for another hour every now and then. The animals wouldn't die if they got fed at seven a.m. instead of six, but it would throw off his schedule for the rest of the day, so sleeping-in days were rare.

Leaning up against the counter, Ethan rubbed the sleep out of his eyes. The smell of fresh-brewed coffee began to permeate the air and Ethan breathed deeply, savoring the feeling of home. Grayson Falls fit like a glove and felt more like home than Nebraska. He loved his parents deeply—and he would always think of them as his parents—but something about being with his blood-siblings was just a different feeling altogether. Of course, he'd never let on to that around his parents. He would rather head back to a warzone than let his parents think they were in any way lacking when it came to meeting his needs.

When Eric Davis showed up at the Donahue farm telling him he was investigating Daisy Dolan—Ethan's biological mother—Ethan was shocked to find out he had two siblings in New Hampshire. It wasn't until he received Eric's full report that he discovered he actually had a total of five siblings from his mother.

Lately, Ethan and Natalie's biological father kept coming to mind. They knew it wasn't the bastard that raised Natalie. Daisy had said he was a hockey player also named Ethan. Zach's father had run down some possibilities he discovered, because when Zach was young, he expressed interest in meeting his brothers and sisters, but Dr. Porter had hit a dead end.

Now, Ethan had Eric and his mysterious resources. He was starting to think maybe if he had closure in certain issues, other areas of his life might start to be less stressful. He didn't have survivor's guilt. He was sorry his friends died, but he wasn't sorry he lived. He tried to live his second chance at life to the fullest. He didn't wallow in the loss of the limb. He vowed to honor the sacrifice of his fellow soldiers by living the best life he could—making sure he had a purpose, which was something he struggled with when he returned home.

The things he saw in war would always be with him—would always haunt him. He went to see the families of his friends that were killed that day. He grieved with them. He did everything you were supposed to do, and yet, the nightmares persisted. By now, he was resigned to the fact that they would always be with him. Perhaps their frequency would change, but some things just stayed with you.

Bravo scratched at the door, and Ethan let him back in then moved to the cabinet, retrieved a mug, and filled it with the magic morning elixir. Ethan took his coffee black. Sugar and creamer weren't always readily available in the desert.

As the latest nightmare faded from his memory, he sipped his coffee and let his mind wander to other things—more pleasant things—like the beautiful, compelling, and confusing woman that was Brooke Larrabe. He knew she was proud of herself for tricking him into going to Over the Hop with her, but the truth was, she wouldn't have gotten him to go if he didn't want to. His need for alone time overpowered everything in his life but family emergencies.

Speaking of which, he took a minute to fire off a text to Sebastian to find out how Megan was recovering and how Sebastian was doing. He felt a slight twinge of guilt when he remembered that as a doctor, Sebastian didn't silence his phone at night and that he would be getting a text alert at quarter after four in the morning. He would also now know that Ethan had trouble sleeping when he saw the time stamp.

The whole ordeal with Sebastian's girlfriend Megan had taken quite a toll on his brother, and Ethan wanted to make sure Sebastian came out on the other side intact—the same way his brother was doing for him. Sebastian only recently moved to Grayson Falls in October, so until recently, Ethan was only really able to get to know him when Sebastian came to visit and through texts and emails. His relationship with him wasn't as strong as it was with Ryan, Zach, and their sisters, but Ethan was making a dedicated effort to strengthen it. He liked all his siblings. None of them were assholes. They could *be* assholes, sure, but none of them were by nature.

His thoughts drifted back to Brooke again. She was something all right. Always put together. Lately, he found himself craving to take her apart. But he feared in doing that, she might deconstruct him in the process. Some parts of him weren't worth seeing. Some parts of him, he didn't show anybody. Some parts of him even he didn't explore.

But he found himself wanting to share those places with her. His instincts told him that she would understand, that she would comfort him, hold him, and heal him. Maybe if he brought them into her light, the darkness might fade.

That seemed like a lot of pressure to put on somebody he didn't know well. He liked her and was attracted to her. But he was definitely out of practice when it came to romancing a woman. Hell, he wasn't sure he ever knew how. When he was in the Marines, women came to him—that whole men in uniform thing. And when he was medically discharged, well, he didn't have any interest in women for a while. All his time was consumed with therapy and then finding his siblings, moving to Grayson Falls, and starting a new life here. In fact, it wasn't until he met Brooke that his hormones stood up and took notice.

As he drained his coffee cup, he glanced at the clock. He had time to bang out some pushups and sit-ups to help burn off the rest of this physical reaction to the nightmare, take a shower, and head to the General Store to be there when Brooke opened for the day. That morning quiet time while she did her daily walk through and power up and he ate his breakfast and drank coffee had come to be his favorite part of the day. It wasn't the calm before the storm because his days were pretty predictable, but it was a peacefulness he didn't get anywhere else. Even home.

When he realized it was because of Brooke's presence, he put a hand down to grip the counter in fear that his knees would give out. Thinking back to how long he had this particular routine, he came to the conclusion that it didn't start until after Brooke came to Grayson Falls. Of course, he had patronized the General Store frequently before she showed up—he tried to shop local as much as possible—but he made stopping there on his way to the farm in the mornings his routine when Brooke had taken over the early shift.

He ran a hand down his face. That was certainly telling, now wasn't it? Pushing off the counter, he put his mug in the dishwasher and moved to the living room for his workout. He tried to keep his mind clear as he moved through his one hundred pushups followed by one hundred sit-ups. He tried to keep his mind focused on counting, but there in the background was the image of Brooke sitting by that big stone fireplace surrounded by Christmas decorations. It wasn't until the end of his workout that he realized the image stayed with him the entire time. He didn't think of the nightmares or go to that dark abyss he occasionally slipped into during highly stressful times. He stayed with her.

Ethan hurried through his shower and getting dressed. He arrived at the store before Brooke did. Usually he timed his arrival to be there after she had a chance to open the door and put the pastries in the oven. Did he look desperate? Maybe she would just think he was hungry. But then wouldn't she wonder if he was that hungry why he didn't just eat at home? Was it too much to hope that she would think he was here so early because he was interested in her? He wouldn't share his epiphany with her. He didn't want to scare her off—not that he thought he could scare her off at this point, what with her setting traps for him to fall into.

Looking over to his dog, Ethan said, "What do you think? Am I being crazy? Desperate?" Bravo's response was to lay down on the seat and roll over, exposing his belly to be pet. "Fat lot of help you are," Ethan muttered but gave in to the dog's request. Bravo groaned at the belly scratches.

Headlights shined in the mirror, and Brooke pulled in next to him. Cocking her head to the side, she gave him an inquisitive look. Yes, it was odd for him to beat her there, but he usually didn't arrive long after she did. She killed the engine on her car, got out, and stood there looking at him expectantly. He rolled down his window.

"Hungry this morning?" She teased.

"Running a little early. Couldn't sleep." Why did he tell her that? Trouble sleeping was a common problem though. People had trouble sleeping all the time. Many things on someone's mind led to sleepless nights.

But she nodded her head with a knowing look in her eyes—almost as if she saw right through her. Wasn't that what he had come for? Wasn't he just thinking that morning that she seemed to see more of him than his brothers and sisters?

She waved her hand. "Come on in," she said. "But it'll be a little while until the stoves heat up and the coffee brews."

Rolling up the window, Ethan and Bravo got out of the car and followed her to the side door of the store. Ethan stopped at the wood pile and grabbed an armload on his way by. While Brooke was going through her morning routine, he'd start a fire in the wood stove and fill up the indoor wood loop. He walked behind her as she disengaged the alarm and began turning on the lights. Because it was so cold outside, the temperature inside felt downright balmy. But as Ethan passed the thermostat, he saw the store was set down at fifty-five degrees. Damn, the girls really turned the heat low at night. His barn thermostat was set higher than that in the winter, but then again, he lost a lot of heat in there. It was insulated inside for the animals, but it was still a barn.

As he walked toward the stove, he saw that the wood loop was already full. Setting the wood on the floor, he opened the stove doors.

"Ryan must have filled it up last night," Brooke said. "He picked Sophie up. The closer it gets to their wedding, the more glued to each other they get. Speaking of which, have you been fitted for your tux yet?"

"I have the same measurements I had when Jackie got married. Can you just use those?" He set to work shoveling the ashes out of the stove and into the metal ash bucket.

Brooke pursed her lips and looked like she was going to argue. Instead, she shrugged off her coat. "It's awfully close to the wedding now to be playing fast and loose with fittings."

Piling the kindling in the stove, Ethan said, "The wedding is still six weeks away. Thanksgiving is next week. Someone on the planet will be able to make alterations still." He heard her huff, but didn't respond. He continued building the fire as she walked around the store.

What was the big deal? He couldn't understand why Sophie was making them wear tuxedos anyway. She and Ryan weren't flashy. Ryan had money, but not like Jackie did. Jackie inherited all her father's money. Ryan did have a trust fund from his father, though, which he used to build his business. Ethan knew his brother was well off, but didn't take him for a wedding tuxedo type of guy.

Sighing, Ethan stood up and left the fire doors open a bit to help warm the immediate area. Bravo curled up at his feet and let out a long breath. What a life that dog had now.

Hearing Brooke walking around upstairs, Ethan strolled behind the food counter and turned on the coffee and hot water pots. Like the wood, the coffee was prepped the previous evening. Walking to the small kitchen, he took stock of the ovens for the pastries. He knew they were prepared the night before, but couldn't see any indication on what ovens needed to be turned on and at what temperature. He walked back over to the fire and pulled up a café chair to wait for Brooke.

"So," Brooke said when she returned. "Why couldn't you sleep?"

"Bad dream." He didn't think, he just answered. He could have come up with anything—leg ached, Bravo was farting, the room was too hot—but the truth came naturally with her.

"Do you get them a lot?"

He could hear her moving around behind him as she popped into the kitchen to turn on the ovens then returned to power up the computers.

"They come and go," he said. "I'll go months without one, and then they'll come every night for a week straight. I don't know what triggers them."

"Maybe the date?" She suggested. He could hear her preparing coffee now, probably his. He should just start doing that himself. He came in every morning. She didn't need to wait on him. "I read that dates can do that, like the anniversary of the accident, or a birthday or something."

Scanning his internal calendar, he pursed his lips in thought. "Nothing springs to mind."

"Do you take anything to help you sleep?"

"That just makes it harder to wake myself up."

His coffee appeared over his shoulder, and he turned around to take it from her. Their fingers touched in the transfer, and he felt a tingle. They looked at each other, each surprised by the physical reaction. But he really shouldn't have been. He had known for a while now that there was something between them. If she hadn't made the move first, he wasn't sure when he would get up the courage to do so himself. He hadn't pursued a woman yet in this new life of his—in this new body of his. As it turned out, he wasn't the one doing the pursuing, but he certainly wasn't fighting.

"Listen," he began.

"That's a great idea." Her enthusiasm was contagious. *Dear Lord, now what did she have in mind?*

"It is?" He asked.

"I'd love to come over tonight and watch a movie. Do you want me to stop at Over the Hop first to grab some dinner and maybe a growler of beer? Will Natalie be there? Should I get enough for three?

"Um, no," he said. "She's working the second shift and won't be home until about ten o'clock. Why don't I stop and get the food?"

"I don't mind. You get it next time," she said. *Next time?* You don't mind if I wear comfortable clothes, do you?" Quite frankly, he wouldn't mind if she wore no clothes at all. But he wasn't going to tell her that.

"No, not at all," he said. And now, he was going to spend the rest of the day wondering what her definition of comfortable clothes was.

Five

BROOKE'S COUSIN SOPHIE popped her head over Brooke's shoulder to look at the computer screen. Brooke was scrolling through Over the Hop's food menu, despite the fact that she knew it by heart. They all did. But the chef said it would be changing soon.

"You're not eating with us tonight?" Sophie asked, sitting down on the stool next to Brooke's. "Or is that for all of us?"

Brooke stopped what she was doing and turned to her cousin. "I kind of, sort of have a date with Ethan tonight."

Slapping her hand over her mouth, Sophie's eyes widened. "No!" she said, removing her hand. "He finally asked you?"

"Well, I kind of tricked him into it." Brooke had the good grace to wince a bit. "I tricked him into going to Over the Hop the other night, and this morning I tricked him into a date at his house to eat dinner and watch a movie."

"Tricked him how?"

Brooke turned back to the computer. "I wait until he gives me an opening and then I pounce before he ever figures out what hit him. I'm two and O."

Laughing, Sophie put her hand on Brooke's shoulder. "I have a hard time believing you have to trick any man into going on a date with you."

"*Any* man, no," Brooke said. "Ethan's different though. He's quiet. He doesn't like crowds, and I think he's nervous of asking anybody out right now."

"Because of his leg?"

"I think maybe his confidence might be a little lacking in that area." Brooke shrugged and made her dinner and beer selection. She pulled out her credit card and paid through the website. Now, she just had to swing by and pick it up later.

"Brooke." The seriousness in her cousin's tone made Brooke stop and turn around. "Go easy with Ethan. He's—"

"Not fragile," Brooke said with just a bit of a snap to her voice. Everyone thought Ethan was going to break. Why didn't they see his strength?

"But there are times when he is," Sophie persisted. "They're worried about him."

Nodding, Brooke turned to take her coat off the hook behind the counter. "He's having nightmares," she said. "I know. He told me. But that's pretty normal for a guy that's been through what he has. It's going to bug him at times. It's true I have no experience with post-traumatic stress disorder and I'm not a doctor. I don't presume to know how his mind works, and I could be totally wrong, but my instincts tell me something different."

Shrugging into her coat, Brooke pulled her knit hat on her head, but before she could pull her gloves out of her pocket, Sophie grabbed her hands. "Brooke, he cut his hand real bad and blacked out. He doesn't remember what happened."

Brooke pulled her hand back, tensing up. "I don't know anything about that," Brooke said. "And I'm certainly not going to talk about it behind Ethan's back. He only shared the nightmares with me today. He'll tell me anything else when he's ready—*if* he's ever ready to. I need to build his trust. I can't go into this with preconceived opinions."

Brows raised, Sophie blinked in surprise. Brooke felt bad about biting her cousin's head off, but for once in her life, she wanted to do something right.

"You really like him," Sophie said.

"Don't sound so surprised," Brooke laughed. "I think of other people now. I know it's shocking, but it's the new me."

"The old you wasn't too bad. Don't change too much," Sophie said. "Don't make yourself crazy trying to be someone you're not."

"It's who I was that's the problem. This life I have now, it feels right," Brooke said, pulling her gloves out of her pockets and picking up her Louis Vuitton bag—some things changed, good taste did not. Granted it was an older bag, but one she didn't want to part with.

Giving Sophie a peck on the cheek, she turned and headed out the side entrance of the store. Her practical, yet fully loaded Jeep SUV waited for her running. Remote start in New Hampshire was a beautiful thing. Grinning as she piled her bags into the passenger seat, she thought of driving this up to her parents' mansion in Boston in her middle-class car. They'd think one of the servants parked in the wrong spot. She had to go visit them at some point, and she wasn't looking forward to it. Her father would breeze in and out between appointments and social engagements, and her mother would constantly lecture her over the downturn her life had taken. It would be a duty visit and nothing more.

Maybe Brooke could get them to change their minds about her going there and have them come down for the New Years' Ball at the ski resort—maybe stay for a bit after Sophie's wedding. It looked breathtaking now and was black tie optional. It could be that event would be enough to reassure her parents she wasn't hopeless now. It was sneaky, but perhaps she could infer that she did more things like that. It would appease their snobbish-ness.

Backing out of the parking lot, she made the short drive over to Ryan and Sophie's house. Things were coming along on her own small house, and it looked like just a few more weeks until it was ready. The contractor brought in multiple construction teams to tackle the various projects quickly. Already, the little house had all new windows, new stone front steps, and new siding. The cabinets in the kitchen were replaced, along with the appliances and floor. Now, the house was being insulated and rewired, while the upstairs dormer was being done. Then the drywall would go up, the wood stove insert put in place, and finally the wood floors.

She was pleased with how fast things were moving. Of course, the monetary bonus had made it all happen, and the irony wasn't lost on her that she had thrown money at a situation for her convenience. She figured she was a work in progress. She was anxious to have her own place.

Turning down the dirt road at the hospital, she drove along past Jackie and Danny's large, log cabin, past Ethan's barn and Ryan's business' headquarters and up to Ryan and Sophie's house. A twinge of emotion always hit her when the house came into view, knowing that Ryan had built it for Sophie before they were a couple. How romantic could you be?

Or how stalkerish, depending on the way you looked at it.

Since she was only going to be home for a little while, Brooke left her car out front. Ryan had created a parking area around the side of the house for his employees to park in so they weren't all outside Jackie's house or in Ethan's way. They could either walk down to the barn or take one of the two golf carts. Brooke knew the employees typically just walked.

Unlocking the front door, she was greeted by Ryan's mutt, Wilson, who was rescued outside the General Store. Wilson was dopey, loving, and always enthusiastic. Raising her knee to ward off Wilson's jump on her, she scratched behind his ears and held him down on the floor while she greeted him. Ryan let the dog get away with murder. Once Wilson was sufficiently satisfied, Brooke picked up her bags and headed upstairs toward the guest room. She admired their grandmother's quilts that Sophie had draped around. The house, though large, was homey and cozy. Sophie picked warm colors for the walls and furniture. The place barely resembled the way Ryan had it before Sophie officially moved in. A woman's touch was everywhere.

Dumping her bags on the chair in her bedroom, Brooke moved to the dresser. She had decided on yoga pants and a hoodie. Two items someone would have never seen her in before—much less a man she was interested in. Even her husband hadn't seen her so dressed down. It was true that she did not go about town dressed this way and only tended to wear yoga pants while she was actually practicing yoga, but Ethan was different. She didn't have to pretend with him. She could leave the skinny jeans and cute ankle boots behind. They wouldn't be comfortable for curling up on a sofa.

And she planned on curling up.

Freshening her makeup, Brooke eyed her toothbrush. While she wasn't planning on having sex, what if she accidentally fell asleep on the couch? Should she stash a pair of clothes and a toothbrush in her car? Was she being presumptuous? Was she overthinking things?

Her soon-to-be ex-husband, Josh, wasn't romantic. The sex between them had been bland, and she was rarely left satisfied. It disgusted her now how complicit she had been in her marriage and just how much she had allowed her life to be dictated. When she found out about Josh's affairs, she had considered just having a few of her own. That's when she knew she had to seriously reevaluate her life choices. When she had the car accident, something clicked inside Brooke.

Ironically, just a few days later, Sophie was in a car accident herself. Brooke took it as a sign, told her husband she wanted a divorce, packed some bags, and left for Grayson Falls. Josh hadn't thought she was serious, and when she didn't return, he sicced her parents on her. But even they hadn't been able to change her mind. She had signed a pre-nup, so she wouldn't get any assets—other than a pre-agreed upon monetary settlement. She did have some money from her grandparents' estate that was split between Brooke and Sophie, but she wouldn't be able to draw on the irrevocable trust in her name from her parents for another few years. It was no matter. She was making her way and would continue to do so.

Deciding against packing anything in anticipation of an overnight, she walked out of the bathroom, grabbed her coat from the bedroom, gave Wilson another belly scratch, and headed out into the night.

Taking a deep breath, she looked up. One thing she loved about Grayson Falls was the number of stars you could see on a clear night. There was so much light pollution over Boston you could hardly see any, but here in Grayson Falls, it was almost as if you could reach up and touch them. Snow crunched under her boots as she walked to her car. Christmas was coming, and with it, Ryan and Sophie's wedding. Her parents had been invited, but Brooke wasn't sure if they would attend. They hadn't responded yet, and she didn't want to ask. She'd let her Aunt Clara, Sophie's mother, handle that.

Brooke and Sophie's mothers were sisters, and two different women you never did meet. While Clara and Brooke's mother, Lenore, had the same middle-class upbringing, Lenore had married into a wealthy family and lost sight of her roots. She rarely went down to Virginia to visit her aging parents, instead sending Brooke down to spend the summers. But for a week's vacation at some amazingly posh hotspot at the beginning of break, Brooke spent the entirety of her summers in Virginia as a girl.

She drove slowly through town, not out of deference to Danny McKenzie, her former classmate and chief of police, but to admire the Christmas decorations spread through town. The lampposts were decorated with wreaths, evergreen bunting, twinkling lights, and bright red bows. Store windows had festive winter scenes displayed.

Grayson Falls was a small, charming New England town where people stopped on the street to talk to each other. They still shopped local, and you could count on the community to see you through a tough spot. It was a town with heart that was always willing to welcome someone new or someone returning with warm, open arms.

Tomorrow was her day off from the store. Brooke would head over to Piper and Zach's to get some work done early on her quilt projects. They were always up early, and Brooke and Piper shared the space and quiet to work comfortably. Brooke could play some music while she worked, and since Piper was deaf, it didn't bother her while she painted. Zach would meander in and out to make sure they were fed and hydrated, but he rarely lingered. He knew better than to bother his fiancé when she was in "the zone."

Brooke pulled into Over the Hop. It was just starting to get busy on this Friday night. Commuters from the train often stopped in for a beer or dinner on their way home from work. Locals would stroll down to socialize and enjoy the atmosphere and friends. The noise level was a dull roar when she entered. It wasn't something she ever paid attention to before, but now that Ethan had said he'd be avoiding the place during the busy hours, she took note. There wasn't a wait to be seated yet, but there would be soon.

Laurie was behind the bar serving up cold beer, good food, and stimulating conversation. She was good at her job and made a point to know what all the locals liked best. She was so good, often your beer would be served as you sat down.

"Well, well," Laurie said as she pulled over a plastic bag holding to-go containers inside. "If it isn't the woman that's captured the attention of a certain brooding farmer."

Knowing Laurie would want all the details, Brooke smiled coyly.

"I was among the camp that thought he was with Nurse Natalie," Laurie continued, "but the way you two were cozying up, I think maybe we were all wrong."

"You are," Brooke said, pulling out her wallet. "Ethan and Natalie really are just roommates." *And somehow related*, Brooke thought, but she wouldn't say that.

"You looked good together," Laurie replied. "I hadn't realized you were a couple."

"We aren't," Brooke said, handing Laurie her credit card. "Yet."

"Confidence, I like that." Laurie swiped Brooke's card on the tablet register and turned the screen around for her signature.

"It's still early on," Brooke said, drawing nothing more than a squiggle line. "I'm doing all the chasing and hoping he doesn't get too freaked out by it. I like him a lot, and I know he's interested. Just not sure yet about the follow through. I'm heading to his house now for a movie night."

"Well, good luck to you then," Laurie said. "That family has been blessed with some fine genetics, and the men are dropping like flies."

Chuckling, Brooke left the pub. Clouds had moved in and a light snow began to fall. The forecast was only for a light accumulation, so she didn't worry. It added to the festive feel. They were a few days from Thanksgiving, but despite Ethan's grumbling, the town was itching for the Christmas season. The church choir was having a fundraiser this year. They had bought Victorian-period costumes and would be caroling throughout the season. What else said Norman Rockwell more than that?

She pulled into what would be her new neighborhood. Ethan and Natalie also lived here, but Brooke's house was farther back and more secluded. The houses were smaller, comfortable cabins that people had remodeled and added on to over the years. It was a working-class neighborhood that she was excited to join. Pulling into the driveway of Ethan and Natalie's little ranch, she killed the engine and took a deep, fortifying breath before getting out of the car.

Operation Make-Ethan-Donahue-Her-Boyfriend was officially launched.

Six

E THAN CLOSED HIS laptop and stared into the fire. He just emailed his request to have Eric Davis look into finding out who his and Nat's father was and whether or not they had any family left on that side. Ethan gave Eric the little information he had from Doug Porter, Zach's father. Ethan Price had been an NHL hockey player for the Philadelphia Flyers and died in a car accident right about the time Ethan and Natalie were born. Ethan had given Eric permission to use his DNA sample to see if it matched anyone in Price's family—should Eric's investigation actually get that far. But Eric Davis could find anyone and anything. Hell, he had found Natalie in the Witness Protection Program, and that was supposed to be impossible. No one knew how he pulled that one off, and Eric wasn't talking.

Of course, Ethan wasn't sure Natalie was interested in finding her birth father. She didn't even officially acknowledge Ethan and their siblings. But that wouldn't stop Ethan from looking into it. He would wait to see what Eric reported and then make a decision on whether or not he would want to meet any family that turned up.

If he did happen to be the son of the famous hockey player, he wouldn't ask anything of the family. Nothing from the estate or any kind of press. Jackie and Sebastian would want him to get a family medical history, and that he could do. But if they didn't want to see him, he would honor their wishes. He just wanted to know where he came from.

Glancing over at the clock, he figured he had just enough time to wash the farm off him and change into clean, non-smelling clothing.

He made his way back to the one bathroom he and his sister shared. It wasn't very big—and it was difficult to maneuver around once he had the prosthetic off—but he had a system. It didn't take long to rinse the day off him. Wrapped in a towel, he made his way to his bedroom, and now he had a decision to make. Usually, he took the prosthetic off when he got home and moved around the house by his crutches, but Brooke had never seen him without the bottom half of his leg. Knowing what it was and seeing it could be very different things, especially when deciding on whether or not to embark on a romantic relationship with somebody.

He decided to leave it off. If she was going to run, it was best she did it now before he got too emotionally involved. He would deal with it straight off. After putting on a pair of cotton lounge pants, Ethan pinned the one leg up at the knee and pulled a hooded Mavericks sweatshirt over his head. This was the real him. She could take him or leave him.

He found himself really wishing she would take him.

Stopping as he left his bedroom, he gave a cursory look at the bed. It was made, of course, and tidily so. He made it every morning just like the military instilled in him, but should he change the sheets?

Are you insane? You're not having sex tonight, dickhead. He had to agree with his inner self. He wasn't ready for sex. Right now, sex between them would be strictly physical, and he needed the emotional. If that made him sound too much like a woman, so be it. His psyche needed more of a connection with someone and deeper feelings than lust. With the nightmares and possible blackout, Ethan didn't need to add anything more to the fire.

He wondered when Natalie would feel comfortable bringing his guns back from Eric's. She didn't know he knew, but he took very good care of his weapons and when he opened up his safe to find them gone, he knew what had happened. His first instinct was to get angry, but Natalie had done it out of love and fear. He couldn't fault her. It wasn't possible to fully assure his siblings he wasn't interested in blowing his head off when there were too many stories on the news of guys eating their guns with the same symptoms Ethan showed.

Eric would give Ethan his weapons back if Ethan went over there and asked him for them, but if it gave Natalie some peace of mind to know they weren't in the house for a little while, he'd give her that. Then again, Davis was so far gone over Natalie maybe he would refuse Ethan just to stay in Natalie's good graces. It was tough to say.

The doorbell rang just as Ethan reached the living room. Here went nothing. Crutching over to the door, he opened it up to Brooke standing there. Her gaze traveled over him, pausing briefly at his missing leg, but outwardly, he saw no reaction.

Leaning up, she kissed his cheek. "Thank you for trusting me enough to show me yourself as you really are." Moving past him, she put the food on a small table in the foyer and began to take off her coat, hat, scarf, and gloves.

Dumbfounded, Ethan stood there at the door. Figuring there would be some kind of awkwardness, he couldn't have imagined she would make it a non-issue. Someone as polished and put together as he knew Brooke was, was constantly cognizant of the way she looked and presented herself to others. Why would somebody like that be interested in an incomplete man?

Once she hung up her coat, she picked up the bag and growler and looked at him.

"So, kitchen?" she asked, stepping closer.

Turning, he looked at her. Damn, she was beautiful, and he was learning she was just as amazing inside as she was outside. Was he really doing this? Was he really about to embark on a romantic relationship with someone? He hadn't been sure that was in the playbook for him.

Before he could lose his courage, he grabbed onto her sweatshirt, pulled her a step forward, and locked his lips on her. She was surprised, but responsive. Bringing his hand up to cup her cheek, he parted her lips and plundered her mouth with his tongue. Dammit, she was amazing. He'd forgotten how incredible a woman could taste—the heat they could wrap you in so quickly. It was as if the horrors slipped away and he was whole again.

Maybe he should change his sheets.

With that thought, he stepped back. He would not let his hormones take over. He didn't give a shit how eager they were.

"Straight back," he whispered.

"Mmm?" She asked, slowly opening her eyes and looking at him in confusion.

"The food." He tucked a piece of hair behind her ear. "You wanted to bring it to the kitchen."

"Yes, right." She said, recovering her senses. But instead of walking away, she put the food and glass jug back on the table along the wall, and they moved to each other.

This time, the kiss was desperate with a tangle of tongue and groping arms as they feasted on each other. Ethan's body sprang to attention, and his earlier thoughts to go slow vanished. Never in his life had a woman made him need this way. She had been reeling him in slowly for the last year, and he fell harder and further each time he saw her and she cast those beautiful eyes on him.

Her hands found their way beneath his sweatshirt, and he hissed when they came in contact with his skin. She ran them around his back and up, clawing at his shoulders. When she tipped back her head, Ethan devoured her neck. Moaning, she ran her hand down his front and cupped him through his pants. He stiffened and buried his groan in her shoulder.

"Couch," she panted.

"Food."

"Can be heated up."

"Right, good remembering that." There was no passionate, sexy, or graceful way for Ethan to get to the couch on crutches. They just had to move fast. Next time, he would consider leaving the prosthetic on. But then again, taking it off is what led to this lust-crazed moment. Who would have thought that could be a turn on?

Who was he kidding thinking he didn't already have an emotional attachment to her? He had been slowly falling in love with her for a year. She saw him as he really was and accepted him that way. He dropped the crutches out of the way and sat down on the couch. As she straddled him, he ran his hands up her back under her sweatshirt as she lowered down.

"Fuck," he groaned, as she rocked against him. "Babe, I haven't been with a woman since before I got deployed and something really embarrassing is going to happen if you keep doing that."

Pausing, she sat back and looked at him. "Really?"

Wincing, he said, "Does that make me more of a freak?"

Sliding off his lap to the side, she slid a finger down his face and through the scruff of his beard. "It doesn't make you any kind of freak. Is that how you see yourself?"

Shrugging, he met her eyes. "Women usually prefer a whole man." Was he testing her now? Hadn't she proven the lack of a whole leg wasn't an issue? What was he trying to accomplish here?

"You think you're somehow less of a man?" She looked at him like he sprouted another head. "Ethan, you got your leg blown off fighting a war. What could be manlier than that?"

She made him pause. "I can't say I ever thought of it just like that."

Shoving him a bit, annoyance crossed her face and now he was angry with himself for upsetting the mood. He was so out of practice.

"Well, start thinking of it like that. Ethan, you have a confidence in yourself that's rare for people who have been through what you have. There is nothing you physically cannot do. Haven't you proven that time and again? Why wouldn't you think that applied to women?" She linked her fingers with his and he squeezed in return. "I'm attracted to you. I want to be with you. How much more obvious do I need to be? We've known each other for over a year now, and I've been trying to get you to ask me out that entire time. I practically had to club you over the head and drag you to my cave."

Tugging her back, Ethan settled his hands on his hips. "You're right." He said. "And I'm not normally so insecure, but I haven't so much as thought of a romantic relationship since the accident. I was comfortable with myself and my body until I started seeing myself through a female lens and all that confidence deflated. I'll do better."

"See that you do." She pushed him again. "Now, why hasn't Bravo killed me yet?"

"He's with Natalie tonight. She's working alone."

"You're very protective of her," Brooke said. "It's sweet."

"She doesn't always think so, and I'm glad you see it that way. I don't know if we'd go much further if you couldn't understand my relationship with Nat."

"I know you're related somehow," she shrugged, standing up and picking up his crutches from where he had dropped them. Ethan froze. He never expected anyone to confront him about that. He didn't know what to do. He couldn't consult his siblings about what to say. He was alone.

"She's my friend," he evaded, not meeting her eyes, and grabbing his crutches. He propped them under his arms and stood up off the couch. He knew she wouldn't buy it. He wouldn't have highlighted his relationship with Natalie if they were just friends.

"Ethan," Brooke said, quietly. "We won't get far with lies between us. I don't know why you don't tell anyone you're related or how you are, but I'm not stupid. For one, you look alike; second, you finish each other's sentences; and third, there's just something different about you that I can't quite put my finger on."

Because we're twins.

"Brooke—" He began, desperate to make her understand, but having no idea how to do it.

"Just don't lie," she whispered. "My husband lied to me, and it's hard for me trust now. Just don't lie."

"Please understand," he found himself saying. "If I could share it with you, I would."

She looked at him, right through his surface to his soul inside. He knew he was laid bare. He never thought he would be in the position to choose between his twin sister and another woman, but that's where he seemed to be right now. She cocked her head to the side.

"She's in danger." Her voice was quiet, nearly inaudible.

Damn, this woman was perceptive. How could she read him so well? Did he need to be more careful now or let himself stay open to her? He nodded ever so slightly in response.

"Oh, Ethan," she whispered. She walked to him and wrapped her arms around him. "I won't say anything. I won't even bring it up to you again, I promise. You can trust me."

He hoped so. He hoped to fucking hell he could. She knew his family's secret now. And there was no going back.

THERE WAS NO PRETENSE of watching a movie. They took dinner and the beer into the living room. Brooke stopped herself at one drink since, theoretically speaking, she had to drive home and it was still snowing. Ethan wasn't a heavy drinker, but he had a couple himself, having the luxury of not having to leave his house. He sat with his back in one corner of the couch and his good knee bent. Brooke sat on the other corner of the couch, her knees up. A cozy fire was going in the fireplace, and Ethan was keeping it low enough that she wasn't sweating from the heat of it.

"What was it like growing up on a farm?" She asked, sipping from a water bottle.

"What was it like growing up rich at a boarding school?"

"I'll answer mine after you answer yours," she said, shaking her head. "I asked you first."

Sighing, Ethan ran a hand down back of his head. "Well, it was pretty good actually. It was hard work, obviously. By the time I left for school in the morning, I had already put two hours-worth of chores in. I came home, did my homework if I had any, and then back out I went for the evening chores. We didn't have a big farm, but we had a successful one. I learned so much about the animals and how to care for them, the agriculture. It was good work, honest work. I knew I was making a direct impact on someone's life, you know? Because of the work my family was doing, people were eating."

Ethan scratched his neck before continuing. "It kept me in shape, too. I had crazy muscles for a teenager."

"I bet the girls liked that," Brooke smiled, nudging his foot with hers. She could just imagine the girls of his high school swooning as he walked by, leaving broken hearts behind him.

Blushing, Ethan looked down at his hands and shrugged. "I don't know about that. I wasn't much of a dater in high school. I wasn't much of anything. My life was the farm. My parents could afford a few extra workers. It's not that I couldn't go out on a Friday or Saturday night, but I was just so damn tired at the end of the day, and I knew I would have to get up early the next morning, no matter how late I was up or out the night before. I never even held a video game controller in my hand until I joined the Marines."

She cocked her head to the side, enjoying how open he was being. "Why did you join the Marines? Why not just continue on at the farm if you enjoyed it so much?"

"Because I wanted to improve it, and there was no money for college," he said. These were the kinds of things that made her sad about her upbringing. Her parents threw money at everything. There was never a lack of money for her. It never occurred to her to think about the kids like Ethan who struggled for everything. She even often forgot growing up that Sophie wasn't from a wealthy family. Her cousin had paid for most of college with scholarships. "I was going to do four years and then take college classes on the GI bill and get a Bachelor's degree in agricultural sciences or a program to be a large animal vet. The closest one to us was hours away. Then when my parents were ready to retire, I'd take over the farm. But they hit hard times while I was deployed and sold it instead. I found out when I returned. They didn't want to worry me when I was overseas, and then after I was injured, they didn't want to add any more weight to my recovery. Their hearts were in the right places, but I would have liked to have the opportunity to take a loan out and try and save it."

"Are you still interested in college?" she asked. "You have your farm now. You could take online classes. It seems every new season you've improved the farm in some way with more crops or animals or repaired machinery."

"I don't know, maybe," he said, noncommittally. "This suits me now. When my parents told me they'd sold our home and were moving to Florida, suddenly, I was at a crossroad. I knew I wasn't moving to Florida. With them and the farm gone, there really wasn't anything left for me in Nebraska. I had literally just gotten my legs under me. I didn't know what else I could do."

"So, what happened?"

"Eric Davis found me, and the rest is history." She now knew the story of how Eric had found the rest of Ryan and Jackie's siblings and that slowly, they'd all come to Grayson Falls to meet each other, ultimately staying. Everyone but ...

Ah, so maybe that's how Ethan and Natalie were related. She was probably their other sister with a different name. Knowing Ethan didn't want to discuss the matter, Brooke didn't ask him if her theory was correct. She didn't know the exact details of his siblings or what Eric had put in his report to Danny. She only had the information Sophie told her, and Sophie thought she remembered a sister Eric couldn't find.

Deciding not to dive into "the rest" Ethan referred to, Brooke took her inquisition to a different area. "When did you find out you were adopted? Did you always know?"

"No," he said, stretching out his full leg. He pressed the palms of his hands together and sunk them in between his thighs. "I kind of wondered here and there growing up because I didn't look anything like either of my parents. Nobody ever told me I had my dad's hands or my mom's eyes. They sat me down when I was thirteen and explained it all to me. They had never planned to keep it a secret, but they wanted to wait until I was old enough to understand."

"How did you take it?"

"Damn, girl, you ask a lot of questions." Ethan said, letting out a breath.

"I want to know you better," Brooke shrugged, not sorry. She wanted to know everything he would tell her. She was fascinated by him since the day they first met at Ryan's house, but he was a tough egg to crack. "And this is the most we've ever talked. I have to strike while the iron is hot."

"I guess." He looked skeptical. As far as she knew, Ethan just didn't talk this much in general. He was quiet, which was why she knew so little about him. "To answer your question, I didn't take it well. I thought it meant that I had to leave—like there was some kind of time limit to how long they were allowed to keep me. I know it sounds ridiculous, but I didn't know anyone who was adopted, and it's not like I could spend a lot of time on the computer. I barely watched television. I screamed at them and ran out of the house, not knowing where I was going, but I wasn't going to let anyone take me away. So, I ended up spending the night in my horse's stall. My parents had found me at some point during the night and covered me with blankets. They must have decided to teach me a lesson, because I woke up itchy as hell with a rash all over me. My skin is sensitive to hay."

Brooke smiled at the thought of a rebellious little Ethan running away. She had a hard time picturing it. Ethan was so polite and well-mannered.

"So, what happened in the morning?"

"They sat me down and gave me a lecture on being disrespectful by yelling at them, rude by walking away from the conversation, and selfish by making them worry. They were frantic trying to find me. Who actually created me didn't matter; they were my parents, and they reminded me of that fact with their lecture. They just thought I should know because I was getting older, and it would be important as an adult. I couldn't give their medical histories to doctors because they weren't my histories."

"They sound like wonderful people," she said.

"They are," he replied. "I love them very much. I didn't have much growing up, but I always had food, a roof over my head, clothes to wear, and two parents that loved me. What more could a kid really want? After I found out about the adoption and I recovered from the shock, I became more appreciative of what they had done for me, giving me a home, loving me. I could have grown up being bounced around the system."

"I hope I get to meet them someday."

He looked at her for a long moment, almost as if he were in the process of making some decision. When he was finished, he tapped her foot with his. "Your turn."

Rolling her eyes, she sat up more and tucked an ankle under her opposite leg. Ethan hadn't moved from his position, and she had just about gotten used to seeing him sitting there without the bottom part of a leg. She was happy and relieved when he answered the door and she saw he had taken the prosthesis off. It was a test, of course—one she felt she passed with flying colors. He'd put it out there, and they dealt with it.

Blowing some hair out of her face, she shook her head, pursing her lips and wondering where to start.

"I was raised by nannies and boarding school. Sophie, Ryan, and I started at Trent Academy when we in kindergarten. It was pretty scary for a five-year-old to be dropped off and left there. My parents actually came that first year to drop me off. After that it was nannies or chauffeurs. I had Sophie, of course, and we roomed together the entire time we were there, but Ryan didn't have anyone. Sophie and I clung to each other. We were always together. She doesn't come from money, but my grandparents didn't want Sophie to be left out of the things I got, so they helped my aunt and uncle pay for the tuition each year. It couldn't have been easy on them.

"The school was okay. It had a lot of things to do. I spent most of the summers in Virginia with my grandmother. Spring break and Christmas break, I went with my parents on vacation. Depending on the time of year, it was Tahoe, Aspen, Switzerland, Paris, Monaco, the French Riviera. I literally spent a handful of days a year in my bedroom. A girl at school once asked me to describe my bedroom at home, and I couldn't do it. I made it up. Ryan and I are alike there. When he wasn't in school, he was traveling with his father on the race circuit. Though he did go home for Thanksgiving, Christmas, and spring break."

A sadness settled over Brooke as she talked of her upbringing. She didn't know there could be a different life than the boarding school route. By the time she realized there was, she had been programed to think she was better than others—to look down upon those that didn't wear the right clothes or drive the right car—basically, people like her cousin, Sophie.

But Sophie was her lifeline, and since she was also at Trent, Brooke could pretend that her cousin belonged in her bourgeois world.

Ethan had seen the war of emotions in her and began rubbing her ankle. "Hey, you okay?"

Brooke shook her head and wiped a stray tear from her eye. It was silly, really. She had made changes for the positive in herself and was proud for breaking away from a life she never felt right in. But as she sat there explaining her life to Ethan, she realized how much she had missed out on.

"Hey, hey, don't do that," Ethan said. He crawled across the couch and pulled her into his arms, shifting them on the couch to lay down. "What happened? What's got you so upset?"

"It's stupid," she said. "I had this elitist life that kids dream of growing up, and I didn't know to be grateful for it. It just was. Of course, I knew my grandparents weren't rich, but I often forgot Sophie wasn't. My whole life anything I wanted was handed to me with no effort. I was spoiled, and I acted like it. It was a big slap in the face when Jackie came to school and Ryan stopped paying attention to me. I didn't even know until recently that he and Sophie had spent most of their lives pining for each other, and there I was going after him hard because he was the most popular, the best looking, just the best in general. I didn't even love him. That's who I was, and I'm ashamed of it."

Ethan stroked her hair and pressed a kiss to her forehead. "Don't be ashamed," he whispered. "Don't ever be ashamed or apologize for who you were or who your parents raised you to be. Everything made you who you are today, and that person seems pretty amazing to me."

Brooke wiped the tears from her cheeks. "No one's ever called me amazing before."

"Another crime."

She gave a half laugh then ran her hand down his side to his hip. She marveled in how well they fit together, despite the lack of the bottom part of his leg. This was comfortable. It was something she never would have done with Josh. It was an intimacy she never shared with her husband, and she didn't realize until now just how much she had craved it.

"You're so good, Ethan," she said.

Shaking his head, his eye clouded over. It surprised her to see pain reflected back. "There's darkness in me," Ethan whispered. "I mostly do okay, but sometimes it takes over and consumes me."

It was her turn to comfort and soothe him. She didn't have much experience in it. "It can never take you over, Ethan. It will never win." She firmly believed that. Ethan did everything he was supposed to do—the therapy, the medication, the communication with his family. This was a man who accepted who he was and the battles he had to fight. He deserved to win. And she would do whatever she could to ensure that happened.

Seven

THE CREEPY FEELING of being watched woke Ethan the next morning. Shifting a bit, he realized Brooke was still in his arms. The fire had burned out, and there was a chill in the room, but during the night they gained a blanket. Natalie must have laid one over them when she came home. Smiling lightly, he pushed hair out of her face. At the clearing of a throat, he looked up to see Natalie staring down at him with an arched brow. He gave her a smirk in return. Rolling her eyes for him to follow, she walked away and into the kitchen.

Ethan gently extricated himself from Brooke and tucked the blanket around her. Bravo lay along the front of the couch on the floor. Ethan's crutches were right by the couch, another thing Natalie must have done for him. Bravo scrambled out of the way when the crutches came down. Heaving himself up, Ethan first hit the bathroom and then his bedroom to retrieve the prosthetic and put it on before joining Natalie in the kitchen.

Natalie was leaning up against the counter with her coffee mug to her face, looking curiously at him over the rim. She didn't have to speak for him to know she wanted all the details of why Brooke slept on their couch last night.

Wordlessly, Ethan walked to the cabinet to retrieve a mug. Looking down while he poured his coffee, he said, "I like her." Once his mug was full, he moved to the opposite counter and stood across from her. "I like her a lot."

"I didn't know."

Ethan shrugged and looked down at his mug. "You don't know everything about me."

"Clearly." Ethan heard the tone of her voice. Was she annoyed at not already knowing this information or at his defensive comment? "For someone who spent the night with a beautiful woman in his arms, I'd think he'd wake up in a better mood. Did you not sleep well?"

Ethan ran a hand down his face. "I slept the sleep of the dead," he said. "I haven't slept that well in months. She—"

She what? What was it about her that made him so comfortable and content? On paper, they were the most unlikely couple on the planet, but in reality, he wanted to spend as much time with her as possible. He wanted her to know him and almost felt safe sharing the ugly things about himself with her. He believed her when she said she changed.

He looked over Natalie's shoulder and out the kitchen window where the first rays of the winter morning could be seen peeking through the trees. The dawn of a new day and a second chance at whatever you needed it for. Maybe they were an odd match, but he had been given a second chance at life, and he was going all in.

"She what?" Natalie prompted.

"She makes the difference," he said. "She's important."

Lowering her mug, Natalie put one hand on the counter next to her and strummed her fingers. "This is a big deal," she noted.

"For me it is," he agreed. "I wasn't afraid when I went to war, Nat, but I'm afraid of this. I came back with more than just the scars she can see. What if it's too much for her?"

"You'll have to let her decide that," Natalie said. "Love is a risk, Ethan. That's why so many people are alone. They don't want to gamble with their heart or give up any control to someone else."

Ethan suspected they were now talking about her more than him. "You don't have to be scared of him, Nat. The man is in love with you. He's so far gone over you, it's almost painful to watch."

"I don't have to make a target of him and his little girl, do I?" She countered. Regardless of what Natalie thought, did, or said, Ethan knew that Natalie likewise had feelings for Eric.

This moment was important for a couple of reasons. First of all, they were admitting to having feelings for people, which neither of them had done before; and second, Natalie had come out and made reference to her status in hiding. It was something they danced around—talked about without using the important words. They each understood the truth and conveyed their real meaning non-verbally.

Ethan locked gazes with his twin and said as evenly and seriously as possible, "If there is anybody that can protect you, himself, and his daughter, it's him. He doesn't take missions anymore to be here for you. His teams are the best. That shouldn't be a deterrent if you love him."

"I'm not sure I do."

"Well, that's something different then," Ethan said. "But maybe he has a right to know that so he can move on? You shouldn't let him hold out hope."

Natalie shook her head quickly at the "Woof!" from the living room. Brooke must have woken up. Bravo entered the kitchen first and sat down between Ethan and Natalie. Brooke smiled sleepily at him, and he sucked in his breath. Good god, she was beautiful, even with her hair mussed up and her eyes half open. On instinct, Ethan held out his arm, and she wandered over and curled into his side. He kissed her on the forehead and she stole his coffee.

After taking a sip, her eyes widened at the strength of the brew. "That'll wake you up."

"I need a higher octane in the morning," he said. She snuggled further into him before saying good morning to Natalie, who greeted her warmly in return. It was important to Ethan that they got along.

He wasn't sure he would be able to handle tension between the girl he was seeing and the woman he shared a womb with.

"Glad I opted for the comfortable clothes," Brooke said, hiding a yawn behind her hand. "I don't think I've ever been so comfortable when I slept in my life."

Smirking at Ethan, Natalie said, "Yeah, that couch just sucks you in."

Brooke looked up at him with those sweet, brown eyes that saw so much more of him than he knew existed. "I think it might have been the company." He rewarded the compliment with a quick peck on the lips before he moved to retrieve a mug for her coffee. He could get used to this—spending mornings with her. Of course, he went to the store for breakfast every morning she worked, but this was different—more intimate.

"Natalie makes the best frittatas," he said, grinning down at her. "Maybe we can convince her to make one for breakfast."

Natalie rolled her eyes. "Way to be subtle. Why don't you just ask?"

"Please, Nat, will you make one of your amazing frittatas?" Ethan pleaded. He was no slouch in the kitchen either. He just wanted an excuse to keep Brooke in his arms for a little while longer.

"I can help," Brooke offered.

"Next time," Ethan said, tightening his arms. Dipping his head, he kissed her as if this morning was all he'd get from her. She melted under his touch and eagerly returned the kiss. Laughing lightly, he pulled away at Natalie's groan.

Brooke surprised him after breakfast with wanting to help with the animals. Ethan suspected it might be Christmas Morning she was keen to see, but he wouldn't mind any help she was willing to give. Having the most experience with horses, Brooke set out to muck out their stalls and feed them. That left Ethan free to take care of the other animals and various chores of the morning. They worked well together. After she finished with the horses, she kissed him goodbye and went about her day. She did a surprisingly thorough job cleaning the stalls.

After ensuring all the animals had water, Ethan cleaned up the tack room a bit, swept up the floor, and threw new hay down for the pigs and chickens. It wasn't long before Eric Davis showed up accompanied by his daughter Emma. The little girl ran right for the pigs, bypassing both Ethan and Bravo. Ethan shook his head. It was rare that he didn't have an armful of Emma when she was around. She absolutely adored Ethan and Natalie. They frequently babysat for her when Eric was called away for work.

"She watched Charlotte's Web last night," Eric said by way of explanation.

Nodding, Ethan put his hands in his pockets and waited for his friend to speak. He assumed Eric had come to discuss his email. Eric looked past him to where Emma was carefully opening the gate to the pigs' pen, walking in, and carefully closing it behind her. All of Ethan's animals loved Emma, so Ethan wasn't worried too much about Emma being hurt by them. But it could be inadvertent, so he and Eric stepped closer.

"Does Natalie know you're looking for your father?" Eric asked.

"Not yet," Ethan said. "I haven't had the chance to tell her." And he would. Despite her not knowing about his feelings for Brooke, Ethan tried not to keep many secrets from his sister.

Eric nodded, but didn't say anything else about Natalie. Eric Davis was a bad ass. He served in Special Forces with Danny in the Army, and then after they got out, they both went into police work. Before coming to Grayson Falls, Eric and Danny were last with the NYPD. When an old hookup ended up on Eric's doorstep, shoving two-year old Emma at him and disappearing, Eric decided to get out of the city and raise Emma in a safer environment—after a DNA test had confirmed that the little girl was, in fact, his daughter.

Now, Eric ran his security agency—a company that took on hostage recovery, kidnapping victim recovery, and other investigations into trafficking cartels. Of course, Ethan knew that the company also took on less-desirable assignments in bad parts of the world, but that's not something that was general knowledge. Ethan often manned the company's war room, while teams were out on missions, and helped with training. Lately, Eric had been consulting with Ethan about adding two dogs that Ethan would train.

"Well, preliminarily, Ethan Price lived just outside Philadelphia. His mother is a retired teacher and his father an accountant—the father died a few years ago. Price was a bit of a hot-head on the ice at least. Nothing so far has shown any sort of citation or arrest indicating that he couldn't control his temper off the ice. He liked fast cars and fast women and he partied hard."

"How hard?"

"Did a few stints in rehab for cocaine addiction," Eric said.

"So far he sounds like a great dad," Ethan said wryly.

Eric shrugged and stuck his hands in his pockets. Emma moved out of the pigs' stall and started walking down the aisle, greeting the horses. "He may not be your father. It could be Daisy Dolan just thought it was him. At the risk of sounding indelicate, she did get around." Ethan supposed he'd be more offended if he actually had any kind of relationship with his birth mother.

"I'd like you to keep digging," Ethan said. "I don't have any specific plan for what I'm going to do if it turns out he is our father, but since he's the only lead we have, I'd like to follow it."

"And if he's not?" Eric asked.

"I don't know that either," Ethan sighed.

"ETHAN!" Emma's shriek came from Christmas Morning's stall. "You got a new horse!" Turning, Ethan saw Emma jumping up trying to reach the horse's snout. Walking over, his feet echoing on the wood floor of the barn, Ethan scooped up the girl he thought of as his niece so she could pet the horse.

"She's only been here about a week now," Ethan said, running a hand along the horse's neck. He had always found comfort in his horses.

"Can I ride her?" Emma asked, bouncing in Ethan's arms. Emma was always enthusiastic and threw herself completely into whatever she was doing. She was, at times, exhausting.

"Soon," he said. "She needs to get used to being here first. I need to make sure she's safe for you. Miss Brooke rode her the other day and did fine, so I think maybe she'll be gentle enough for you."

"What's her name? Can I name her?" Emma asked.

Smiling at the girl's precociousness, Ethan held out his hand and stroked the horse's silky mane. The horse's trusting eyes were on him. Though she came from an abusive situation prior to Grayson Falls, the mare could already see the good in her new owner.

"Well, I suppose we could think about a new name," Ethan said, knowing he had no intentions of doing so. "But I think her name is pretty great already."

"What's her name?" Emma asked. "Is it Princess Persephone?"

"No, not exactly," Ethan said, chuckling. "Her name is Christmas Morning."

Emma's eyes widened and her face filled with utter delight. What could be better to a little girl than Christmas?

"I need to hug her," Emma said. Ethan leaned forward so Emma could hug the horse's neck. The mare didn't have much of a reaction, so Ethan was encouraged. Emma and Brooke certainly seemed in love, and he enjoyed the idea of watching two important females in his life get to know the horse and shower her with love. He was looking forward to one day showing his own daughter the horses. He always wanted a family of his own when the time was right, but this was the first time he was able to visualize it. It looked pretty good.

SETTLING INTO HER BORROWED corner of Piper's studio, Brooke arranged her work area to accommodate what she wanted to accomplish that day, laying out her scissors, seam ripper, and pins closed by. She was working on Christmas stockings. After the New Year, she hoped to start another queen-sized quilt, but now that she was spending time with Ethan, that might be slow going. She had other things ready to go—laptop sleeves, e-reader sleeves, purses, and a power cord holder. They were her own patterns that she had meticulously written out and copyrighted. Maybe if they ever added the quilt shop to the store, she would share them.

Smiling, she thought back to that morning when she woke up on Ethan's cozy couch. Though Ethan had already gotten up, his masculine scent lingered, and she snuggled down under the blanket to savor the last wisps of him.

Before Bravo barked and got her moving.

Ethan was affectionate. Now all she wanted was more of him, but she sensed they would have to move slowly. That was fine. Now that they were stepping forward, it was okay with her to move at his pace.

She thought of the things he revealed to her—the darkness he felt he had inside of him and how he feared it consumed him. Her heart broke for the way he suffered. Why did someone who did everything right have to hurt so badly? She suspected he would never be totally free from nightmares, but she did hope she could help him tamp down the darkness.

Was it arrogant of her to believe she could cure such a serious issue? Some veterans killed themselves because they couldn't reconcile the things they'd seen and done. Post-traumatic stress disorder was nothing to play around with. She had read everything she could find about the warning signs and treatment. Ethan's siblings rallied around him. They kept a very close watch on his moods. Ethan was lucky to have the support system he did.

She would become part of that support system.

Brooke looked up from her machine when Zach and Piper entered the studio. Zach was walking directly behind Piper with his hands splayed over her stomach, nibbling on her neck. Obviously, he was trying to convince her to put off painting for a bit. When Piper turned in his arms, Brooke looked down at her hands and back up again. That was some kind of kiss they were having considering Zach wasn't actually going anywhere.

She admired their passion. Zach had learned sign language so he could communicate with Piper. In fact, much of the town did. Danny and Jackie learned it, and Zach's brothers and Sophie were also taking classes to help them communicate better with her. Piper was beloved in Grayson Falls. Born and raised here, she had lost her hearing in college. The town rallied around her to help her succeed.

Piper wasn't helpless though. She had apps on her phone she used to speak with people, and she could also use her voice, though she just wasn't comfortable doing so. It was a very rare occurrence to hear Piper speak, so when she pushed Zach away laughing and said, "Go!" pointing her finger at the door, Brooke knew Piper was finally comfortable enough with her presence and was now part of Piper's inner circle.

Piper turned around and rolled her eyes at Brooke. In response, Brooke signed, *"He loves you so much. The way he looks at you is beautiful."*

"You have someone special that looks at you the same way."

Piper knew of Brooke's attempts to get Ethan to notice her over the months—or more than notice, to respond to her. Piper was the first person Brooke texted when Ethan didn't back out of the Over the Hop so-called invitation.

"How was the movie?" Piper asked.

Brooke smiled slyly. *"We never watched one. We talked all night and then fell asleep on the couch together. We didn't even have sex, and it was one of the best nights of my life."*

"I love nights like that," Piper signed. *"Intimacy is so much more than just sex. Sex is great, but it's not what drives all relationships. If you don't connect with someone in your heart, you'll never truly connect with them with your body."*

Piper was by far the most insightful person Brooke had ever met. She was always watching people and observing. She saw things other people never picked up on. She sat down on the stool in front of the canvas she was working on, and Brooke went back to work.

When her phone rang, she frowned when she saw the contact for the events department at the ski resort. Praying nothing was wrong with Sophie and Ryan's wedding reservation for Christmas Eve, Brooke answered.

"Hello?"

"Is this Brooke Larrabe?" the female voice on other end of the line asked.

Squinting her eyes shut, Brooke pressed two fingers to her forehead. "This is she." *Please let nothing be wrong. Please let nothing be wrong.*

"This is Robin in the events department at The Summit Ski Resort. I worked with Marcy Stone."

"Worked?"

"Yes, ma'am. Marcy is no longer with us," Robin said. "We've run into a jam."

"Please don't tell me there's a problem with the Van Stewart/Willis wedding," Brooke said. "My cousin has her heart set on a Christmas Eve wedding, and if she loses that venue she might go into some sort of suspended animation."

"Oh, no," Robin said. "Everything is fine with that. We're all set there. It's the New Years' Ball that we're having a problem with."

What? What did that have to do with Brooke? "Would you be willing to come up and talk with me? You're doing such a beautiful job on the wedding that we thought you might be able to step in and help us with the ball. I'm afraid Marcy has left us in a bit of lurch."

Stunned, Brooke open and closed her mouth. "I don't understand."

"We want to hire you, dear, to finish the planning and organizing for the ball. The wedding is going to be high-class elegance. We're so impressed with what you've done. It's exactly what we wanted for the ball, but Marcy wasn't quite getting us there. Now that she's gone, we were hoping you could pinch-hit, so to speak."

Plan the New Years' Ball? It was the biggest event of the year in Grayson Falls—even bigger than the fall Pumpkin Festival. It acted as a fundraiser for the Special Olympics and from Brooke's understanding always had a very large turnout. People from all over the state attended. She had even heard about it in Boston.

Brooke had planned events before, obviously. After all, it's what she was raised to do. She could organize an army of volunteers like a drill sergeant. And the ball was large, but not the largest event she had planned. But she wasn't a professional event planner. Was she? Was she dabbling in that now? Did she want to?

"You have impeccable taste, dear," Robin continued. *Well, of course, that's true.* "I'd consider it a personal favor if you did so. Is tomorrow afternoon a good time to meet?"

Brooke found herself in the strange position of accepting the invitation to at least meet. She would withhold acceptance of the job until she found out just what they needed and how much work was left to do. The ball would be coming on the heels of the wedding, so it would be a lot of work to take on.

But it would be fun, she thought. And many of the things she was doing for the wedding could easily carry over to the ball, which is probably why Robin called her. She made the appointment and hung up the phone. For a girl who supposedly had everything she wanted growing up, she suddenly had more options than she ever had before.

Eight

WHEN ETHAN HEARD Danny's voice, it was as if he was listening through a tunnel. Danny's words sounded hollow as they rang through his head. He blinked his eyes in an attempt to clear up his vision. He was sitting on the floor of the barn facing Christmas Morning's stall with his elbows propped on his knees and no recollection of how he got there.

His body shook. His chest felt like it was closing in on itself, and he tried to control his breathing, which was coming in harsh pants. After scratching his hands in his hair, he ran them down his face, itched roughly at his beard, and gulped for air. Danny eased down next to him to assess the situation. A former medic in the Army, Danny was not without his skills. When Ethan's breathing began to level out, Danny mirrored Ethan's position.

It wasn't comfortable on the floor of the barn. It was cold and dirty. But something inside directed him to the floor, and there he stayed. Had he blacked out again? Assessing himself for injuries, he was relieved that at least he didn't need stitches after this episode.

"Did I ever tell you about the time I got shot?" Danny asked.

"We all know the story," Ethan said, between breaths. "You and Davis ran down an alley after a perp; crazy Cooper Eden shot you; you landed in Jackie's ER, and lived happily ever after."

"That was the second time," Danny said, ignoring Ethan's sarcasm.

Rubbing his chest with one hand, Ethan pressed his other fist to his forehead. He was all right. He was home in the States, and he was safe. He wasn't injured. He and Bravo had made it home alive and were healing. Nobody said it would be easy. Ethan became cognizant of his loyal canine lying next to him and pressing his head against Ethan's leg offering whatever comfort he could. Sinking his hand into Bravo's fur, Ethan comforted his companion in return.

"We got ambushed in the Hindu Kush Mountains," Danny continued. "We worked counter-intelligence, but had bad intel. That mission was, and to the best of my knowledge, still is classified. Man, the whole thing was a clusterfuck. By some stroke of divine intervention, we had only lost two guys, but most of us were injured in some way and fighting through it. I took one in the chest and thought I was a goner for sure, but somehow Davis was able to patch me up enough to move. The walking wounded had to carry the rest of us out. It took us three days to reach a safe location. It was muddy, rainy, cold as fuck. We were low on ammo, out of food, and low on water. I have my share of nightmares from it."

"And in those nightmares, have the people in your unit ever been replaced by the people you love?"

"Well, I loved those guys," Danny replied. "But I know what you mean. And yeah, Jackie's been in the middle of that a time or two, coming to save me. She never makes it out. I wake up sweating and panting. But there she is right next to me sleeping like an angel, safe in our bed. It helps a lot to be able to touch her then. Things got better after I found Jackie again. My purpose became clear. I've been home for years, and the nightmares are infrequent now, but there was no life of leisure for me. Even before I went into the Army, I was never going to take a desk job. That's why I went into police work, to keep my moving, keep sharp. By focusing on helping people, I think less of what I saw over there. Here, I *know* I'm making a difference."

Ethan shook his head and looked down at his dog. "I don't want the edge anymore, and I don't want to keep moving. I never really craved that. I just joined the Marines to pay for college so I could improve our farm. Even then, I went to work with the dogs. I'm not sorry I did it. I was proud of the work I did. I just wish that now that

I'm home, I can *be* home. I can be present and not stuck over there. I'm getting there."

Danny stretched out one leg and rested his elbow on the bent one. The sounds of the barn—the soft rustle of the horses, the clucking of the chickens just outside the door—began to comfort Ethan. "I'd try to reassure you that you'll get there, but we both know that's bullshit," Danny said. Ethan appreciated Danny's candor. He didn't try to throw sunshine at Ethan like others might. Danny had been there and understood, and that helped.

"What are you taking for the nightmares?" Danny asked. Ethan answered and Danny nodded his head. "It doesn't sound like it's right for you, and I think it's making you faint."

Ethan paused. He hadn't thought about the side effects of his medication. He just thought things were getting worse, but Danny might be right. It was definitely worth exploring.

"You might want to think about having your doctor take you off of that."

"It's a good suggestion," Ethan said. "I'll make the appointment." Standing up, Danny offered his hand down to Ethan, who accepted it and lumbered to his feet. "Was there something you came in for?"

Scratching the back of his head, Danny winced and said, "You're going to hate this, but I came in to check on you."

"I guess this time I'm glad you did," Ethan replied.

"It's got to be frustrating, the way everyone's been hovering," Danny said.

"Sometimes." Ethan shrugged. "But their hearts are in the right place, and it's true, I have been struggling a little. I try to stay grateful I have a family that cares."

"That's what sets you apart from other guys that have issues similar to yours," Danny said. "You try to stay positive. You could have put yourself in a wheelchair and turned to the bottle, but you didn't."

Ethan didn't respond. He didn't need accolades, though Danny was really just stating the obvious. "What were you going to say if you walked in here and I was just going about my day?"

"I don't know. Thanksgiving is in a few days. I could have come up with something." That's what Ethan liked about Danny. He was honest and unapologetic. Clapping Ethan on the back, Danny gave a spread fingered wave as he walked away, looking over his shoulder.

Turning back to the barn, Ethan looked around him. A barn had always been his safe haven. The smell of the hay, the comfort of the animals, the feeling of home, and the memories of an easier, more innocent time did far more to soothe his soul than anything else could.

Ethan walked toward Christmas Morning and raised his hand to stroke her snout. His breath made small puffs of air in the frigid barn, but the sun shining through the open doors illuminated the floors and the horse, giving her a heavenly glow. The mare nuzzled into Ethan's neck—two broken souls recognizing each other, accepting each other.

Leaving the barn, Ethan adjusted the thermostat and closed the barn doors. He'd be back later to settle everyone in for the night, but for now, he gave them a nice, comfortable, and especially safe home.

BROOKE WALKED THROUGH the store, her boots clicking on the hardwood below. She was dressed up today because she already had the meeting with Robin that morning, and they had entered into a contract for Brooke to finish the planning of the New Year's ball. When Robin had given Brooke the figure the resort would pay her, Brooke immediately agreed. She hoped she hadn't looked desperate. What they were going to pay her would almost cover the costs of the renovations on the house.

"Hey, Soph!" Brooke greeted her cousin, who stood behind the register on the computer. Sophie was likely reviewing the inventory for the Christmas season, like she planned to do today.

Nodding her head in the direction of the café, Sophie greeted her back. Brooke looked over to the café to see what Sophie wanted her to look at, and Ethan sat at a table, staring down at his linked fingers with Bravo sitting next to him, resting his nose on Ethan's thigh. Ethan hadn't looked up, so Brooke supposed he didn't hear Sophie's greeting. Brow furrowed, Brooke looked back at Sophie in silent question.

"He's been here for hours," Sophie whispered. "I told him you wouldn't be in until later, but he wanted to wait. I'll cover for you. Why don't you go see what's wrong? He's barely interacted with me."

Brooke approached Ethan, heels clicking on the floors. "Ethan?" she asked, as she drew nearer. Bravo gave a whimper, and Ethan's head snapped up. Her heart turned over at the lost look in his eyes. "What happened?"

Wordlessly, he stared at her for what she thought was nearly a minute before answering her. "Can we go somewhere and talk?" His voice was rough. *He doesn't want to see me anymore. He's going to step away, and I'll be crushed.*

"Is everything all right?"

Shrugging, Ethan shook his head and looked down again.

"Okay," Brooke said slowly. "Why don't we head back to Ryan and Sophie's so I can get changed? The house is empty now."

Nodding, Ethan stood back up. When Brooke turned to head back outside, he grabbed her wrist. Tentatively, she turned. When he tugged her hand, she stepped forward and opened her arms. Sinking into her, Ethan buried his face in the crook of her neck and breathed in deeply. She began to suspect something else was at play here, and it didn't have anything to do with the status of their budding relationship. Rubbing his back, she held tight and let him take what he needed. He rubbed his bearded cheek over her shoulder, then squeezed her tighter. He smelled of the outdoors, of wood and leather. Around them, swirled the piped in holiday music and the creak of the floors as customers walked along them. When he pulled away, she cupped his cheek and pressed a kiss to his forehead. He ran his hands down her arm and stepped back.

"See you later, Soph!" Brooke called as they passed the register.

"You're on dinner," Sophie replied, agreeing to work the double shift for her cousin, Brooke knew it wouldn't come without a price, but she could handle dinner. Maybe she would make her grandmother's white sauce, and they'd have pasta. It didn't matter now. What did was getting Ethan somewhere quiet and finding out what was going on.

ETHAN FOLLOWED BROOKE inside his brother's house where they were greeted by Ryan's mutt Wilson, who bowed his head to Bravo before scurrying over to his bed by the fireplace. Wilson was not unfamiliar to Bravo, so the big dog left the little one alone and stuck by Ethan's side.

"I'm going to go upstairs and get changed," Brooke said. "Do you mind if we talk in the kitchen? I'd like to start prepping my Thanksgiving sides for Jackie and Danny's. Unless you'd rather go in the living room?"

Ethan thought about it and decided that he'd rather not have her eyes on him for the entirety of this conversation. It was enough for her to listen. "That's fine."

"All right," she said. "I'll be right back."

Ethan watched her jog up the stairs. When he saw her disappear, the house seemed empty, just like he felt. A cavern inside with thousands of nooks and crannies and sound reverberating off the walls.

While the worst of the morning's anxiety attack was over, the tension still lingered within him.

At home in his brother's house, Ethan walked to the kitchen and surveyed the contents of the refrigerator and freezer. Pulling out a couple of steaks, he set them on the counter and went about pulling contents for a marinade. If Brooke had to prepare some sides for Thanksgiving dinner, then the least Ethan could do was take care of the dinner preparation.

Entering the room in yoga pants and a hoodie, Brooke still managed to look polished. She made everything look sexy and this time, his heart sped up for other reasons.

Moving to the cabinet to start pulling out bowls and pans for her meal prep, Brooke asked over her shoulder, "What are you working on over there?"

Scoring the meat, Ethan said, "Steaks for dinner. I'm going to make a marinade and let them sit. You don't have to do all the work yourself."

Pausing before stepping over to him, Brooke placed a sweet kiss on his cheek. "Consideration. That's a rarity in the world I come from." Wrapping her arms around his waist, she rested her head on his shoulder. He turned his head to hers, and their lips met. It was soft and sweet, not with the crazed passion they had previously shared. This kiss was about intimacy and closeness, and was just the comfort he needed from her now.

"Enjoy getting used to it," he murmured against her lips.

"Mmm," she said. "I think I will enjoy getting used to this." She nearly made him forget why he came to find her—and maybe that was a good thing. Wouldn't it be amazing if she could ground him this way? Instead of medication, he could turn to her.

Except while she might want him right now, she might not want him forever. What better way to shake up the family and ex-husband then by dating a practically poor farmer and technically disabled veteran? It could be she was just getting a little rebellion out of her system.

But she seemed genuine, and that's what drew him to her. He wouldn't believe she was capable of that sort of treatment. She gave him one more kiss before she pulled away. Finished with his marinade, he returned the steaks to the refrigerator. Leaning up against the counter, he crossed his arms.

"I didn't have such a good day," he began. She stopped whisking and turned to him, leaning up against the opposite counter. He was hoping she would continue with her work so he wouldn't have to make eye contact, but as he was learning, Brooke was someone who gave her full attention to a conversation when it was important. And given the way he started off, he had indicated this one was very important.

"Why, what happened?"

"You know I have PTSD from the explosion," he said, thankful when she just nodded for him to continue. "Well, there are different ways it manifests itself. I mean, more than just nightmares. I blacked out once and put my hand through the glass of my tractor." Holding up his hand, he showed her the healing wound that Sebastian had stitched up for him. "I don't remember doing it."

"Oh, Ethan," she said softly, placing a hand over her heart.

Ethan looked away. *Why wasn't she moving around the kitchen anymore?*

"I don't tell you any of this for pity or sympathy," he said. "It happened again today. I woke up on the floor of the barn after an anxiety attack, and Danny found me. He thinks I need a medication change."

"Sounds reasonable," she said.

"After the worst of it passed, I came to the store looking for you." He drew in a deep breath as he tried to figure out how to word what he needed to say. "I wanted to be near you, with you. I forgot about the ski resort thing, so I waited. I need you to understand what you're getting into. I'm not like other men you know." He made sure to make eye contact with his next words. "I'm scarred, and there's a darkness in me that can overtake everything. It's unpredictable. I feel myself getting emotionally attached to you, and I need to know if I should step back. If this is just a fling or a little rebellion against mom and dad, that's cool, but I need to know. I can't allow myself to become emotionally dependent on you and have you just drop me. It's a lot for you to take on."

Dropping her hand from her chest, Brooke stared at him. The wait for her to speak, probably only took a second or two, felt interminable. He held his breath and became attuned to the white noises around him that seemed to echo in the silence—the light drip of the faucet, the soft sum of the refrigerator, a small click as the heat kicked on. All things that were the normal background noises of life were blaring in his head as he waited for her response.

Slowly, she nodded her head. "I see." Turning away from him, she returned to her task of food prep. Ethan let his breath out when he couldn't hold it anymore. He could tell by the tension in her shoulders and her now aggressive whisking that something wasn't right. "You don't think I've changed at all. You still see me as a spoiled little rich girl, playing games. Maybe I've gone slumming, huh?"

Speechless, Ethan gaped at her. "No," he said. "I don't think that at all."

Slamming down her wooden spoon, Brooke spun on him. His chest tightened when he saw the tears in her eyes. The tears *he* put there. "Don't lie, Ethan. That's exactly what you just asked me. I deserve it, I guess, for my past sins. It's too far-fetched to think that someone of my supposed stature can actually care about you. I must have some sort of superficial motive."

Ethan pressed his palms to his eyes and resisted the urge to roar. He made a mess out of this. That's not what he thought, but she was right, it was exactly what he said, or at least implied.

"You didn't deserve that," Ethan said. "You've been nothing but a good friend to me, and I got ugly. The truth is, I'm scared. You're the first woman that's meant anything to me since I was deployed. I don't know what to do. I don't know what you want. I only know what I need. And what I need to know most is," he shrugged his shoulders and dropped his hands to his side, "what I need to know most is that you're serious about this ... about me ... about *us*."

Brooke crossed her arms and glared at him. "You did get ugly about it," she said. "I'm glad you're talking to me and being open about it, but there's a better way to word things. Promise me you'll work on that, and I'll stop being mad about your presentation."

Nodding his head, he said, "I'll probably mess it up, but I'll try."

Walking over to him, Brooke wrapped her arms around him. "I'm in this for as long as you'll have me, Ethan."

Burying his face in the crook of her neck, he bound his arms around her. He took a deep breath in and slowly let it back out again. "That might be a long time."

"Sounds good to me," she said. "And I like that you came to me. I'm getting emotionally attached to you, too. If I'm being honest, I have been for a while now."

"Yeah?"

"Yeah."

"That's nice to know," he said.

Pulling back, she placed a gentle kiss on his lips. "We've both come so far but still have a long way to go. Maybe we can get there together."

Tipping his head against hers, he closed his eyes. Rubbing her arms, he stepped back. "Tell me what's in the fridge that I can use for some side dishes with dinner. I'll work on that while you're doing your Thanksgiving dishes."

He was relieved when she allowed the topic change. He handled the conversation badly. He wasn't used to opening up quite as much and especially to a woman. His last meaningful relationship was before he was deployed, and he split up with the girl before he left. While he was away, he found out that she met someone new and got married, solidifying that he had made the right decision not to leave anyone other than his parents behind.

After prepping his potatoes and green beans, he walked out onto Ryan's patio to start the grill. When he returned, he did what he could to help Brooke, taking things out of the oven, straining boiling pots, going wherever she pointed him. They worked well together, never getting in each other's way. It reminded him of the way he and Natalie orbited each other when they worked in the kitchen together. Was it possible he and Brooke understood each other on a level he shared with his twin? Could he be that lucky?

Bundling up in his coat, Ethan grabbed the steaks and a beer and headed out back to put dinner on. Ryan found him out there a few minutes later.

"Hey, you didn't need to make dinner," Ryan said.

Shrugging, Ethan poked at the steaks. "Gave me something to do."

"Did you need to talk to me about something?" Ryan asked. Ethan shook his head. "Sophie?" Again, Ethan shook his head. Silence stretched between them. "Ah," Ryan said when he finally spoke again. "So, Brooke is the girl you're interested in. I should have seen it sooner. The sexual tension between you two is combustible."

"There's more to her than her sex appeal."

"I know," Ryan said. "She lives with me, remember? She's certainly not the girl I used to hook up with in school."

"And if we could never mention that again," Ethan said. "That'd be great."

Ryan held up his hands in peace, a bottle in each one, and handed Ethan another beer.

"You were concerned about starting anything with a woman," Ryan said.

"I just feel comfortable around her. I find that I *want* to tell her all the things about me that I don't share with anyone. She gets me, and she's patient. She told me about the past version of her, but that's not who she is anymore. She listens, and she doesn't judge."

Ryan clinked his beer bottle with Ethan's. "If you're happy, I'm happy."

Ethan took a long pull of his beer before he nodded his thanks. He was happy. He just hoped it stayed that way.

Nine

ALL OF ETHAN'S siblings were in attendance at Thanksgiving dinner with their significant others, along with Ryan's father, Zach's father, Sebastian's sister Shannon, Eric Davis, his daughter, and Brooke—Megan and Sebastian even stopped by for a little while before they left for Megan's family's gathering. Brooke and Ethan had made it a point to arrive together. It was sort of their little announcement to the family that they were an item, but no one seemed to think anything of it. The only strange look received was when Jackie cocked her head to the side and gave Brooke a curious look, but she said nothing. Brooke thought that perhaps Jackie was remembering how she was in school and wondering what her motives were with another one of her brothers. Brooke and Jackie had buried the hatchet before Jackie's wedding, but they certainly weren't besties.

After the controlled chaos of dinner, as dishes were passed, toasts were made, and stories were told, Ethan picked up a guitar and sat next to Danny, who was already playing. The football game was on the television on mute—Zach, Eric, and Dr. Porter were the only ones paying attention to it. Everyone else was drinking, talking, and picking at the food that remained on the table. Brooke stayed close to Ethan as he played the guitar. It was a side to him that she hadn't seen yet, and she found that musician Ethan was just as hot as farmer Ethan, horse riding Ethan, and morning Ethan. Danny and Ethan were a pretty tight duet and Brooke knew that they played together often. She smiled as she watched Ethan's fingers strum over the strings. That was the guitar she bought for him. Granted, she was replacing the one Sophie clubbed over the head of one of Cooper Eden's goons, but it warmed her to know he played it.

Inevitably, talk turned to Ryan and Sophie's wedding and then Zach and Piper's. Brooke was genuinely happy for her cousin as Sophie gushed about the details of the wedding and the honeymoon to follow. Ryan was keeping the trip a surprise for Sophie. Brooke agreed to pack Sophie up so she wouldn't know if they were going to a warm or cold climate. Brooke was the only person that knew Ryan was taking Sophie on a three-week tour of Europe. Sophie, of course, would freak out about being away from the store that long, but Brooke would handle it. They had a part-time worker, as well, who would pitch in to cover for Sophie when Brooke couldn't be there.

While Ethan seemed lost in the music he played and tuned out to the boisterous conversation and barking dogs that swirled around them, Brooke took the scene in. Sophie and Brooke were the only grandchildren on their mothers' side of the family and holiday get togethers were small and quiet. This one was busy and everywhere.

She watched as Piper curled up next to Zach on the couch. What did Piper feel like in gatherings like this? She couldn't hear what was going on around her, but someone always gently nudged her to draw her into the conversation.

Ryan's father, Toby, cooed and played with his honorary granddaughter, Jackie and Danny's baby Ally. Eric's daughter, Emma, propped herself up on Bravo and brushed her doll's hair. Jackie, Sophie, and Natalie were looking over paint colors as Jackie talked about remodeling the downstairs guest bedroom.

No one was cleaning up and Brooke took the opportunity to take a break from the mayhem.

Ethan found her putting food in containers in the kitchen. He knew she had only taken the task on herself to escape the overpowering family dynamic in the living room. She liked these people. They were her friends and family, but she always got a little overwhelmed when everyone was together.

"Hiding?" Ethan asked her. He turned and leaned against the counter next to where she was working, crossing his arms over his chest.

"Just for a little bit," she admitted. She would always be sure there was truth between them. After living the lies of her marriage, she refused to go into any relationship not being truthful. "Does that make me a bad person?"

"They're my family," Ethan said. "And they overwhelm me at times too. It's not unusual for me to pop into another room or outside to recharge." Pushing away from the counter, he took her wrist in his hand. "Speaking of outside, I need to check on the animals and bed them down for the night. Why don't you come out and help me?"

Taking the life-line he was offering, she finished putting the mashed potatoes into a plastic container and stored them in the fridge with others full of cinnamon nutmeg apples, potato and bleu cheese tart, parmesan asparagus, and other delicious dishes they all created. Stepping back from the fridge, she took a second to marvel at how easily this group of people worked together to create something amazing. Something as easy and as complicated as Thanksgiving dinner.

Shaking her head, she closed the refrigerator and turned to Ethan. He was part of the enigma that was this fascinating family. He offered her his hand, and when she took it, he raised it to his lips and kissed the inside of her wrist. She was quickly approaching the point of no return. Giving her a gentle tug, his other hand wound up the back of her neck and she stepped forward, feeling the heat from his body. Their lips met in a sweet stolen kiss. The sounds from the living room faded away, and he was the only thought left behind.

"I'm telling you, brussels sprouts, no matter how they're prepared, smell and are disgusting." Ethan's brother Zach entered the room talking over his shoulder, breaking the moment between them.

Pulling away just slightly, Ethan and Brooke kept their eyes only on each other. "Oh, whoops. Sorry, dude." Zach said as he noticed his bad timing.

Ethan stepped back and looked at his brother. "We were just heading out to the barn to settle the animals in for the night."

Zach put the dish on the counter and turned to them. "Is that what the kids are calling it nowadays?" He raised his fingers into air quotes. "Settling the animals in for the night?"

Rolling his eyes, Ethan began to lead Brooke out of the kitchen. "You're such the comedian, dickhead."

"And you're going to go get it on in a hayloft," Zach called back as they left the kitchen.

"Sorry about him," Ethan said to Brooke.

"I don't know." She said. "Getting it on in a hayloft sounds kind of exciting."

Ethan stopped next to the dining room table, still strewn with flatware, glasses, and plates. Most of the food had already been cleared but some was still out. "It's not all it's cracked up to be. Getting stuck by straw is annoying. It smells, and there might be snakes. But if you want to give it a whirl, I definitely recommend waiting for warmer weather."

Brooke's jaw fell open before she snapped it back shut. Now she had *that* in her head. So far, they had only kissed—heavy at times, gentler at others—but the thought of being with him anywhere at all had her heart racing and her blood warming. She broke away from his intense gaze and walked to the coat-rack to retrieve her cold weather gear.

Charades had begun in the living room, and the teams were set. Emma lay on the floor with Wilson and Bravo, the dogs patiently allowing her to curl up and snuggle with them, but when Bravo saw Ethan reach for his coat, he bounded up and trotted over. Reaching down, Brooke scratched behind his ears. Bravo replied with a small wag of his tail. He knew her to be a friend, but hadn't yet embraced her into his tight circle of those he loved. That was all right, she thought. He was like his master—slow to trust and moving at his own pace.

Once Ethan was likewise bundled up, they stepped out onto the front porch, closing the door on the laughter and loud voices now muffled in the peace of the cold, New England evening. Inhaling deeply of the fresh air, Brooke walked down the front steps and looked up at the night. Diamonds splashed all over the black canvas of sky. She had missed this in Boston. Looking up there, you only ever saw a small spattering of stars, but here in the Great North Woods, you saw them all.

Ethan held out his hand, and she took it. Bravo took the lead as they had a short, easy stroll to the barn.

"It's so quiet and peaceful out here," she said softly, breath coming out in little white wisps. "I'm still not used to the big family. I didn't have that growing up."

"None of us did," Ethan said. "Except for Sebastian, we were all only children. This is still kind of new for us, too. Sometimes the noise gets to me. And when we're all together, the space can get tight. They're used to my disappearing act."

They approached the barn, and Bravo ran up to the door. A single flood light shined overhead. Sliding the door open, Ethan walked in and turned on the overhead lights, three large industrial lights hanging from the ceiling. They provided a dim glow over the mammoth space. Ethan slid the door closed again once they were inside it. It was slightly warmer in here, but not so warm she could take off her coat. It was just a more comfortable temperature for the animals. The scent of hay filled her nose, and even the barn had a calmness about it. Darkness still filled the corners of the stalls. She knew there was a hayloft, but she couldn't find it in the inky black, even with the lights.

Bravo curled up on his red plaid pillow, and Ethan moved to the pigs first. He had a routine. She learned it during the few times she had helped out. The wood floors creaked under her boots as she approached Christmas Morning's stall. The mare's head poked out just as she got there. Brooke's hand immediately came up, and she stroked the horse's snout.

"Hey there, beautiful," she whispered. The horse swished her tail and nuzzled Brooke's hand again. There was something about this horse that drew her in—the wisdom and soul she saw in her dark eyes. She was a creature that knew pain and was a survivor. Despite the cruelty of her past, her big heart remained intact.

Brooke grabbed the shovel leaning up against the wall and the blue muck sack by its handles. The stall had already been cleaned earlier in the day, but a quick clean now would make less work later.

Ethan was definitely rubbing off on her.

She shoveled the manure into the sack. This was the unglamorous part of being an equestrian, and at school, someone else did the job. Once that unpleasant task was complete, she checked Christmas Morning's blanket. Ensuring it was secure, she moved to the feed bag and replenished the horse's food and water. Moving to Ethan's basket of apples, she gave the horse an evening treat before moving on to the next stall. There were four horses in all. When Ethan had finished with the pigs and chickens, he took care of the last horse.

Once she was finished with the third horse, she walked back to Christmas Morning. There was some sort of gravitational pull that always drew her in. She wondered if the horse also felt the connection with her or if it was only on Brooke's end. When the horse nuzzled Brooke's face, she thought that the feeling just might be mutual.

"That horse sure does like you," Ethan said, approaching them from behind.

"The feeling is entirely mutual."

"I like you, too." The words were spoken softly. A chill ran down her spine. Slowly, she turned toward him, her breath catching at the look of vulnerability on his handsome face.

"The feeling is entirely mutual," she whispered. She felt as exposed as he looked. Two people hurt so badly in different ways, but given a second chance at the life they wanted. She wanted to heal him. She hoped they could heal each other.

"Come home with me tonight and stay," he said. She nodded. There was no other answer but yes, and words failed her.

He stretched his hand out to her again, and she took it. The electricity between them now hummed in anticipation of what they'd silently agreed to do. Ethan closed up the barn, Bravo by their side again.

"I need to get some things from Ryan and Sophie's," she said. "Do you mind walking down there and back to the car?"

"A stroll under the stars with a captivating woman? What is there to mind about that?"

She knew his leg pained him in the evening, but he didn't spend much time standing today. Other than the normal care of the animals, he hadn't done any work on the farm.

Solar lights ran along the dirt road leading from Jackie's house to Ryan's. Dense forest and blackness were all around them. It spooked her out a bit, but she watched Bravo closely for any sign that a bear or other animal was near. Bravo merely trotted along, sniffing here and there, raising his leg a few times, nothing concerning.

A single lamp burned in the front window as they approach her cousin's mountain-chic home. Security lights lit up the yard as motion was detected. After having his house broken into, Ryan took no chances on Sophie's safety. Brooke took out her key, and they entered the house. She disengaged the alarm, knowing that even then Eric Davis would be a getting an alert on his phone that someone had entered Ryan's house. Eric handled the security for all of them, and it was something he took very seriously. She tried not to think that by doing so, he knew all their movements, all their normal schedules. It should give her comfort, but quite frankly, sometimes it creeped her out.

There were two dog beds in the living room. Despite only having one dog, Ryan was enough of a sucker to leave an extra bed for when Ethan or Zach's dogs came for a visit. After Bravo had run through the whole house—checking it for anything amiss—he investigated both beds, made his selection, and dropped down with a cross between a groan and a grunt.

After removing their coats and shoes, Brooke walked up the stairs toward her room, Ethan following behind. The energy between them cracked. Maybe it was just overactive phenomes, but they were alone, things around them were quiet, and she didn't want to wait another minute to be with him.

ETHAN HADN'T INTENDED to follow Brooke upstairs. But when they entered the house, the quiet surrounded them. Bravo settled in for some sleep. Things just began to feel different. With the way Brooke had moved, trailing her fingers along the bannister on her way up the open staircase, his feet just went into motion. Her curves called to him, dared him to follow, and he was helpless to do otherwise. The invisible tether connecting them pulled him along. She sent one look over her shoulder—lush lips parted, sultry eyes heavy—and he knew she felt it too.

The air between them exploded. As soon as she stepped over the threshold of her bedroom, she stopped, facing away from him. He lay his trembling hands on her hips, bringing her back against his body, already tight and coiling to spring. The shaking spread out and rolled through him. This was the moment he both feared and awaited since he had been injured. It was always a faceless woman that rejected him, preferring no man to one who wasn't whole. His heart knew she wouldn't turn him away, but part of his mind thought differently.

Settling against him, she tipped her head to the side, and he lowered his lips to her smooth, soft skin. He heard the sharp intake of her breath as he trailed his open mouth up her neck to her jaw. Her breathing became heavy, and he glided one hand over her rib cage, coming to a stop just under her breast.

Fighting against the terror inside and overall feeling of inadequacy, his other arm came across her chest, and he hugged her to him, dropping his forehead to her shoulder. Inhaling deeply of her scent, a shuddered breath came out again.

Her hand slipped up his neck and into his hair, cradling his head in place. "I want this, Ethan," she whispered. "I want *you*."

Eyes watering, he squeezed his lids shut. Of course, she knew just want he needed to hear, just how to comfort and encourage him. He took a moment to get ahold of himself. He wouldn't—couldn't—break in front of her. Ethan eased her simple green Henley up and over her head. Once freed, she shook her hair out and waves of luscious russet fell down her back.

His hands came up then to her breasts as his mouth sucked, nipped, and kissed his way around her neck, her jaw. She turned in his arms and began to unbutton his shirt. He stayed her hand out of reflex. "You may not like what you see there," he warned.

Fire jumped into her eyes, and he cursed his words. He meant to warn her of the patchwork quilt of scars on his chest and back, but he knew then she had taken them to mean she was looking for the perfect specimen of man. Though he was loathed to have that look directed at him, it was that fire he craved. He wanted to be consumed by it, blinded by it.

"I only want to see *you*, Ethan," she hissed. "I don't want anybody else. I don't expect you to be or look like anyone but you. When will you see that?"

Helpless, he shook his head. "I don't know," he whispered, the pain evident in his voice. This was not the passion he wanted to show her—the show of strength he *needed* to show her.

She looked at him, whiskey eyes moving rapidly back and forth, a decision being made. *Please God, let me not have ruined the mood.*

"Then I'll just have to show you," she said.

Gripping the ends of his shirt tight she ripped the fabric open the rest of the way, buttons popping off and shooting in different directions. His control snapped. Suddenly, it didn't matter what she saw. It didn't matter that his body was flawed. He needed to get at that fire. The spark she had ignited in him turned to an inferno.

Fumbling, they unfastened each other's pants, pushed them over hips, and stepped out as they turned, tripped, and finally fell onto the bed with him on top. She slipped her way up to the pillows and like a predator with cornered prey, he stalked her. He was just about to settle down over her when his prosthetic got caught on the quilt covering her bed.

Reality crashed down around him. Sitting back on the mattress, he looked at his leg hanging over the side. What did he *do* with it? Did he try to keep it on or fumble his way through without it? The time for a decision had come.

Brooke came up behind him on her knees and kissed his bare shoulder. "Whatever makes you comfortable, Ethan," she said. "We'll try it with it on and with it off."

Ethan blew out a half laugh and smiled, turning his head toward her, hands clenching the quilt underneath them. "You're already planning on another time?"

"I'm planning on many times," she grinned. "Sitting, standing, top, bottom, shower, with, without it." Her hand slid up and cupped his cheek. "We'll find our rhythm. Any way it happens will be perfect."

His chest filled. Oh, how she empowered him. He could only pray he returned the same to her. Decision made, he released the pressure and removed the prosthetic, leaning it up against the nightstand next to the bed. She eased back into the pillows and held her arms open to him. He lowered to his knees and paused waiting for some kind of pain or mishap, but there was none. He crawled after her and hovered above, looking down to her eyes that were dark with lust but bright with emotion. Running a hand down the side of her body, he took her in. He knew she'd be perfect, not a blemish to be found. Hills and valleys of milky white skin, legs that went on for days.

She raised up and began kissing along his shoulders, his chest, his pecs, running her tongue around his nipples. She hooked an ankle around his and pulled him closer. Propped up on his hands, he slowly lowered himself down to her with a muscle control stemming from hours of activity and the back-breaking work of a farm.

Their lips met as he began to grind against her. Sliding his hand behind her back, he unsnapped her bra with a quick snap of his fingers. Frantically, she pulled it away to offer her freed breasts up to his touch.

And touch he did.

He palmed them, ran his thumbs over her nipples, covered them in kisses, first one then the other before finally taking the pebbled peaks into his mouth. She jackknifed off the bed and called out his name. He stopped suddenly, raising his head and meeting her blissful gaze. And if in that moment she wasn't the most beautiful thing he had ever seen, he didn't know what else could possibly compare.

She let out a giggle. "I didn't know that could happen just from this."

"That was the best thing ever," he said. She laughed and brought her hands to his shoulders.

Taking advantage of her sensitivity, he slid his hand down between her legs and found her ready. He looked over his shoulder to where his pants lay on the floor and realized with horror he had forgotten one tiny but important detail.

He really was out of practice.

Dropping his forehead to hers, he groaned. "Don't kill me. I forgot about a condom."

"Bedside table drawer."

He picked up his head and furrowed his brow. "Just how many guys have you been entertaining in here?"

"Just you," she said with a laugh. "They're for you. I brought them back from the store. I figured, you never know, right?"

Reaching over, he pulled the drawer open. "You're certainly more prepared than me." He found the box, removed the condom, ripped open the foil packet, and sheathed himself as quickly as he possibly could.

As he slid inside her, propped on his knees, he thanked God the injury hadn't taken his entire leg. While she probably had to get used to not feeling one of his legs where it should have been, so far, everything was working.

Once he was fully buried inside of her, he dropped his head to her shoulder, squeezing his eyes shut against the tears that had returned. He had never felt like this before—this feeling of contentment, of belonging, of knowing he had found his other half. She brought her hips up to encourage him to move, but he needed just one more minute to absorb the moment.

Finally, he began to slowly move his hips—slow, long thrusts. She threw her head back into the pillow and he opened his eyes to watch her as he moved—enthralled by the sheer beauty beneath him.

Beauty and the Beast.

But he didn't feel like a beast. He felt invigorated, strong ... whole. His leg hadn't been a hindrance.

Slow thrusts turned into a maddening frenzy of speed. She chanted his name in an ancient. Delirious with the sensation building up inside him, he continued on, reaching, reaching for glory at the end of the line, and realizing that his arms were already full of the prize.

This time, his name came out of her in a breathless whisper. His release exploded out of him, and he felt himself break into pieces. It rolled through him in wave after wave, filling all the little dark crevices inside with a light brighter than he had ever felt. She did that. She was the light. This girl who had showed up on his farm in stiletto boots and designer jeans and reinvented herself because she didn't like who she'd become.

She destroyed him.

He collapsed on top of her before rolling to his side and pulling her close, dropping a kiss on her temple.

"Thank you," he said.

"For?"

"Bringing me back to the land of the living."

"Oh, it was my singular pleasure," she said. He smiled.

"I need to take care of the condom," he said.

"Well, that's not sexy." He kissed her then, long and lazy. When he lifted his head, her eyes were heavy and her grin stupidly happy. "Hurry back."

"I'm going to stop in Ryan's room for something to wear." He pushed himself up and realized he didn't have his crutches. He would have to reattach the prosthesis and take it off again when he climbed back into bed. It was inconvenient and he briefly wondered if he should leave an extra set here.

Brooke rolled to her side and ran a hand along his back. She pushed herself up and kissed his shoulder.

"We did good," she said.

"Good?" He arched a playful brow at her.

"Amazing." He couldn't agree more. "Let's get some rest and then do that again. Bring the garbage can from the bathroom back so you don't have to keep getting up."

He reattached the prosthesis and stood up, naked before her now, tattoos and scars on display. Her hungry gaze took him in from head to toe. He knew what she saw—ripped muscles and a lean physique—covered in the scars of war. He took care of his body, ensuring that the rest of him made up for what he lacked.

He went into the bathroom, disposed of the condom, and returned to put the garbage can discreetly next to the bed before heading to Ryan's room. Not being as familiar with his brother's room as he was in his brother's kitchen, he pulled a few drawers open before he found a pair of flannel pants and a New England Maverick's t-shirt. Back at the bedroom door, he whistled for Bravo, who came bounding up the stairs. Ethan led the dog into the room. While Ethan was gone, Brooke had picked up their clothes from the floor and changed into a silk pajama set. It wasn't in any way revealing, but made his mouth water all the same.

Closing the door, he walked back to the bed as she pulled down the covers. After removing the prothesis again, he slid between the flannel sheets with her, and Bravo curled up on the floor. Brooke reached over and turned off the light before curling down into his arms.

This was home, he thought. *This was peace.*

Ten

BROOKE AWOKE TO violent flailing and thrashing. Sitting up, she reached over and turned on the light. Bravo jumped up on the bed and whimpering, lay across Ethan, who was enthralled in a nightmare. Wary of what would happen if she didn't wake him, she reached over and tried to shake his shoulders. She called his name. A fist swung out, and she ducked, narrowly missing a right hook to her jaw.

Her heart raced in fear. *What if he hurt himself?*

Seconds after Ethan let loose a thunderous "No!" the bedroom door flew open and Ryan was there. She looked helplessly at him. Seeing Brooke struggling to bring Ethan out of the dream, Ryan ran into the bathroom and returned with a cup of cold water, which he tossed into Ethan's face. Ethan stilled a fraction of a second before opening his eyes and sputtering, wiping at the water dripping down his face.

"What the hell, man?" Ethan growled.

"You tell me," Ryan said, keeping his voice calm. "You looked like you were having one hell of a nightmare. Brooke couldn't get you out of it."

Ethan turned to her and grabbed her shoulders. "Did I hurt you?" he asked desperately. "Please tell me I didn't hurt you." Speechless, she shook her head. "Don't lie."

"You didn't hurt me," she whispered.

But he almost did.

She wouldn't tell him. The agony in his eyes would only increase if he knew he had come close. He might decide to leave, and she couldn't bear that. Scooting closer, she rubbed his back in what she

109

hoped were soothing circles as Ethan struggled to get his breathing under control.

Sophie appeared at Ryan's side and took hold of his hand. "Come back to bed, Ry," she said softly. "Brooke has things well in hand." Did she though? She wasn't so sure.

Brooke looked up at Ryan hoping to see some encouragement there, but Ryan looked as helpless as she felt. She couldn't fight these demons. Only Ethan could.

"E?" Ryan asked.

Ethan held up his hand. "Go." His voice was hoarse, and he was taking deep breaths.

Ryan waited and watched before finally letting out a sigh. "Wake me up if you need to talk," he said. Ethan nodded. "Wake me up if you need anything at all."

"Just go back to bed," Ethan snapped. Taken aback by the harshness of his tone, Brooke looked up at Ryan. Ryan's jaw clenched. She knew him well-enough to know that his first instinct was to snap right back at his brother, but Ethan wasn't in a good place. Reason won out. Without another word, Ryan spun on his heel and left the bedroom, closing the door behind him.

Ethan gave Bravo a nudge, and his trusty companion jumped to the floor. He sat next to the bed and rested his face on the mattress. Brooke took her cues from the dog. If Bravo wasn't comfortable that the worst was over, neither was she.

Ethan scrubbed his hands down his face and started to rise. "I have to go." She reached for him as he stood, but missed, causing him to lose his balance. He grabbed onto the nightstand and she launched to her knees, grabbing him around the waist and throwing her body toward the bed, tumbling to the mattress. She didn't think either one of them could handle it right now if he fell.

Breathing heavily, they both stayed there—her back pressed to the mattress, his body dead weight on top of her. She stared at the ceiling, woefully unqualified to handle a situation like this. He didn't need *her*. He needed his therapist.

"I don't want to be here," he said softly, his voice laced with emotion.

"That's a lie," she said forcefully. "And if you leave now, you'll drive a wedge between us. I'm all in this. You leaving will tell me you're not."

He pushed back from her, and her breath caught at the glimpse of the darkness within him—the ugliness that unleashed itself in his dreams.

His face turned to pain when he looked at her. "You're breaking me apart," he said with such raw emotion it caused tears to form in her eyes. "I don't know if I can do this."

Her heart cracked in two. The tears slipped from her eyes and down her cheeks. Oh, her brave Ethan. She had no idea of the true struggle within him. Nothing she had read prepared her for the reality of him.

Tentatively, she crawled over to him and settled herself in his lap, wrapping her legs and arms around him. "Let me be there for you, Ethan. Let me be the one you turn to in the night when the ugliness comes." Binding his arms around her, he sobbed once into her shoulder. His arms tightened, and she said not a word. She just let him hold on.

WHEN ETHAN AWOKE WITH the early fingers of dawn slipping through the curtains, the first thing he noticed was the luscious, warm body draped over him. He spent hours staring up at the ceiling before he fell asleep again. She said he didn't hurt her, and he believed her. But the fear he saw in her eyes said he'd at least come close.

Gently, he brushed the hair from her face with his finger. She didn't consider being called beautiful a compliment, but she was—inside and out. It had been a long time since he took comfort from anyone but his dog. He acknowledged it from his siblings, but he never *took* it—never absorbed himself in the compassion of another person—at least not recently.

She had broken him last night. First, when they made love and then again when she clung to him as if she could pull the demons from his soul and vanquish them herself. If only she could.

She had fought for them last night. She was fierce. He didn't want to stay and fight. He was going to run, lick his wounds in the darkness of his own bedroom, and then avoid her. When he realized he'd been caught up in a nightmare that she witnessed, it hit the panic button inside him. He was mortified. He'd woken up the whole house and then snapped at them for showing concern.

Though he wished to pull the covers up over his head and hide from the world today, he knew all too well he couldn't. He had animals that depended on him, and it was time to face the music. Gently extricating himself from Brooke and sitting up, he swung his legs over the side of the bed. After scrubbing his hands over his face, he rolled up his pant leg and picked up his prosthetic. Last night was a milestone in his recovery. He had once again proven that there was something he could do just as well as he used to before the injury that took the lower part of his leg. He was feeling pretty good about things when they went to sleep.

And then the nightmare hit. This one was different. He was clearing an open space of mines with Bravo in the desert—the sun beating down, the oppressive heat visible in the shaky air and making the seventy pounds of gear on his back feel like he had the entire weight of the world on his shoulders. A small house sat in the distance, and he remembered feeling a burning need to get to it as soon as possible. Slowly, quadrant by quadrant, he and Bravo worked to clear the field in front of them. They were alone. There was no sign of his unit, or even a vehicle that may have brought them there. In the dream, that didn't seem odd to him.

Steadily, they moved, flagging the spots where Bravo alerted. The front door of the concrete house opened, and Ethan immediately went for his rifle, swinging it over his shoulder and sighting in less than a second. Bravo snarled and barked at his side.

It was a woman, shrieking and running toward him, and his first thought was that she was a suicide bomber. As she drew closer, he realized she was screaming his name, long brown tresses streaming along behind her. With horror, he realized it was Brooke and swung his gun back over his shoulder, holding his hands out.

"Baby, stop! Don't move! Let me come to you!" He screamed until his voice was hoarse, but she didn't listen. Maybe she couldn't hear him. White hot terror was on her face as she drew closer, and he continued to yell at her to stop moving. Just when he thought he might be able to reach her—that she was only steps from his arms—fire shot from the ground like a geyser.

"NOOOO!" he screamed, then fell to his knees, agony crushing through him, ripping his chest open. He stayed there on his knees weeping until it started to rain. He woke up to cold water on his face, sputtering. The second he saw Ryan's worried face, he had spun on Brooke to make sure she was all right—to ensure she was all in one piece, and he hadn't hurt her.

That one would stick with him for a while.

"Ethan?" A soft hand ran up his back. Her raspy morning voice was sexy as hell.

Leaning back, he pressed a kiss to her cheek. "Go back to sleep. I'm going to head to the farm to take care of the animals."

Pushing up on her hand, she said, "I'll come with you. Then maybe we can go get breakfast."

"If you don't fall back asleep, you can come. I'm going to go downstairs and get some coffee." She dropped back into the pillows, and he was pretty sure she was asleep before he got to the door. He picked up his clothes and patted his thigh for Bravo to follow. Ethan ducked into the hall bathroom to change and take care of other morning necessities, before plodding downstairs and opening the front door for Bravo to go out.

A light burned from the kitchen, and the smell of fresh coffee wafted out. He knew he was about to deal with Ryan, Sophie, or possibly both. Crossing over the threshold of the kitchen, he saw his brother leaning up against the counter with a mug to his face.

Gentlemen, start your engines. Ryan slid along the counter so Ethan had access to the mugs and coffeepot. Silently, Ethan retrieved a mug and filled it. He took a sip and nearly burned his lips. Ethan took up a spot opposite his brother, and they held each other's eyes, each assessing the other.

"I'm assuming you don't want to talk about it," Ryan began.

Ethan shrugged and raised his coffee to his lips. "Nothing to talk about. It was a bad dream. Everybody has them."

"It was a nightmare. And not everybody has them like that. You screamed, and she couldn't wake you up," Ryan said.

"There's still nothing to talk about," Ethan replied. "They come, and they go."

"Okay, fine," Ryan waved off. Though his brother seemed like he was dropping that line of conversation, Ethan was sure he wouldn't hear the last of it. "You and I had a conversation in my office about *other* things. You're cozying up with Brooke in my house."

"I'm not *cozying up*. We're in a relationship." Ethan said. He felt a strange release of pressure when he said that—a calmness he needed to offset the chaos of the night.

"And? Do you still have concerns?" Ryan asked.

Ethan took a deep breath and let it out. His brother was only following up on issues that Ethan had dumped in his lap. "Some," he confessed. "But it's good. It's really good. She gets me. Sometimes it's like she knows what I'm thinking."

"That's the way it should be when you're in love," Ryan said, lifting his mug and drinking.

Ethan rolled that around in his head. It didn't scare him or make him nervous like he may have thought before. With Brooke, it felt *right*. There was a woman out there that wanted him, thorns and all. But could she *love* him? He realized then in his brother's kitchen, as dawn was rising after a hellish night, in those quiet hours of the day when anything seemed possible, that he had been falling in love with her since the day she showed up on his farm in stiletto boots.

"When I was overseas, I wasn't afraid of dying," Ethan said. "I was afraid I'd get my dog hurt, but for myself, I had a job to do. Fear of death was counter-productive when you worked with bomb sniffing dogs. But I'm afraid to hurt her. It terrifies me to get in this deep and then lose her. I'm not sure I can survive that."

"You're the strongest person I know, E." Ryan said. When Ethan opened his mouth to object, Ryan held up his hand to cut him off. "I know you hate the hero label. But what you've survived, what you overcame and continue to battle, there's nothing you can't do."

His brother was wrong, of course, Ethan thought. He couldn't beat this illness that threatened to eat him alive. There was no cure for PTSD. There was only managing it. He had an appointment with his therapist to talk about changing his medication, and hopefully that would work. But this was his life, and it would only ever be degrees of this. It was a lot to ask a person to take on.

Finishing his coffee, he stepped out of the kitchen just in time to see Brooke hurrying down the stairs, bleary-eyed, hair a nest on top of her head, zipping up a hoodie. Sitting down by the door, she bypassed her comfortable Uggs and went for the more utilitarian boots she wore around the barn and when she went riding.

"I'm ready, I'm ready." She hurried, leaning back and tugging on her boots.

Amused, Ethan watched her. Where was the polished princess now? This girl was a hot mess and damn if he didn't love her for it. "Can I get you a to-go cup?"

Pausing, she looked up at him, and blowing the bangs off her forehead, she said, "Oh, dear lord, yes."

Chuckling, Ethan turned back into the kitchen and made up her coffee for her while she tugged on her coat. Smirking, Ryan turned away from his brother. When Ethan had Brooke's coffee ready, he walked to the door get his own coat on. She gratefully took the coffee from him.

Once they stepped outside into the frigid, cloudy morning, Bravo ran up to them, and they started the walk back to the farm, leaves crunching under their boots.

"Smells like snow," Brooke said.

"Yup." Ethan looked to the cloud-covered sky. "The October storm was a bad sign for winter." Linking her free arm through his, she dropped her head to his shoulder and yawned. "I told you to stay in bed," he said.

"I needed to make sure you were okay this morning," she said. "I'm told people in a relationship do those kinds of things for each other."

"I like being in a relationship with you. I'm all right though," he said, leaning over to press a grateful kiss to her forehead. He tried to keep his voice light. "I'm sorry you had to deal with that."

"I'm not," she said. "It means you weren't alone. I hate to think of you going through something like that with nobody there, even if it's just to hold you and not speak. Though, I guess Natalie has been there for them."

"She doesn't always know about them." Ethan kicked at the dirt with his good foot as he walked. "I only know I call out in my sleep when she comes in. They're really not that frequent, and I always have Bravo."

"He seems to know exactly what to do."

"So, are you working at the store today?" He needed to switch gears. He wasn't used to sharing this much about the ugly side of his life. Just by being who she was, he found himself wanting to tell her things, but there was only so long it could last before his mouth dried up and his heart started to race.

"Later," she nodded, bringing her mug to her lips. "I'm headed up to the ski resort to talk to the events coordinator about the New Years' Eve ball. Their planner left, and she likes what I'm doing with the wedding. So, she asked if I'd be interested in pinch-hitting."

Ethan furrowed his brow. "That sounds like a lot to take on during the holidays, especially with Ry and Sophie's wedding."

Shrugging, she said, "It should be fine."

They arrived at the barn, and Bravo ran right up to the door. The buried behind gray clouds, and small flakes were beginning to fall. Lifting her face to the sky, Brooke closed her eyes, absorbed in the moment.

God, she was beautiful. And for now, she was his.

Eleven

O N HER WAY BACK from the ski resort, Brooke stopped by her house. The only thing left to do were the floors and the dormer upstairs, and she wanted to see it all nearly finished. It turned out the dormer was slightly delayed because that crew had been struck down with the flu, but Brooke didn't need that finished to move in once the floors were completed.

As she pulled into the driveway, the new gravel crunched under her tires. The snow that morning never materialized into anything of significance. Now, she sat and admired her house from the car. The contractor would come back in the spring to pave the driveway. The stone exterior had been cleaned, and the siding painted a deep brick color. The new windows made a huge difference in the overall presentation of the house.

Tingling with anticipation, Brooke approached the new wood door and thought of the day Ethan came by with the brownies. It was only a few weeks ago, but a lot had happened since then. This morning she had been given a contract by the ski resort to finish organizing and planning the New Years' Eve Ball for a decent amount of money. They asked if she would be interested in joining their staff on a part-time basis to start as they had some spring weddings booked. Brooke said she would let them know after the ball when she had a better gauge of how much time would be involved. After all, she was a business owner herself, and she also had Stitches by Sadie to consider. She didn't want to spread herself too thin, especially with this new relationship with Ethan.

Unlocking the new door—which opened just fine now—she stepped into her very first house and gasped. Tears sprang into her eyes as she saw it was everything she had hoped it would be. The painted knotty pine on the walls gave the house a cottage feel, which she adored. She wandered through the rooms, taking in the smell of the fresh paint. As she crossed into the kitchen, the Travertine floor took her breath away. It was absolutely stunning with the cabinets and marble countertop she chose. The recessed lighting made what was once a dark space welcoming, and the cave-like feeling the kitchen had previously was gone. She walked out onto the porch that overlooked the lake. This space was a perfect blend of stone and slate. Even without the heat turned low in the house, she could feel that the new windows were working. It wasn't drafty anymore.

Walking through the downstairs bedrooms, she was satisfied with how they turned out. A bit on the small side, but she had her eye on space-saving furniture to make the most out of the room she did have. She had originally thought of putting her bedroom upstairs with the dormer, but while Ethan could maneuver the stairs, it would be difficult with crutches, which he preferred to use around the house. She found herself considering beds with storage underneath in case he wanted to leave anything at her place—or one day, move in.

Pausing at the door that overlooked the lake that would have been her studio, she now considered it as a bedroom. It already had a closet, which she was going to use as storage for her supplies, but now she saw the room as something different. Lazy mornings in bed with a backdrop of a brilliant summer day or an iced-over lake. She imagined them returning to this house after taking care of the animals to crawl back into bed and look out over the lake—earthly colors splashed over the leaves and acorns falling from the trees.

The image was so perfect—*so happy*—her eyes watered. That was as sure a sign as any that her studio was going upstairs when the dormer was finished. Why hadn't she thought of this arrangement before?

Because you didn't have anyone to share it with before.

But now there was Ethan, and everything was different. The wood floors were on track to be finished next week, so she would schedule her furniture delivery and move what she had accumulated already from storage. Her excitement grew at unpacking the dishes she'd purchased and setting up her kitchen, arranging her furniture, hanging curtains. *Her first home.* Not some echoing museum done by a decorator strictly for the essential purpose of showing off. But somewhere she could leave her muddy boots at the door, put her feet up on a coffee table, or leave her coffee mug in the sink.

Hell, she could walk around naked if she wanted to.

She would be her own cook, her own maid, and she'd answer her own damn door. No one would know her secrets—whether she was eating or not eating, whether she was having sex or not having sex. Her life would truly be her own.

The notification of a text message drew her out of her thoughts. The message was from Sophie, who was supposed to be at the store.

"Get here. NOW."

Brooke frowned. She couldn't remember Sophie ever not being able to handle any issue that came up. Brooke messaged back, *"Is it busy?"*

Three little dots floated in front of her indicating an incoming response. *"JOSH IS HERE!"*

Frozen, Brooke stared at the message. Such a pleasant, cozy daydream she was having that ended with a bucket of ice water thrown over her head.

Brooke locked her front door and walked to her car. Why on earth would her soon-to-be ex-husband come all the way here? That took effort—something he never bothered to give her before. He didn't even chase her when she left him a year ago. He just let the lawyers hash it out. Part of her wanted to leave him standing there indefinitely. She didn't owe him anything. But she wouldn't do that to Sophie. If Brooke didn't show up, Josh would just harass Sophie.

As she pulled into the lot for the store, a shiny, new Lexus coup stood out in the line of dirty SUVs, covered in white salt from the last snowstorm, mud caked to the tire flaps. The fact that Josh even drove himself here was stunning in and of itself. Josh had a driver to take him to the office or anywhere else he wanted to go. He often didn't understand Brooke's own need to drive herself. No matter what Brooke had agreed to when she married him, she refused to lose all of her independence and freedom.

She walked through the side door and stopped dead in her tracks as she entered the café. Ethan sat at one of the tables eating a sandwich. He hardly *ever* came in during the day. Mornings were his routine. Of course the one day she would want him to stay far away, he was there. For a brief second, she considered that Sophie might have texted him, as well, but dismissed it. Sophie wouldn't want to cause unnecessary drama.

When he looked up, a devastating smile spread across his face and he rose to meet her. She refused to flinch away or in any way show him her inner turmoil, but he must have sensed in in her kiss.

"What's wrong?" He asked, frowning. How well he could read her. She must have overcompensated.

Lowering her voice and scanning the immediate area with her eyes, she said, "My soon-to-be ex-husband is here somewhere."

"Ah, so that's who that guy is," Ethan said. "He's sort of obvious in his expensive-looking suit and coat. "I thought he was a lawyer."

"Business executive."

"What does he want?"

"I don't know," Brooke said with a lift of her shoulders. "Sophie sent an SOS text, and I came right over."

Ethan ran his hand up and down her arm. "Do you want me to go?"

Her answer was immediate. With a shake of her head, she said, "No. He might make it awkward, but I have nothing to hide from you. Remember, I promised you truth." And she would *always* give it to him, no matter how uncomfortable it might be. "I don't know what he wants. I'll probably need moral support ... or bail money."

He pressed a sweet kiss to her forehead before stepping back. "All right. I'll be right here if you need me. And I have an in with the chief of police."

He couldn't know what it meant to her that he had her back. Historically speaking, there weren't many people in Brooke's corner, and she loved his loyalty.

Walking behind the counter, Brooke stashed her purse near where Sophie was standing and removed her practical parka. "Where is he?" She asked her cousin. Scanning the area immediate around them, Brooke zeroed in on Joshua Mars coming upon their apparel section.

"Meandering around ... *judging*."

"*You* made this store what it is. People love coming here. This is something we can be proud of, and he can kiss our ass." Sophie laughed at Brooke's candor. Her southern manners often prevented her from voicing her real thoughts, but when she was of a mind, she could slay someone.

Brooke's heeled-boots clipped along the scarred wood floor. She was dressed up for her meeting at the ski resort. She had planned to go home and change first before coming in later that afternoon, but Sophie's text sent her right over. Oddly, the polished urbanite look *wasn't* what she wanted to project to her ex. She wanted him to see who she really was now.

As she approached, she saw him gingerly fingering the sleeve of one of the Fair Isle sweaters they sold. It was beautiful work and one of their more popular items. The fact that he was looking at it with distain rattled her. That was *her* not too long ago. The woman of her previous life would never have shopped at a place like this. A chunky sweater? Really? Was it the '80s? Even the Brooke that showed up on Ryan and Sophie's doorstep over a year ago wouldn't have bought something like that.

Now, she owned two to them and found them very comfortable and warm—perfect for the harsh New Hampshire winters. Oh, how she longed to be wearing one of them at that moment.

She cocked her hip and folded her arms. "Joshua."

Tall, dark, and devastatingly handsome, her husband looked up and pierced her with his steel gray eyes. Instantly, he flashed his most disarming smile. That smile had women falling at his feet—or into his bed.

"Darling, you look amazing, as always." He stepped forward, presumably to give her a hello kiss, but the slight shake of her head and glare in her eyes had him coming up short.

"What are you doing here?"

"Is that any way to greet your husband?"

"*Ex*-husband."

He grinned, but it didn't reach his cold eyes. "Not yet." Brooke's blood went cold. This visit was calculated. He wanted something, and he was here to negotiate for it. Whatever it was, she wouldn't give it to him. She owed him nothing.

"We finalized the settlement, Joshua," Brooke said. "It's as good as over."

"I haven't signed off on anything, and before I give you a significant amount of money—"

"Please," she scoffed. "What you're giving me is nothing to you. It's change on the floor of your car. Write the check so we can move on."

"As I was saying, I need something from you first. Can we go somewhere more private and talk?" Derision covered his features as he looked around them—the candy, the toys, the stacked snow shovels and deicer along the wall—all thing Joshua Mars didn't have a need for.

"No." Brooke refused. "Anything you have to say you can say right here." The store wasn't busy, but there were a few customers milling around. Since it was a small town and gossip traveled fast, the few that were around had one eye on them. This whole encounter would be on Norrie's Facebook page for the whole town to absorb before it was even over. Brooke was happy to give them a show. She was determined to come out on top. It took a while for this town to warm up to her. She refused to lose the ground she had gained.

Josh put his hands in his pockets and rocked back on his heels. "I have a business proposition for you."

"Not interested." Brooke dropped her arms and began to walk away. Josh followed her through the apparel section, on to home goods, and to the candy section where Brooke stopped short. Ethan was facing them, leaning up against the counter next to Sophie. Neither even pretended they were doing anything else other than watching them.

"I'll triple the settlement payment." Brooke stopped and slowly turned on her heel. Dammit, she didn't want to be lured by money, but she and Sophie could do a lot with the store with that kind of cash infusion. That offer made the payment well into the seven digits. It could even set her up for life. She wasn't that girl. This was her test. "Interested now?" She didn't answer him. She stood where she was in silence.

"All I need you to do is stay married to me for another year and attend several public events. I'm not asking you to move back home. Just do what you do best—look beautiful, charm the buyers, and put on a hell of a show."

It was like a slap in the face. He just belittled her entire existence. She had no other value to him. Of course, she knew going in that it wasn't a marriage of love, but she thought he at least had a higher regard for her than that. All she had ever been was just another asset for him to call upon when he needed.

"Go to hell, Josh," Brooke seethed.

"Yes!" Sophie cheered from behind her. It bolstered Brooke's confidence. Was Ethan still there? Did she have his support, too?

"I'll even let you keep your farmer." Josh said. Brook's hands clenched. "This time, you get to have your side projects, too. It's a win-win."

"Not for my dignity, it's not," she said. "I walked away from you to change my life, and I did that. I have people that care about me here. I'm doing work I'm proud of, and one day, I might even make a difference in someone's life. The girl you married? Yeah, she liked all those things. She was good at them, but that's not me anymore. You can take your offer and shove it up your ass." Despite the fact that her chest heaved and her body was tense, she also felt freed.

"You should reconsider," Josh said. "Triple the money and your own farm boy."

"War hero," Brooke snapped. "He's done more than you ever have, and his name is Ethan." She heard the distinctive sound of Ethan's gait coming up behind her. She needed him.

"Is that a limp he's got?" Josh cast his eyes over her shoulder.

"You don't get to judge him," she hissed. Oh, how she hated the judgmental ass. "He lost the bottom part of his leg in a war, Josh. He knows what it is to sacrifice."

"Interesting," Josh said, looking back at her. "You've got your own little Beauty and the Beast thing happening here."

"Get out." She said, flinging her arm out and pointing toward the door. "This conversation is over. Get out or I'll call the police."

"Think about my offer," Josh said, stepping toward her. "Think long and hard."

"I believe the lady asked you to leave." Ethan's low and threatening voice came from directly behind her, then the menacing growl of

Bravo by her side. Brooke couldn't help the self-satisfied smirk that spread across her face. Josh had looked smug during their short conversation, but now he looked down at Bravo, who bared his teeth. Now, Josh looked scared.

But that was Josh, after all. When the bullied fought back, he didn't have the spine to follow through.

"Oh, Josh," Brooke said sweetly. "This is Ethan's dog, Bravo. They served together in Iraq. He's trained to sniff out terrorists and all-around assholes. Believe me when I tell you, you won't want him to escort you to the door. He's been known to drag creeps around by the neck."

Looking back up at Brooke, Josh sneered at her. "You're making a mistake."

"Already made it and learned from it."

Josh gave Bravo a wide berth as he moved to leave the store. Bravo followed him out, hackles raised, snapping and snarling at Josh's heels.

Brooke let out a long breath when Ethan's hands came up and started massaging her shoulders. "Breathe," he said quietly next to her ear. "You were amazing. And that guy was a dick. Was he always an asshole to you?"

"No, he mostly ignored me." Brooke said. "I literally was nothing more than a business asset to him, which is what I raised to be. He'd buy me fantastic jewelry and the latest couture when I needed to be on his arm somewhere."

"I can't compete with that."

Stunned, Brooke turned to face him. "You can't compete with *him*? He's a cardboard cutout in an expensive suit. *He* can't compete with *you*, and he knows it." Bravo trotted back in and sat down next to Ethan watching the byplay like a tennis match. She raised her hands to his face. "I'm with the person I want to be with. Didn't you hear me tell him no? I had all the money I could ever dream of—every material thing my heart desired—and I walked away from it. Twice now." She took one hand and laid it over his heart. "*This* is where you win, Ethan."

Rising up, she pressed a kiss to his lips. Even in heels she was shorter than him, but she loved the way they fit together.

"Perhaps you two could go somewhere more private." Sophie's southern drawl was more pronounced when she was being sarcastic. "Our apparel department does not sell intimate wear."

Ethan smiled against Brooke's lips before breaking away and turning to Sophie. "Too bad that apartment isn't still upstairs."

Rolling her eyes, Sophie waved her hands at them like she was over it. "Go. Shoo. I've got another employee here today. We don't need you."

Brooke and Ethan turned back to each other. "Sounds like a good plan," she ran a finger down his cheek. "What do you say, farm boy? Care to take this elsewhere?"

Wrapping his arms around her, Ethan pulled her up against his hard body. "Wherever you lead, I'll follow."

Twelve

ETHAN FUMBLED WITH the keys to his front door while Brooke's roaming hands drove him to distraction. The nightmare had ruined any other chances for sex last night, and he had a driving need to be inside her again. He needed to get back on an even keel—back to that place of wonder and, dare he say, new love.

He loved her. He was so in love with her she became part of his breathing—part of his heartbeat. A lesser woman would have taken Josh the Dick up on his demeaning offer, but Brooke stood up for herself—for *him*. He hated when people called him a war hero, but damn if he didn't like it tossed in that asshole's face.

And Bravo—he loved that dog. Bravo was an excellent judge of character and acted entirely on his own. Ethan could have called him to heel—could have stopped his threatening behavior at any time, but why bother? The guy was an asshole and didn't leave when Brooke told him to. Bravo merely gave him an escort.

The dog whined at his feet now and scratched at the door.

Giggling, Brooke ran her hand inside his jacket and along his waistband. "Need an extra set of hands?" Her voice was husky. Her hand dipped lower, and he gulped and prayed nothing embarrassing happened while he was trying to get the damn door unlocked.

"I like what your hands are already doing." Did his voice just squeak? He'd already had sex with this woman, and he was acting like a nervous teenager on prom night. Or he supposed teenagers were nervous on prom night. He didn't actually go to his prom.

Finally, the lock gave and the door swung open. Bravo bolted into the house and did his usual run through check. Grabbing Brooke by the hand, Ethan jerked her over the threshold. His lips fused to hers as they grabbed and pulled at each other's coats—then their shirts. As Brooke's black ribbed turtleneck came over her head it exposed the sexiest black lace bra he'd ever seen. His mouth pooled with saliva just from the sight of it—the way it pushed and formed her perfect breasts nearly finished him off right there.

She trailed her finger gently along his cheek before hooking it under his chin and bringing her eyes up to her heavy-lidded gaze. "Do you like it? I wore it for you." All Ethan was capable of was nodding his head. He was like a teenager blinded by his first look at a pair of breasts. Slowly, she turned, and he was treated to the sexy, fine lines of her back—the way her form tapered at her waist and then flared out at her hips. Looking over her shoulder, she let her hair down, shiny chestnut waves falling along her back. He didn't know hair could fall gracefully, but somehow, hers did.

She looked over her shoulder as her hair fell and covered part of her face, turning her into a sexy pinup girl like the mechanics put around Ryan's garage. "Would you mind getting the zipper of my skirt?" He looked down at the zipper in question and then back up to her as an idea came to him. Could he do it? He'd been on his knees before. There was only one way to find out.

He unzippered his jeans and pushed them down his hips, yanking off his boots and then tugging the pants over his prosthetic foot. There was just never going to be a sexy way of doing that. When he stood there in his boxers, he walked her forward until she stood before the back of the couch. He stayed her hand as she reached down to the zipper of her boots.

"Those stay on," his voice was husky and more authoritative than he intended, but the fire that sparked in her eyes told him she liked it.

Here went nothing.

Leaning forward, he ran his tongue along the plane of her spine as he slowly lowered himself to his knees.

"Ethan—"

"I'm fine." He allowed her to turn around and slowly brought the zipper of her skirt down. Hooking his fingers at her waistband, he slid her skirt and panties down her legs then gently lifted each booted foot and tossed the clothing aside. Her breathing was heavy now and his heart raced. When she threw her arms out to grab a hold of the back of the couch for support, his control broke. He brought each of her legs over his shoulders, leaned in, and feasted.

Brooke threw her head back and cried out. Bravo barked and whined. Ethan didn't care. The taste of her was heaven. She writhed and squirmed. If his knee was sore, he didn't know it. The only thing that mattered to him was the woman who was coming apart around him. He was thankful his sister wasn't home because Brooke was *loud*—moaning his name, gasping, and finally screaming.

He held her steady as she recovered, gently putting her feet back under her and carefully standing up.

"Holy shit, Ethan," she breathed, bringing her hands up to his face. "No one's ever done that to me before. I thought my head would explode."

Chuckling, he leaned in for a kiss. It started playful, but turned heated. He devoured her as she pushed his boxers down over his hips and he stepped out of one side. No need to chance the other side and end up toppling over. Talk about a mood breaker. He wanted to show her his strength now, not his weakness. He needed to solidify for her that she made the right decision in rejecting Josh the Jerk and choosing Ethan.

In one powerful swoop, he brought both her legs up and around his waist. She started to object, but he cut her off by shoving his tongue down her throat, walking a few steps and pushing her up against the hallway wall. He pulled his lips from hers and absorbed himself in the fire of her eyes. That's what he craved, that fire, the luminescence that promised him paradise. He thrust up into her and a scream tore from her lips. Again, Bravo barked and whimpered. Ethan drove into her with blinding need, chasing the light as it stayed just out of his reached. She bit into his shoulder. His fingers burrowed into the soft skin of her luscious thighs. Her mouth fell open in a haze of passion. His mind began to spin. Who was this man delirious with lust?

The light was there getting larger, brighter, going from warm to an inferno. He rushed toward it, pulling little cries from her as he sucked on her neck and pounded into her harder, faster. She deserved tender, but she wouldn't get that from him now. She took all of him—everything he possibly had to give her.

"Come with me, Ethan." Somewhere in the frenzy, he heard her whispered command and it broke him. The sunburst was there, and he dove for it head first. Every nerve in his body exploded and a roar tore from his lips. Had he ever had that kind of reaction to an orgasm before? He couldn't remember. He couldn't remember anyone before her now. The glow enveloped him slowly. He could visualize them in a bubble of it. Just the two of them. Against the world.

Lifting his head from her shoulder, he looked into her eyes. They were glazed with tears, her cheeks were flushed, and she wore a goofy smile. "Hey," she said softly.

"Hi," he said back, pressing a gentle kiss to her lips.

"Wow."

"The black really did it for me."

"I guess so."

Bravo began to bark as the front door opened. Ethan imagined his face mirrored Brooke's mortification. Natalie was home. Out of his periphery, Ethan say Natalie move into the living room.

"Ethan? What's with the clothes ... oh, my God ... oh, ew! ETHAN!"

Cackling and holding onto to Brooke tight, he hurried down the hall toward his room, the sounds of his prosthetic foot squeaking gave his path away. Brooke squealed. Ethan wasn't quite fast enough carrying Brooke with his pants still around one foot.

"Is that your ASS!? Oh my, God! I just saw your ASS, Ethan!" Natalie screeched.

Pulling back his comforter, Ethan dropped Brooke onto the bed and fell down next to her, barely covering up before his enraged twin appeared in the doorway. Brooke pulled the blanket over her head.

"You dumbass, Ethan! Is that Brooke under there? Show yourself, you coward!" Ethan couldn't take it. He burst out laughing as Natalie glared at him, her eyes shooting daggers at him.

Brooke popped only her head out from under the blanket.

"You!" Natalie pointed her finger at Brooke. "I expected you to have more sense!"

"I thought you were working," Ethan said.

"I was working. My shift ended, and now I'm home and in desperate need of mind bleach!" Natalie spun on her heel, slamming the door so hard it popped back open.

Still laughing, Ethan reached down to the bottom of the bed to retrieve his flannel pants and t-shirt. After pulling them on, he turned and gave Brooke a smacking kiss before following after his pissed off housemate.

Once he reached the living room, he leaned against the archway going into the hall and crossed his arms. Gathering up the clothes, Natalie shoved them at Ethan. "I don't ever want to see evidence of you having sex in this house again!" Ethan laughed and wrapped his hands around the bundle in his arms. Natalie stomped toward the kitchen, muttering, "There is not enough wine in the world to erase this from my brain."

Ethan walked back to the bedroom and dropped their clothes on the bed. "Rifle through my drawers if you want something more comfortable. I doubt she's going to be inclined to share her clothes with you right now."

"Oh my, God, Ethan!" Sitting up, Brooke clutched to the comforter to her chest. "I want Natalie to like me!"

"She does like you."

"I don't think so."

"She's just being dramatic, I promise. Get some clothes on, and come on out. You'll see." The skeptical look Brooke gave him told him otherwise, but he left her to her own devices, closing the door behind him to give her privacy.

As Natalie slammed around the kitchen, grabbing a bottle of wine, a glass, and an opener, Bravo sat nearby with his ears back and head hung as if *he* was in the wrong. As Ethan passed him, his faithful companion gave him a low growl, clearly telling his master what he thought of the whole situation. Ethan raised his eyebrows at the dog as he walked to the breakfast counter and sat down with a loud groan.

Now that he was off his feet, he felt just how badly his stump ached. He decided it was worth it. He would need to take the prosthetic off and use his crutches.

Natalie turned to him as she aggressively opened the bottle of wine. "Don't you dare sit there looking at me all happy and glowing and smug! I don't think I'll ever get the sight of your hairy, white ass turning into your bedroom out of my head. It'll be there every time I walk down the hall."

Ethan leaned in and lowered his voice. "We shared a womb."

Natalie got right up in his face and hissed, "That doesn't mean I want to see your *ass*, Ethan!"

His sister spun back and poured her wine, filling her glass up nearly to the top. "Don't I get some? Brooke might want some, too. After all, she thinks you don't like her."

Furrowing her brow, Natalie got out two more glasses and set them in front of Ethan with the bottle of wine. "Why does she think that?"

"Oh, I don't know," he said as he poured two glasses. "Probably that epic display you just put on."

"That doesn't mean I don't like her." She took a long swallow of wine. "That just means I don't like what the two of you did in our living room so close to me coming home."

"In my defense," Ethan said, holding up his glass. "I lost track of time."

"That's no defense," she snapped, then softened her tone. "By the way, Norrie has you all over the town Facebook page. There's a picture of you standing behind Brooke with your hand on her shoulder staring down some guy. The caption says something about your arousing show of protection for the new filly in your life then poses the comment that things must be over between us."

"That was Brooke's ex-husband. He's a bit of a douche."

"He looked like one." Natalie leaned back against the counter and sighed. "She makes you really happy." He nodded as her face fell. "I don't think I'll ever have that. I just can't do that to somebody."

Before Ethan could respond, Brooke came in looking contrite, but adorable in a pair of his flannel pants and a Maverick's t-shirt. She put her hair up in a messy bun and shuffling across the floor, she took the stool next to him. Ethan slid her glass toward her and Brooke happily drank.

Ethan wanted to revisit Natalie's comment but would have to wait until they were alone, and since he planned on begging Brooke to stay, that would have to wait until tomorrow. He wanted things to be easier for his sister. He just wasn't sure how to achieve that.

LATER THAT EVENING, Brooke and Ethan were tucked away in his room—banished by Natalie was more like it. Ethan had changed out of his pants and shirt and into just a pair of boxers. Still dressed,

Brooke was sitting lower on the bed admiring Ethan's strong body on display.

Tentatively, she reached down and brought his stump into her lap. He looked at her apprehensively. She knew he was still unsure of her feelings about him missing a part of his body. Where he might see that as a weakness, she saw only his strength.

He hissed when she began to massage, and she shot her gaze to his, immediately stopping. "I'm sorry. It hurts to do that?"

"No, it feels good. It's sore."

"Maybe no more up against the wall action, less time on your knees."

Vehemently shaking his head, Ethan said, "No deal. It's nothing Tylenol and the massaging won't fix. I might put a hot compress on it, too. Only things that require an actual narcotic get ruled out. That was worth anything I might have to deal with, especially if you sign on to do this after."

"I could be convinced." She grinned and returned to her massage. It was important to him that he be strong and test his limits. She'd learned this about him in the time she'd known him. He managed well, and she was truly coming to believe there wasn't anything he couldn't do. People with amputations ran marathons. It was all about the human spirit and what you were willing to do to overcome the loss. Did you let it break you or did you rise from the ashes?

"You have a lot more tattoos than I've seen," she said, working her fingers into his skin, around the stump, over his knee, up his thigh, and back down again. "Do they hold special meaning?"

"Some do," he said. She admired the art over his chest and shoulders. She knew he had some on his back, as well. "Some are covering scars. Those are the ones that are names of my friends that died. Others hold meaning from different points in my life." Brooke ran her fingertips lightly over the names intertwined over an American flag over his shoulder, feeling the ridges in the skin that made up the scars beneath.

"You're like a walking memorial," she said. "It's amazing."

"It's important to me to honor them, their sacrifice, their friendship with me. They were my brothers. I got out. They didn't. I think about them every day."

Focusing on her hands, she said, "I don't know what that's like—to have that deep-rooted loyalty. The only constant people in my life were Sophie, my grandparents, and Ryan. We may have been on again, off again, but he was also always there growing up. It was a love/hate relationship over the years. Now, it's like he's my brother."

"Were you ever in love with him?" The question was quiet, and she almost didn't hear it.

"I wanted to be," she said honestly. "He was good-looking, popular, rich, everything I was supposed to want. Maybe a little bit wild, especially once we hit our teenage years and he'd come back to school after the summers and tell us all about scoring with girls on the race circuit." She rolled her eyes. "I pretended to be mad and irritated over it. I wanted to be. I wanted somebody other than Sophie and my grandparents to love me—to put me first and shower me with affection. It was never Ryan."

"It's kind of weird sometimes, knowing you have a romantic past," Ethan said. "It's hard not to compare."

Leaning forward on her hands and knees, Brooke pressed her lips to his for a kiss. "I told you, he's like a brother to me. I never felt even half for him that I feel for you. There's no comparison. There's no comparison between you and Josh or any other man. You're the one I want. You're the one my heart is full of."

His arms banded around her, and she touched her forehead to his.

"I love you, too," he said softly.

Tears pooled in her eyes and slipped down her cheeks. "Really?"

"I'm the one that will put you first," he said. "I'm the one that will shower you with affection."

A sob formed in her throat and escaped. "I love you, Ethan."

She poured all her love into that next kiss, and she felt his love in return. She couldn't believe this was happening—couldn't believe she had found what she'd always been searching for. Falling in love with Ethan was the easiest thing she had ever done—as easy as breathing. But she believed his words—reveled in them—let them slide over her like his soft caress. Finally, *finally*, she was home.

Thirteen

E THAN WAS MUCKING out the horse stalls when Eric Davis showed up in the barn. Just from his friend's stance, Ethan knew Eric had news for him.

"You got something?" Ethan asked. He propped the shovel he was using up against the wall of the stable.

"Ethan Price was a direct hit," Eric said. "Congratulations, you've got yourself a father."

Ethan thought he was prepared for the news Eric would eventually have to give him, but his body tingled. His breathing became short. A biological father, albeit a deceased one. Something inside him cracked, and his breathing started to come in pants. He rubbed his chest and sat down on a wooden rocker he kept in the barn for when he needed breaks to get off his leg.

"I didn't expect it to hit me like this."

"A light breeze could have knocked you over when I told you about your mother and siblings," Eric said, shoving his hands in the pockets of his jeans. "Price's family wants to meet you."

"Jesus," Ethan looked up at his friend. His ears were ringing. Eric was right. This was the exact same reaction he had when he found out about Daisy Dolan, his biological mother, and his brothers and sisters.

"I told them you didn't want anything from them but a medical history if they were willing to give it—that you didn't want to bother them or cause any disruption, that you just wanted to know. They want to meet you, if you're up for it. I didn't tell them about Nat. They didn't know about you, so I saw no point in bringing her up.

You have a grandmother. No other siblings, but aunts and uncles, some cousins."

Nodding his head and still rubbing his chest, Ethan said, "Yeah. Yeah, I want to meet them."

"Okay," Eric said. "I'll give you their contact information and you can set it up. They're spread out around the Philadelphia area."

Ethan took a deep breath and pushed himself up from the rocking chair, making sure he was steady on his feet. His breathing was returning to normal. Taking in the barn around him, he allowed the atmosphere that always comforted him to do its work. The smell of the hay and horses, the sounds of the animals rustling around their stalls, the sight of the equipment he meticulously stored in its corner, and the presence of the hayloft where he promised Brooke a tumble when the weather got warmer. He took it all in.

"I've got more," Eric hedged.

"Christ, really?" Ethan wasn't sure he could take much more.

Nodding, Eric said, "I'm going out of town. Nat's agreed to take Em."

"I thought you didn't take missions anymore."

"I'm taking this one." Eric's eyes darkened his features turned to granite. "For the past year, my teams have trained and gathered intel on Juan Espinoza's cartel. We know where they are. Espinoza was found dead in his cell day before yesterday. With the support of a government Black Ops team, we're going in to take out the rest. Three days from now, the threat to Natalie will be completely gone."

Ethan blinked in surprise. He had no idea Eric was putting in this kind of effort for Nat. He handled her security—their house was wired to heaven and back—but working with the government in Central America and wiping out a major drug cartel? To think, soon Natalie could openly be their sister, no more putting up the front that none of them believed anyway, no more dancing around the issue—just their finally completed family.

"I want in," Ethan said suddenly. He may be a little rusty in skills, but he *needed* to be in on taking down the people that terrorized his twin sister and sent her scared and on her own into hiding.

"No." Eric was firm in his answer. "I need you in the command center. I'll have my full teams with me, and you're the only one I trust for this. Also, I need you to stay behind in case anyone makes their way up here. I don't think that will happen, but I need to be ready for it. I've already talked to Danny. He'll be in the command center with you."

"Are you going to tell her?"

Eric shook his head.

"No. I don't want her to know my part in all of it. The Marshall service is part of the team. They've had a guy on the inside for a while now. They'll let Natalie know when she's safe, and then she'll have some decisions to make."

"She'll want to know it was you," Ethan said. "She'll probably figure it out anyway."

"That doesn't mean she gets confirmation."

Sighing, Ethan ran a hand down his face. He would never understand the complexities of Eric and Natalie's relationship. But maybe now, Natalie will be comfortable finally getting together with Eric. Ethan had never seen a guy so far gone over a woman as Eric was. It must be agony to have the love of your life right in front of you but out of reach all the same. Ethan had denied he was attracted to Brooke over the time that he'd known her, but he didn't realize he was in love with her until recently, when she had already taken the bull by the horns and moved them forward. He'd be forever grateful for her courage.

"I disagree with you on that point," Ethan said. "But I'll respect your wishes. I won't lie to her though if she ever asks, though, so be prepared for that. I won't ever lie to her—not for you, not for anyone."

Turning, Eric looked off toward Jackie and Danny's house. "She looks at me differently when I get back from these trips. Sometimes, it almost feels as if she's disgusted by this part of my life. It's one of the reasons why I backed off from missions. I told her I was going to look at a helicopter."

The pain on his friend's face was on display. Everyone always thought that Eric was invincible—indestructible—but Ethan knew one tear from Natalie or Emma would put Eric on his knees. While his sisters and soon-to-be sisters-in-law were capable, independent women, Ethan knew their men were in the background ensuring their safety and making sure they wanted for nothing.

"She's afraid of getting in too deep with you," Ethan said. "Nat doesn't want to bring trouble to your door." Eric turned and looked incredulous. Ethan held up his hand. "Before you say anything, she knows you can handle anything that comes your way, but Emma concerns her. She doesn't ever want to make a target of Em."

"Emma lives in a fortress," Eric said forcefully. "With my current and past line of work, I would never risk my daughter's safety or Natalie's. She *knows* that. She saw first-hand what I'm capable of when Cooper Eden's thugs came to your house."

Ethan shrugged. "She doesn't want you to have to deal with it. I'm just telling you how she thinks. Maybe taking out the rest of the cartel and removing the price on her head will help your cause, but she has scars inside. Men haven't always treated her well. It even took a while for her to warm up to her brothers. Don't forget it was an asshole boyfriend that sent her to Mexico to begin with."

Eric ran a hand down his face then over the back of his head. "Maybe I just don't deserve her."

"That's for her to decide." Ethan said, lifting his hands.

"All right," Eric said on a sigh. "I'll email you the contact info for Price."

As Eric walked away, Ethan called out, "When I come over, I'm taking home my fucking guns." Not turning back, Eric raised his hand and gave Ethan a thumbs up. With the medication change his doctor submitted that morning, Ethan thought things were moving in a positive direction for him—as long as the medication worked. He had Brooke now, and he never wanted to disappoint her. He never wanted to see the fear hiding in her eyes that he did Thanksgiving night. He'd do whatever it took to make sure that never happened again.

He finished mucking the stalls and caring for the animals. With snow on the ground, there wasn't much else to do, but tomorrow when Brooke was done with work, they could take the horses out for some exercise. For now, he planned on retrieving Bravo from the house and heading over to Brooke's new place. The floors were done, and her furniture and belongings from storage had been delivered. He intended to give her a hand with the unpacking. Whistling for Bravo, Ethan held the door open for his furry friend to jump in and after making sure Bravo was secure in his harness, walked around to the other side, started the truck with a roar, and headed down the snow-packed road.

When he pulled up to the little house, he could already see the little touches she had added that made it a welcoming sight—curtains in the windows, lamps shining with a homey glow as twilight turned toward darkness. The motion light turned on when he pulled up behind her Jeep.

The stone steps no longer crumbled as he walked up them to the new wooden front door with a decorative glass pane in the middle. The door was unlocked, though she had given him a key just in case. Bravo rushed ahead of him to check out the house, but when Ethan heard his dog's low growl coming from the kitchen, he rushed forward with his heart hammering.

Ethan found Brooke in the kitchen, cookie sheet in hand and held up as a shield. He looked around the room. Perhaps a bird had gotten loose or a large, ugly spider was crawling up the wall.

"Baby, what's going on?"

Brooke's eyes stayed focused on the counter. "I'm pretty sure the pressure cooker is about to blow up my kitchen."

There on the counter sat a shiny, stainless steel pressure cooker making whooshing noises. Gently, Ethan pried the cookie sheet from Brooke's fingers. "It's just pressurizing, baby."

Brooke eyed the small appliance warily. "Are you sure?"

"Yes," he said with a small laugh. "Nat and I have one. We use it all the time. Those are normal sounds." Ethan slid the cookie sheet onto the counter and took Brooke's hands in his to lead her out of the kitchen. Brooke sent a suspicious look over her shoulder.

"What are you making?" Ethan asked.

"Chicken cacciatore if that thing doesn't explode."

"Sounds delicious," he said, leading her back past the dining area and into the living room. His heart turned over when he saw Bravo curled up on a big blue plaid pillow. She made a place for his dog in her home. Boxes, crates, pillows, blankets, and clothing were stacked around the small space, but Bravo's spot had already been clearly set up. There was a full water bowl nearby and a basket of toys and bones next to the fireplace. When Bravo switched from the curled ball he was in and rolled onto his back, Ethan saw the pillow was even embroidered with his name. She made his dog her own, and he was embarrassingly moved by it.

"You got him a bed," Ethan said, a catch in his throat.

"I know you have to stay with Natalie right now," Brooke said. "But one day, I hope you might consider moving in here with me." Ethan's breath hitched as he realized she wanted him permanently. What was even better was that—though Brooke didn't know it—in a few days' time and if all went well, Ethan *would* be able to move in with her. She mistook his silence as apprehension and hurried on. "It's just I see you and Bravo here everywhere I look. I moved my bedroom to the back room to face the lake because it would be easier for you to get to when you use crutches. I see us there in that bed with the changing of the seasons, reading, with newspapers spread about, sleeping, and making love. Bravo is on the bed or curled up on the floor on his pillow. This is *already* your home."

Impossibly moved and afraid if he spoke, he might cry, Ethan pulled her into his arms, holding her tight. He could see that, too. And though he felt she wasn't ready to hear it, he could also see little brown-haired children tearing up the place. But he would keep that little nugget to himself for now. Things were moving faster than he anticipated, and he found himself not at all spooked by it. She would need to meet his parents soon. They made him the man he was, and he wanted them to know each other.

Taking a deep breath, he answered her, speaking into the crook of her neck. "As soon as I'm able, Bravo and I will absolutely move in with you." He picked his head up and saw the happiness on her face. Pushing the hair back, he said, "I was afraid of you—of what you would do to me if I ever let you in. I was afraid you'd break me apart, but instead, you're holding me together. I wasn't prepared for that. I don't know if I'll ever be able to show you just how much I love you."

"I think you just did." She pressed a soft kiss to his lips just as the finish alarm sounded on the pressure cooker. "Shall we see how our first meal in the new house turned out?"

Taking her hand, he followed her back to the kitchen. "I'm game for anything."

Fourteen

E THAN ENTERED HIS house in the late evening hours. As usual, Bravo ran ahead of him to do his security check. Natalie was still awake in the living room with a glass of wine and a book, curled up on the sofa under one of quilts from the general store. Natalie didn't know the identity of Sadie, the quiltmaker, and he wondered what she would think when she found out it was the woman Ethan was in love with.

Walking to the fireplace to retrieve his crutches, he moved back to the couch and sat down, putting the crutches on the floor for easy access.

"I thought you would have spent tonight christening your honey's new house," Natalie said, taking a sip of wine and pulling up her knees to give him more room.

Ethan pulled up his pant leg and removed his prosthetic, sighing at the relief. His leg was still sore after the wall sex, but he wouldn't ever admit it out loud. He just resolved to save that kind of fun for special occasions.

"I needed to talk to you alone," Ethan said. As well as he knew his twin, he still couldn't say how she would react to the news that Eric had found their father.

Arranging himself on the couch so he could elevate his stump, he now faced Natalie. She looked concerned, chewing on the bottom of her lip and clutching the glass in her hand.

"Eric confirmed with my DNA sample that Ethan Price, the hockey player, was our father," Eric said. There was no easing into it. He just laid it out and waited for her to absorb it.

Dropping her book to her lap and lowering her wine glass, Natalie stared at him. Ethan continued, "I didn't tell you because I didn't want to freak you out. I need to know where I come from, even if it's just to have the knowledge. There are no other siblings, just a grandmother, and a couple aunts, uncles, and cousins. They want to meet me. Eric didn't tell them about you, only me."

Natalie put her wine down on the coffee table then wrapped her arms around herself. "I guess a medical history would be helpful."

"I have their contact information. I'll wait until after the holidays to meet them. I'll probably see if Brooke wants to come with me for support." Ethan wouldn't mention that hopefully by then, Natalie would be able to accompany him, as she wouldn't have to hide anymore. Even so, it would be her decision. Ethan would never take away a choice from her. Nat's life was controlled by a government agency. When the need for that protection was gone, he would ensure that all her choices were her own.

"Why does meeting them now matter?" she asked. "I know you grew up an only child, E, but your parents are wonderful. Now, we're crawling with siblings. You need more family?"

"I don't *need* them, no," he said. "And I really hadn't planned on meeting them. I just wanted to know who my father was. They want to meet me. Maybe it'll give them some kind of closure, I don't know. I can do this for them."

"And if they want more than that?" Natalie said. "They lost a son, a brother, Ethan. What if they decide they can get some of him back in you? Are you ready for that?"

No, he wasn't. He may have opened Pandora's Box with this, but he would give them one meeting. That could be all they wanted. Maybe they just wanted to *know* like he did—to see him once. He could hear his dad's story—find out if he even knew Daisy was pregnant or if she also bailed on Price, as was her standard procedure. He went to see Daisy out of curiosity and his need to know, and he left with the knowledge that Natalie was his twin sister. He certainly hoped the Price family didn't have any bombshells they were going to drop on him.

"I'm just going to take it one day at a time," Ethan said. "They asked for a meeting, so I'll meet them."

"And this is Eric's work."

This sounded like a landmine if he'd ever heard one. "Um, well, yes?"

Leaning in, she lowered her voice. "Is this place bugged? Be honest. Is he listening?"

"No," Ethan said, emphatically. Ethan was very firm with Eric that he could not listen or look in. Ethan checked the house himself routinely and never found any listening devices or hidden cameras. Ethan knew Eric's heart was in the right place—if it was Brooke, Ethan would be desperate to do everything he could to protect her—but Ethan would not allow his and Natalie's privacy to be invaded.

"He has a hand in everything," Natalie said in frustration. "He knows everything I do, everywhere I go."

"He's just trying to keep you safe, Natalie," Ethan said, gently. "You mean a lot to him and Emma. That's the only way he can show he cares."

"It's become stifling," she snapped. "And kind of stalkerish. You know, I got home tonight, changed into pjs, grabbed a glass of wine, and sat on the couch. Then I get a text, *lock your doors.* I don't need to be micromanaged."

Wow. Things were not going good for Eric.

"He cares about you," Ethan tried again.

"Controlling my life isn't a good way to show it."

"It won't last forever," Ethan tried to assure her.

"Ethan, you're the only reason I haven't moved away from here," Natalie said bluntly. "I love the others, but I can keep in touch with them by text and email and occasional visits. You're the only one I *need* to see. All I have to do is tell the Marshall Service I feel threatened and bam! I'm gone. Off to Duluth or Boston or Alaska." This would not be a good time to tell her that Eric would only find her, so Ethan held his tongue.

"Have you told Eric you need him to back off a bit?"

"Ha!" Natalie scoffed, picking her glass back up. "He doesn't see it as being intrusive. He sees it as him doing his job. It doesn't matter that *I've* never hired him to do anything. He doesn't work for me, and I'm not a client of his. He ran roughshod over me when he rigged this place up. He took advantage of the fact that I was in a precarious position and scared."

Warily, Ethan eyed the wine glass she was tossing about. He had seen her frustration before, sure, but this was anger—real, raw anger. The kind of anger that made people say things they regretted later.

"I'll talk to him," Ethan said, rubbing her leg, hoping he was soothing her in some way. When she hurt, he hurt. Despite being apart for most of their lives, when they found each other, their connection was strong. He could read her well, and she could do the same for him. They could have conversations without saying a word. After being an only child growing up, having this tether to someone else was, quite honestly, weird. But he wouldn't change it.

Falling back against the pillow behind her, Natalie let out a long breath. "Could you? I feel like it's a cop out to have you do it, but at the point I'm at right now, I might say something I can't take back. I like him, Ethan. I really, really do. But I can't be smothered, and I'll tell you, he'll have *no* chance with me if he goes on this way. I just can't handle another controlling man in my life. I've had too many. I need my life to be my own. I have the Marshall's service. I have you and Bravo."

Leaning back against the couch, Ethan smiled, "If you wish it, I'll make it happen. That's my job."

"I wish I could sic my other brothers on him, too."

"You can," Ethan said. "I get why you try to stand back, but Nat, everyone in our family knows. You know they know. They will do anything to protect you, as well. It's their job. Just as they know you'd do anything for them. And who knows? Maybe if all four of us confront him together, he'll get the message. It's not like he can shoot us."

"Maybe, we'll see." Snuggling down farther, Natalie brought her glass to her lips. "He respects you, your abilities, what you've overcome. He understands that. I think coming from you will be all he needs."

Ethan liked to think that she was right, but he was ready to bring their brothers in, if need be, and even Danny. Eric and Danny definitely spoke the same language and were tighter than brothers. It was worth thinking about. Propping his legs up on the coffee table, Ethan let his head fall back into the cushions. His life had taken some sharp turns in the last few years—most of them for the better.

He thought of Brooke and her offer tonight for him to move in with her. She accepted him so easily. He could see himself living there with her. The vision she gave him appealed to him so much, he craved it. Until she offered it, he didn't know he wanted that kind of commitment from her. But he didn't just want cohabitation. He wanted everything.

A broken solider and poor farmer wasn't exactly the most appealing marriage prospect for a girl like her. Her parents were sure to disapprove. He'd be seen as after her money. Ethan didn't want her money and didn't need it. He did okay. He wasn't *actually* poor. Between his Army pension, savings, and what he made off the farm, he made enough to support himself. Once he started the police dog training and horseback riding lessons, he'd do even better. The market stand he ran when the weather was good did a consistent business. The farm was a tax write-off for Jackie, so when he needed things—such as the capital for Christmas Morning—Jackie funded him. It was a small life, but a fulfilling one.

Grayson Falls felt right from the first day he stepped foot in it. It fit. He connected with Ryan and Jackie quickly. He had no desire to live anywhere else.

BROOKE STOOD AT HER work table in Piper's studio and critically picked through the Christmas stockings she made, deciding which would go to the store and which would go to the children's hospital in Boston as a donation. The stockings always sold out quickly at the store. She made a limited number of stockings and tree skirts, and she never made the same pattern twice in one year. Much to the disappointment of Sadie's customers, Brooke did not take orders. This was a project she took on to honor her grandmother and her influence in Brooke's life. She did it because she enjoyed it. She didn't ever want that feeling to change.

This afternoon, she was boxing up her supplies and finished products to move back to her house. Piper and Zach had been more than generous, but now that Brooke had her own space, she wanted to get down to her new routine. There was no reason to take up any room in Piper's studio. As she filled boxes and closed them up, Zach took them out to her Jeep. Nearly finished, Brooke closed the box that would be mailed to the store for Sadie's latest inventory delivery. Brooke planned on revealing to Sophie that she was Sadie with Sophie's wedding present—a wedding quilt that Brooke painstakingly ensured was perfect and warm enough if Sophie wanted to put it on her bed instead of displaying it.

"Oh, hey, Soph!" Zach's voice carried from the front of the house. It was a warning for Brooke, but Sophie would recognize Brooke's Jeep in front of the house. There was nothing to do to avoid her cousin. Why did she have to pick today of all days to spontaneously drop by?

Turning around, Brooke prepared to go find her cousin. It was best if she didn't hide. But once she looked up, Sophie was standing there silently with a garment bag draped over her shoulder. *Brooke, you idiot. You* knew *the bridesmaids' dresses were ready. Why on earth didn't you take Piper's to deliver to her?*

"Hi," Brooke said lamely.

Wordlessly, Sophie walked over to the box on the table and saw its contents. Her eyes roamed over the remaining supplies on the table, which included Brooke's sewing machine. Winding her fingers together to keep her hands from shaking, Brooke's heartbeat increased and she felt warm. She honestly didn't know how her cousin would react to finding out Brooke's secret.

"Of course," Sophie murmured. "Sadie was grandma's dog. Why didn't I see it sooner?"

When Sophie looked up at Brooke, she cringed internally at the hurt look in Sophie's eyes. Betrayal, disappointment—little arrows into the center of Brooke's heart. "Why didn't you tell me?" Sophie asked, hurt apparent in her voice.

Deciding the truth was best, Brooke made no attempt to stop the tremor in her voice, "I was scared."

Eyebrows up, Sophie jerked her head back. "Of what? My reaction?"

With a heavy sigh, Brooke said, "Of not being good enough." Brooke was encouraged by the softening of her cousin's features. "Think about it, Soph. Put yourself in my shoes. I wasn't raised to do things like this. And I also hadn't done any quilting since the last summer I spent at grandma's. I wasn't even sure I would be any good at it. And I was terrified of what people around here would think of the big city girl taking on such a domestic hobby. I wanted people to get to know Sadie's work first." Just the thought of her mother finding out made Brooke cringe. This was not a suitable hobby in Lenore Larrabe's eyes.

"It's beautiful work," Sophie said. "No wonder it reminded me so much of grandma."

"That's a high compliment," Brooke said, warming inside. "I was going to tell you when I gave you your wedding present. I wanted that to be a surprise. I never intended to deceive you, and I certainly didn't mean it to go on so long. I know you're mad."

"I'm not mad." Sophie lowered the dress off her shoulder and draped it over her arm. "I'm just disappointed that you didn't trust me. I would have encouraged you. I never would have thought you couldn't do it."

"I'm so sorry," Brooke said earnestly. "I didn't handle it well."

"Your work is why so many people have asked if we were going to start carrying quilt supplies," Sophie said. She ran her fingers over the completed Christmas stockings in the box. "I've had some people ask if we could see if Sadie was interested in teaching classes."

"She absolutely is *not*." Brooke said. "I have so much on my plate right now I hardly have time to make new inventory for the store. We don't have space or supplies for classes. Maybe one day in the future, but I don't see that as happening though."

"That would be a very big expansion to the store," Sophie said. "We should take a look at it. Maybe we can bring in guest teachers or something. Or we can think about maybe a second business."

This was not the reaction Brooke expected. Of course, she *had* thought about expanding the store to have a quilt section, but with its current finances, it wasn't really feasible. With the launch of the online store, they were definitely doing better, but a major expansion was not in the numbers. Still, if Sophie were interested, they could look into it—maybe raise the capital for it. On Christmas Eve, Ryan would technically become a part owner. He wasn't rolling in money like Jackie was, but Ryan *did* have a trust fund and a rich father.

Maybe Sophie would be okay with tapping that source. Brooke could guarantee her parents wouldn't be interested. God forbid they support something so menial.

"It's something we can think about," Brooke said. "Maybe we can start looking into it after you get back from you honeymoon."

"It makes me crazy that I don't know where we're going." Sophie huffed. "I don't suppose you'll tell me to make up for the fact you didn't tell me about Sadie."

"Oooh," Brooke said, feeling a twinge of guilt. "That's a tough position to put me in. I want to make sure everything is all right between us, but Ryan is *really* excited about this trip and making sure you're surprised. He wants it bad."

"Dammit," Sophie said with a fake frown. "I can't let him down. And yes, of course we're all right. I am a little hurt that you didn't trust me in the beginning, but I do believe you're genuine when you say you were going to tell me soon. Mostly I can't believe I didn't figure it out sooner."

"Sorry," Brooke said again wincing.

Sophie waved her hand in dismissal then patted the garment bag on her arm.

"I'm just going to leave this for Piper. Ryan and I are coming to your place for dinner Thursday night, so make something yummy, and make sure Ethan is there. I want to see the new place." Before Brooke could utter a word in response, Sophie swept out of the studio.

Switching gears, Brooke immediately went into hostess prep mode. It would be nice to have a cozy couples' dinner with her cousin and Ryan. Ethan really did prefer more intimate evenings rather than crowds they might see out and about. Most nights, they stayed in and cooked together. He started leaving Bravo home with Natalie on the nights he stayed over, and Brooke missed the big lump of fur. But if

Ethan was leaving his trusted friend behind, maybe it meant that the nightmares and anxiety were lessening.

Either way, Brooke had preparations to make. In order for everything to be perfect for Thursday night, she needed one small but essential detail.

Fifteen

"CHRISTMAS TREE SHOPPING?"

Ethan scrunched his face as he watched Brooke brush out Christmas Morning in her stall. She sure did love that horse, he thought. It warmed his heart when he saw people make such strong connections with animals. Some people found horses intimidating because of their size and power, but Ethan had always found comfort working with his horses.

Brooke's request that Ethan accompany her to purchase and decorate a Christmas tree by Thursday evening had taken him by surprise. It also made him painfully aware that not only hadn't he gotten her a Christmas present yet, but he had no clue what to even get her. What did you give a woman you were in love with who had already been given the world? Talk about pressure. Anything he could give just seemed so ... inadequate.

The perfect gift wouldn't be something seen as generic. He couldn't get her jewelry or clothes or a gift card. It needed to be from the heart—something specific to her that showed not only how much he loved her, but how much he *knew* her. That would be important to her. That was something she likely didn't have too much of growing up. He suspected her grandparents would have gotten her such gifts, but her parents and husband likely just threw expensive presents at her.

Ethan was *not* going to be getting her a shiny new Lexus with a big red bow covering the hood.

He also wasn't sure what her expectations were in the gift department. Was she expecting him to give her a gift? He was confident that she would be giving him a present. Should they talk about what they wanted? Put a price limit on the gift? No, he definitely wasn't going to be doing that. That would just make him look pitiful and highlight how much money he *didn't* have. And if he asked her what she wanted for Christmas, it would look like he didn't know her enough to come up with the perfect gift on his own.

Christmas was stressful as fuck.

"Ethan?"

Ethan shook out of his thoughts at her voice. "Why don't we take the horses out on the trail and see if we can find something you like on the property? There's plenty of smaller pine and evergreen trees out there. If you find one, we can hitch it to one of the horses and drag it back."

Brooke cocked her head and pursed her lips in thought. *Damn, she looked cute.* "That sounds like fun!" She turned to Christmas Morning. "Is it okay if I take her? She seems like she's doing okay."

"Of course you can," he said. *Like he would deny her anyway.* When her face lit up and her eyes sparkled with hope, there was nothing he would deny her. The tingling feeling that rolled through his body when he made her happy was still new to him. It didn't happen when he made his parents happy or one of his brothers or sisters. Sure, that gave him pleasure, too, but it didn't make his heart clench.

He was caught in a trance watching her prepare the horse to ride. She lovingly ran her hands over the horse as tenderly as she did over him. He realized then why he didn't die in Iraq. It was because he hadn't met her yet—hadn't had a chance to fall in love with her. *She* was the reason he lived. This beautiful being—inside and out—was made just for him. The struggles they had to overcome before the universe could put them in each other's orbit made them who they needed to be for each other. It was as if God made her from Ethan's own rib just for him.

He would spend the rest of his life worshipping her. Loving her. Taking care of her every need.

The trick to that, though, was to make that happen *without* taking away her newfound independence. He could never do that to her, but his need to care for her, to always ensure everything was right with her world, was so overpowering he didn't understand it. How did he let her spread her wings and soar and still satisfy nature's most basic desire in a man? It would be a delicate balance he would spend a lifetime mastering.

"Are you okay?"

Head foggy from abruptly being yanked from his thoughts, Ethan looked up at Brooke. She was standing there, brow furrowed, concern in her eyes. "You look a little ... freaked out."

On the contrary, he'd never felt more at peace in his life.

"I was just thinking about how much I loved you." It was cheesy, and he felt like a fool admitting it, even if only to her. Like any second Danny or Eric would come and revoke his man card. But it was the truth, and he would always give her the truth. Besides, the smile that spread across her face, reached her eyes, and illuminated her entire being was worth it. That smile was worth anything.

Walking over to him, her nearness made his breath catch and his heart jump. He'd already had her. She was his. But the newness of these feelings, of being with her, never failed to bring him metaphorically, and sometimes physically, to his knees.

He would kill for this woman.

Wrapping her arms around his neck, she fit her body to his. The way they came together was perfect. How could they be made for anyone else? His arms came fast and hard around her. Her breath caught at his force, and she searched his eyes. There was no masking the desire she would see there—the raw lust that coursed through his body. It was too consuming to hide from her.

Leaning forward, he nibbled along her jaw. Her body squirmed against his. His hand ran over the curve of her ass. Squeezing, he pulled her close. Core to core. Her eyes sparked with desire—eyelids growing heavy with her increasing lust.

His mouth connected with hers in a kiss made to punish. Punish her for what, he had no idea, but he needed to stake his claim on her. At its most basic, the most primal urge to be with his mate.

Moaning, she dropped her head back so he could feast on her neck, her scent overriding his most basic thoughts.

"I have to have you," he said against the smooth flesh of her neck. Moving along to the sensitive spot under her ear. "Now," he growled.

Who was this man? He was gentle with her—loving. Things between them were beautiful. But in that moment, he needed dirty. He *had* to do things to her that would make her scream—split her in two. The carnality of the moment was intense. But when she reached down and palmed his raging erection, he knew she caught up to him, wanted him—desperately needed him as much as he did her.

"The hayloft—" she panted.

"Is not as hot as you think." He finished her sentence with a light chuckle. "There's a couch in my office, space heater, clean blankets. The hayloft won't be as fun when you have straw sticking you in the ass."

Her eyes widened at his crass words. But her lids grew heavy again, and her eyes darkened with need.

Grasping her hand in his, he tugged her to the office.

"Not against the wall, Ethan," she decreed. "I know that hurt you for days."

The fuck? Fine. He didn't have time to argue. He was ready to detonate, and he needed to be inside her when he did.

Slamming the office door behind them, he heard Bravo's whimper and bark. His faithful companion would be fine. There was a bed out there for him. The feeling of his dog's wet nose on his ass would only kill the mood. Nothing could stop him now but the end game—the trophy at the end of the race, the conquest at the top of the climb.

Unless the word *no* fell from her lips. That would be the ball-game. *That* would stop him like a bucket of ice-cold water poured over his head. Never would he do anything that made her uncomfortable or scared her.

Pulling her behind his desk, he cleared everything off it with one powerful sweep of his arm. Setting her in front of him up against the desk, he sat in the chair. By the time his butt hit the seat, she was already pulling down her pants until one leg was free. She stepped toward him to straddle his lap, but he gently urged her back against the desk. Nudging her back until she understood he wanted her to lay down.

When she was situated to his liking and laid bare before him, he leaned in between her legs and feasted. Her gasp turned into a sob as he worked her with his tongue, his fingers, the scruff of his beard. Writhing under his fingers, her skin grew hot and flush. And still, he worked her until she trembled around him, seized, and finally screamed his name. An *oh, fuck!* tore from her lips. The way she crashed around him spurned the frenzy on. He stood in a lustful haze, yanking his pants down and freeing himself.

"Hurry," she panted. "Ethan, I need you."

Jesus, what she did to him.

He pulled her to the edge of his desk and dove into her with one powerful thrust. She screamed his name, and he heard it over and over in his head like a mantra—the carnal prayer of her mating call to his. Her tight, wet core clenching around him as the haze engulfed him. He pounded into her, rough and needy, blinded and senseless. She took everything he offered, everything he gave, everything he commanded. This wasn't like any of the times before—gone were the gentle caresses, the tender whispers. And in their place was a wanton lust that he wasn't sure could be sated.

That was until the tension begin to coil inside. Her pants, her moans, her cries spurring him forward until the pleasure made him delirious. Until the passion broke and he came apart in her arms. Bursts of light exploded behind his eyes, and an oblivion of pleasure claimed him. His name tore from her lips and was replaced with soft sighs and a light chuckle.

He lifted his face from where it fell into the crook of her shoulder. He couldn't form words, but he could raise his brow in question. "I don't know what I did, but you'll have to tell me," she said still riding the high. "That was the craziest sex I've ever had in my life."

Raising up on his elbows, he brushed the hair from her angelic face. "I've never felt that way before," he admitted. "Something overtook me, and I had to have you. Now. Nobody has ever done that to me before."

"I don't want to be like all the other girls," she whispered.

Shaking his head, he said, "You never could be." Still connected, he picked her up and carried her to the couch where they eased down together. He yanked blankets off the back of the couch and covered them, cocooning them in the heat they generated. Now that the haze of insanity cleared, he realized his leg throbbed. But the pain was exquisite—worth every single moment of his claiming of her. His marking that she was his and always will be.

It was then he realized he hadn't stopped to use a condom. It was the furthest thing from either of their minds. He wasn't worried about catching anything from her, and the only thing she could get from him was a baby. And that thought didn't scare him. No. That combination of each of them didn't scare him at all. But he didn't know her feelings on the subject.

"I'm sorry," he whispered. "I didn't stop to protect you. I swear I'm healthy. I've *never* done that unprotected before."

She was quiet for a long moment before she finally spoke. When she did, she broke his heart. "Joshua used a condom every time. It wasn't because he had any diseases. He just didn't want children with me. When I found out he was unfaithful, it was because one of his mistresses was pregnant. He was okay with having a baby with a mistress but not his wife. How stupid I was."

Ethan rolled her toward him so they were eye to eye. "Not stupid. You were doing what you thought your parents wanted. You were a different person. But, baby, you were strong enough to break free. What you view as mistakes, I see as necessary steps you needed to take to get to me. I hate that you hurt, that you felt trapped, but that made you who you are today, and this person is the most amazing woman I've ever met. Beauty and the beast."

At his words, Brooke tossed her leg over his and sat up. "*You* are not a beast, Ethan. The man I see has no limitations. The man I see sets goals and conquers them. The man I see has the ability to feel and love. *The man I see is the only one for me.*"

Moved by her words, he pulled her down and cradled her against his chest. Was it any wonder he lost his heart to this woman? That he gave his soul over to her. She owned him. He didn't have much to give her, but what he did have, he laid down at her feet.

"I guess we both still have some demons to slay," he said softly. She moved down to his chest, and he tugged the blankets over them.

Ethan rubbed her back, enjoying her in his arms as he pressed a kiss to her forehead. The uncontrollable necessity to own her, dominate her, was now abated, and he was left with the most serene sense of peace. A calm no one had brought him before. How could she destroy him one minute and build him back up the next? It was a whiplash he couldn't get enough of. His future was clear to him as he imagined going down to one knee and swearing his allegiance, his eternal protection and love to her. It was a peace he searched for since the explosion, yet finally was able to claim.

AS IT TURNED OUT, THEY were able to find the perfect Christmas tree. The smell of sap and pine permeated the air as they trudged through the snow. Brooke rejected tree after tree, but Ethan had begun to look at them in a different light. Just because they weren't the perfect tree for Brooke didn't mean they weren't what another family was looking for. He decided he'd come back out on his own and flag the trees that he deemed worthy to sell. Jackie's property was vast. Zach had already bought a few acres of it to use for a baseball training camp for disabled and underprivileged children, but even with that part developed, there was still plenty of room to set up a tree farm. He would discuss it with his sister, and in the spring, he'd come back to plot where the existing pine and evergreen trees stood that could be sold. There were still defunct fields he hadn't tilled yet, and they would make the perfect spot to plant new trees. Smaller ones he found in the woods he could transplant. He was still realizing the potential for this land, and he reveled in what he was creating, nurturing.

Kodak towed the tree back to the barn. As it happened, Christmas Morning wasn't very amenable to being a work horse. She preened, swooshed her tail, and tossed her head back, shuffling out of the way whenever Ethan tried to harness her. Chuckling to himself over the mare's prissiness, he moved to Kodak, who was only too happy to be of service.

After wrapping the tree in netting and storing it in the bed of Ethan's truck, Brooke had convinced him to stop into Over the Hop for an early lunch. Now he was by the fire in the moderately busy brew pub sipping Irish coffee with a steaming bowl of chili in front of him. Piped in Christmas music, sparkling lights with traditional decorations and trees made him think he'd stumbled into a Norman Rockwell painting, such was the character of Grayson Falls.

Bringing her hot mug to her lips, Brooke asked, "What are you thinking of the Christmas season now?"

Leaning toward her on his elbows, Ethan said, "I like spending it with you."

Mimicking his movements, Brooke leaned across the table and placed a kiss on his lips. "This is turning into my favorite Christmas of all time."

"And it's not even here yet."

Brooke sat back in her chair, and Ethan returned to his chili. "My parents forewent my annual Christmas visit, since they'll be down here for Sophie's wedding on Christmas Eve."

"I bet they'll like what you've done at the ski lodge," Ethan said, savoring the flavor of the chili. *What on earth did Jonathan put in this stuff?*

Shrugging, Brooke's eyes wandered around the room. "You'll meet them, won't you?"

Ethan paused. Of course, this was something couples did. When they were with someone they loved and were serious about, eventually they introduced their significant other to their parents. The thought itself didn't turn him off, but the thought of *her* parents did. What would they think of him? With the prosthetic foot he used now, he walked without a limp. Unless someone said something to them, they would have no idea that he was missing half his leg.

But that wasn't even the part that bothered him. What did was the fact that he wasn't bathing in money. Would her parents approve of a military veteran and farmer for their daughter?

Did he care?

He realized she was looking at him for an answer and his silence was making her concerned when she rolled her bottom lip between her teeth. Reaching across the table, he linked his fingers with hers. "Of course. My parents will be there, as well. It will be the perfect occasion for everyone to get to know each other." Her shoulders sagged and she let a breath out. If she was concerned about what her parents would think of him, she didn't show it. He knew his parents would adore her. If he loved Brooke, that said enough about her character for them. His parents measured people by what they were able to create and accomplish on their own—their integrity and how hard a person was willing to work. Brooke would pass their litmus test.

And did he really need to tell them about her privileged upbringing? It wasn't what was important to her today.

"Looks like it's starting to get busy," Brooke said looking around the pub. "Do you want to get going?"

Looking around, Ethan saw that she was right. Quite a few more people had been seated around them since they came in, and more were waiting at the door for a table. Ethan and Brooke had the most coveted table in the place during the winter. Being too busy enjoying his time with her, he hadn't noticed the crowd—never felt anxious. In her presence, he was calm.

He wasn't surprised one bit.

"Sure," he said, rising and dropping a few bills on the table to cover their light meal, drinks, and tip. Once Brooke was bundled for the bitter temperature outside, she held out her mittened hand, and he grasped it with his gloved one, leading her through the restaurant. Locals didn't look as surprised to see them together anymore, but from the crowd, it was mostly ski resort patrons today. Locals didn't have to look at the menu.

Once they pushed their way outside, a small group was gathered in a semi-circle right outside the door. Ethan's head snapped to Brooke when she gasped.

"Oh, Ethan, carolers!" Her face was alight with the Christmas spirit. Following her gaze, he saw members of the Episcopalian church choir dressed in Victorian era costumes and singing *God Rest Ye Merry Gentlemen*. Brooke was transfixed by the sight of them, so he wrapped his arms around her and watched the small concert. When they began *O Holy Night*, Ethan rested his chin on her shoulder and sighed at the way she continued to center him, even with people walking in and out of the restaurant, teenagers having a snow-ball fight in the parking lot, cars driving by, and the general hustle and bustle of the holiday surrounding them.

They stayed and listened to the carolers until the choir moved on. Tucking her arm in his, he led her back to his truck and toward her house—the one he already considered home.

Sixteen

ETHAN PACED ERIC'S war room slowly—hands on his hips, head bent, listening to the communications coming from Eric's team in Mexico as they moved into position. Danny sat at the command station—three large computer screens in front of him, monitoring the movement and communications of Eric and his men. They weren't patched into the black ops unit that traveled with Delta Security or the Marshall Service, but they were getting accurate reports from Eric and his team.

The war room was Delta Security's command center. Though Eric usually worked in the concrete building himself the last six months or so, this mission was personal to him, and he deployed with the men he carefully selected to join his business. The interior of the room was bright, but there were no windows. Leather couches sat in front of a television that took up most of one wall, maps spread across the rest. A conference table in one corner was surrounded by more leather meeting chairs. The structure also held an office, kitchenette, and full bathroom. Behind one of only two steel doors was a food pantry with enough food and water for ninety days of sustainability and a large weapons locker.

A small princess bounce house sat in a corner near a smaller television with a DVD player and stacks of Disney movies, a twin-sized bed, and toys for Emma. Between that and the brightly-colored area rugs on the floor, the room also had a homey feel instead of a place so serious and intimidating. It was important to Eric that Emma not fear this room—despite the type of work that went on in here.

Eric's entire operation was on this assignment. It wasn't often that Danny or Ethan were called in to staff the command center, but this time, they were both here.

"It's going to be a long night," Danny said, leaning back in the chair. It was late afternoon, and the raid would begin in the total darkness of a Mexican jungle night. Ethan could imagine how hot his brothers-in-arms were down there. Though in Mexico the humidity kept your clothing moist, but the bugs in both climates were murder.

"Does Jackie know what you're doing?" Ethan asked.

"No," Danny said. "She'll find out with the rest of your brothers and Nat. I didn't want to worry her. I work overnights from time to time, so she didn't think anything of me being out tonight." Jackie was the mother hen. She'd be a basket-case if she knew what was happening.

Leaning up against the large oak conference table, Ethan crossed his arms and feet. "You feel guilty about that?"

"A little," Danny shrugged. "She'll understand when it's explained though. If the rest of them knew, they'd only worry and harass us. I take it Bravo's with Nat."

Ethan nodded. "He would be even if Em didn't insist her favorite dog stay for their girls' night. I think Nat assumes I'm at Brooke's."

"And what does *she* think you're doing this evening?" Danny arched a brow.

"She thinks I'm hanging out with you," Ethan said. "She didn't really ask what we were doing. She knows something's up with Nat though—that we're hiding something. She knows we're related somehow, but she doesn't press because she figured out that Nat needed protection."

"I think she's always been smarter than I used to give her credit for," Danny said. He stood up and walked over to the coffee station, preparing the second of many cups that would get them through the long night ahead. "She was so different then. She, Ryan, Sophie, and I were there since kindergarten. We got along when we were younger, but as we got older, that crowd didn't want anything to do with the likes of me, despite the size of my bank account. I didn't look like them, dress like them, act like them. Given it was my mission to get kicked out of there, I was usually in trouble. Your brother was my nemesis—until Jacks showed up. Then we became very unlikely allies, but we still hated each other's guts. Ah, my fond memories." Danny and Ryan had buried their differences when Danny and Jackie reconnected, but there were moments they still snapped at each other—though those moments were more entertaining than anything else.

Chuckling, Ethan also moved to make himself another cup of coffee. "Did Brooke have a lot of boyfriends growing up?" Ethan turned his back on Danny. Not only did Ethan not want to Danny to see what was in his eyes, but Ethan wasn't sure he wanted to see the expression on Danny's face.

"No," Danny said, slowly. "You probably already know she only had eyes for Ry."

"It's been mentioned a time or two." Grumbling, Ethan turned around. Of course, Danny was right there looking amused.

"Like I said," Danny said. "She was a very different person back then. Her dislike for me was mutual. She hated Jacks on sight. Ryan dropped everything and everyone to take care of his sister. Their flirtation was fun for him, until he had a sister to take care of. Our senior year, he was singularly focused on Jackie. He knew then something wasn't right about Jimmy's accident. But I think Brooke's proven she's not that girl anymore. People change, they grow. Sometimes they don't grow into something good, but most usually change for the better."

"She wants to introduce me to her parents at the wedding."

"Oh ... them." Danny said. "Yeah, they're assholes. Her parents and my father shared the same parenting theory, which was make someone else do all the heavy lifting."

"I'm concerned they won't like me," Ethan confessed.

Danny retook his seat behind the computer monitors, leaned back, and with his coffee mug in hand, kicked his feet up onto the desk. "They're not going to like you." Danny said bluntly. "It's best to just reconcile yourself with that going in. They can't stand me, and I have more zeros in my bank account than them. I don't fit their mold, and frankly, neither do you. But that's their shortcoming, not yours."

Taking a deep breath, Ethan let it out then moved to a leather recliner that faced the desk Danny sat at. Ethan raised the footrest and got comfortable. "I don't want to be a burden to her—something else that causes tension between her and her parents."

"That's not on you," Danny said. "They're responsible for their mess with their daughter. It's up to them to fix that shit. And at some point in every couple's life, one is a burden on the other. That's what 'in good times and bad, in sickness and in health' means. It's your love for each other that gets you through."

"Yeah, I guess you're right," Ethan said. He had spent most of his life not really caring about other people's opinions. It wasn't until he was on his way to meet Jackie and Ryan that Ethan realized *their* opinion of him was going to matter more than anyone else's in the world.

Until he met Brooke. Her thoughts desperately mattered.

Danny ran a hand down his face. "I sound like a woman." Ethan laughed, but cut it off when they heard the radio come to life.

"Team two, LZ is hot. Team one is taking fire. Over." The communications were a series of disembodied voices—professionals trained to deal with any situation that presented itself.

"Target was tipped off. Orders? Over."

"Wait for air support and return fire."

"What the fuck happened down there?" Ethan asked, propelling himself off the recliner. Danny was frantically taking down the time of the communications as backup to the computer. Ethan moved to the computer's mouse and brought up satellite photos of the area, scouting for options to retreat to, if need be. While the Delta Security teams were in position, the black ops team assisting needed to scramble to get to the target early now. But though unexpected, this wasn't a unique situation for any man down there.

"Eagle is in route." Eric's voice came over the radio. He sounded calm and serious. Ethan knew Eric had prepared for this scenario. He had prepared for *all* scenarios. Eric never failed in a mission, and Ethan knew failure was especially not an option in this one. This was an operation Eric brought to the government. Any benefits Natalie gained from a successful mission was a happy byproduct. Both the American and Mexican governments wanted the Espinoza cartel eviscerated, and Eric had been all too eager to see it done.

"Is everyone in position?" Eric asked.

"Affirmative."

"Affirmative."

"Affirmative, but Douglas is down. Not sure how bad he is yet."

Ethan met Danny's serious eyes. One man was out of commission. Both of them knew what it was like to be injured in a war zone, far from a hospital with only the resources of a field medic to save you. Hell, Danny *was* that field medic when he was injured. Ethan's skin began to tingle, but he ignored it. Now was no time for a flashback. Eric needed him. *Natalie* needed him. There was nothing he wouldn't do for his twin sister.

He swallowed and scrubbed his hands through his hair and down his face. Conjuring Brooke's face in his mind, he thought about how he would go home to her when this was finished. *He* wasn't the one in battle. He was safe, and she was waiting for him.

Fuck all, he wished he had his dog with him.

"You with me, E?" Danny asked, not turning back.

"Yeah." Ethan bent back down and flipped through satellite images, keeping Brooke's image at the forefront of his mind while he worked alongside Danny.

"Where did all these fuckers come from?" asked a voice on the radio.

"Just throw a fucking grenade and let's get past this," came another.

Danny pushed himself out of the chair and began to pace. Ethan took his place in the chair and ran the comms, tracking the teams' movements, plotting their positions on a map.

On they went for hours—Danny and Ethan took turns manning the command desk, pacing, getting more coffee, pacing some more. Radio communications continued. The black ops team arrived. Air support arrived. The Americans forged forward. Eric's voice came on sporadically. Other men came on. Progress was reported. Ethan kept his demons at bay thinking about Brooke, the work he was doing, and his assurances to himself that he was safe. He actively kept his breathing steady.

The radio crackled again before the next transmission came through.

"Davis is down. Gunther! Davis needs a medic. He's not getting up!" Ethan felt his blood chill.

"On my way."

Come on, come on. Don't check out, Eric.

"He's near the ordinance set to detonate in two. Move fast, Gun."

"Got him. Unresponsive. Fuck! Cover me! Heading to the rendezvous."

Danny slammed down the pencil he was using and popped out of the chair. Ethan watched Danny scrub his palms down his face. He took fast, short, paces. Monitors to princess castle, princess castle to monitors. Monitors to princess castle, princess castle to monitors. The radio was silent. Ethan's own breaths came thick as if they were choked by desert sand. The radio transmissions echoed around him.

Danny stopped and turned toward him. Ethan could see his brother-in-law's rage. His grief. Still Ethan eyed him. They couldn't think of their injured friend. They needed to continue the job they were asked to do.

Finally, Danny nodded and sat back down with a heavy exhale. "This mission was FUBAR from the fucking start."

"Guess we better wake up Sebastian and tell him he's got incoming wounded."

Danny picked up the pencil and forcefully threw it down again. Ethan stepped forward. His stump ached. He forced himself to remember it was because of his rendezvous with Brooke, not from the warzone this time. They spent the rest of the night working in silence. The only sound was the disembodied voices of their men—their friends—in the field.

IT WAS LATE AFTERNOON the following day when Ethan and Danny gathered at the hospital for Eric's arrival. The team medic had removed the bullet in the field and cleaned and dressed the wound the best he could, but there was no exit wound. Sebastian would be operating on Eric to ensure there was no shrapnel or any other foreign body in the wound and that no damage had been done to Eric's organs. The shot had gone in just over Eric's hip bone and he had hit his head when he fell.

Ethan had hoped that Natalie wouldn't be on shift when Eric was brought in, but of course, the universe wasn't on his side. He watched as Danny and Jackie met the helicopter on the landing pad next to the hospital and Eric was unloaded. Crouched low, Danny and Jackie maneuvered the stretcher through the snowy parking lot and up the ramp to the hospital door.

As Eric was wheeled in, sedated for the journey, his ashen face made them all pause. Danny and laid his hand on Eric's forehead. Eric was a giant, and now their friend was vulnerable. Ethan had told Jackie and Sebastian that morning that Eric was injured on a mission and would be coming to the Grayson Falls Hospital—someplace he didn't have to answer a lot of dicey questions by the authorities about why he was rolling in with a gunshot wound.

Jackie got pissed. Real pissed. Sebastian merely went to prepare the OR.

Ethan moved quickly to Natalie when she arrived. He had specifically not woken her up after her long overnight shift the evening before to tell her what happened. There was nothing for her to do but worry until Eric arrived. Now, he held onto her as he told her what happened. Her eyes widened and the blood drained out of her face. He tightened his grip when he thought her knees might give out. When she caught a glimpse of Eric over Ethan's shoulder, she stiffened, nodded, and announced she would join Sebastian in surgery to assist him. The glare she tossed Ethan's way as she walked out was deadly. Danny wasn't the only one in hot water.

"He should be at a trauma center." Jackie hissed at her husband. "I don't like all the commando doctoring."

"No trauma center," Danny said. He reached out to his wife, but she stepped away. A bad sign, Ethan thought. He didn't think Danny anticipated his wife being this irate. Annoyed, yes. Livid, no.

"You're a cop, *Daniel*. You're supposed to be reporting things like this."

"It was a government-sanctioned operation, *Jacklyn*." Danny fired back in a harsh whisper. Norrie and her Facebook page had eyes and ears everywhere. "He was field treated and transferred here for care. He wanted to be near his daughter so she would be able to see him and know he was going to be okay. He's here. You have a patient. Now go deal with it."

Silence descended on the ER as everyone warily looked around at each other. "Deal with it?" Jackie's voice was low. Danny looked a little surprised at his own harshness but said nothing. "I'll show you how I *deal with it*, chief." Spinning on her heel she swung out of the small exam room.

"You're a fucking idiot," Sebastian chuckled at Danny as he watched Natalie push medication into Eric's IV.

"I'd punch you in the face for talking to my sister like that, but I'm too exhausted from the lack of sleep." Ethan added. Danny gave them both the finger.

Natalie didn't weigh in. Nor did she speak to anyone other than Sebastian, and that was only in reference to Eric's care. Along with the irritation he saw in his sister, he also saw her worry and pain. Her hands slightly shook, her face was pale, and she never took her eyes from Eric, constantly touching him in some way. Ethan sincerely hoped Natalie and Eric would be able to work out their differences. The love and tension that radiated off both of them when they were in the same room was palpable.

"All right," Sebastian said. "Let's get him to pre-op. Betsy and Teresa are there to finish his prep while we scrub in."

Natalie and Sebastian wheeled the hospital bed out of the exam room. Natalie pushed the rail with one hand and held Eric's hand with her other one. Danny and Ethan were left in the eerie silence that followed.

"Need a place to crash tonight?" Ethan asked with a smirk.

"She'll never be *that* pissed at me." Danny said. "We've been through too much to push each other to alternative sleeping arrangements. She may not speak to me for the rest of the day, and I'm pretty sure she'll be withholding sex until she deems me punished—"

Ethan held out a hand. "Don't ever use the words 'punish' and 'sex' in same sentence when referring to my sister again."

"We'll be fine." Danny assured. "I'm going to go home and get some sleep. You should too while Eric's out. When I wake up, I'm going to plan my groveling strategy."

That sounded good to Ethan, only he didn't want to sleep in his own bed. Despite Brooke working at the store that day, Ethan went home, grabbed a change of clothes and his dog, and let himself into Brooke's house.

After changing into flannel pants and a Maverick's t-shirt, he removed his prosthetic foot and dropped into her bed followed by Bravo. Surrounded by her scent, a beautiful winter view of the lake, and his trusty companion, he fell into an exhausted, and blessedly dreamless, sleep.

Seventeen

A S ETHAN ENTERED Eric's hospital room, a nurse—who wasn't Natalie—was just leaving. Eric didn't look awesome. His face was still pale white after so much blood loss. His usually clean-shaven face was now sporting the beginnings of a hipster beard, which just looked odd, and his eyes were distant. Ethan knew that look. It was the same one he had for months after his accident.

Eric looked over when Ethan entered. Hospital rooms creeped Ethan out—even the comfortable rooms in the Grayson Falls hospitals that were more like bedrooms since the hospital was in a converted Victorian home. Shoving his hands in his pockets, he stepped forward. The hardwood floors creaked under his feet. He leaned against the bed.

"You actually look better than you did when you came in." Ethan said by way of conversation opener. "How do you feel?"

"Exhausted." Eric spoke through cracked lips, closing his eyes briefly.

"That's probably from the blood loss." Ethan nodded. "I remember that feeling."

"Other than that, Sebastian seems to be pretty liberal with the pain meds for the moment. I can't feel anything else." He sounded as tired as he looked. The confident, strong man Ethan normally knew Eric to be was currently on a hiatus. Eric tried to adjust his position and winced, sweat breaking out on his brow. Eric's strong, muscled arms were useless to him now. It was tough to see someone that was usually so strong, confident, and virile, laid low by an injury that could have killed him. Ethan had visited hospital beds like this too often in the military.

"They taking good care of you?"

"She doesn't come in here." Eric said, his gaze moving away from Ethan, the disappointment clear on his face.

"Yes, she does." Ethan said. "She just does it when you're sleeping. She was here when you came in, and she treated you with Sebastian. She insisted on being his nurse assistant in surgery. They probably should have denied her, but outwardly she was calm and collected. Inside she was a mess."

"She tell you that?" A little bit of hope tinged his rough voice.

Ethan shook his head. "She didn't have to. I'm her twin. I see things that others don't. And because of that, I need to tell you to step back now."

The spark Eric's eyes normally held briefly appeared but then was replaced by resignation and what Ethan thought looked like heart-break. "You think I should give up."

"No." Ethan assured quickly. "But you need to step back. Leave only the basic security on the house, no more texts reminding her to lock the doors and windows. She *needs* the freedom and indepen-dence, dude. She's never had that. I know you care about her, but she's feeling stifled."

Gritting his teeth, Eric pushed himself up just a bit on the bed. "I don't *care* about her, Ethan. I'm balls deep in love with her."

Ethan cringed at Eric's analogy. The very last image Ethan want-ed in his head was Eric balls deep in his sister. That was going to be seared onto his brain now. Ethan held out his hand. "Let's not go there with those images, if you please." He said. "She's very frustrated and feeling smothered. You don't want to push her in the wrong di-rection. I like you, I respect you, and I like you for her."

"But?"

"We shared a womb. My loyalties are to her."

"I can respect that." Eric said with a small nod. "Does she know the mission was a success?"

"She knows *the* mission was a success, but she doesn't know what the mission was." Ethan replied. "I don't know how she'll react, but I do know she'll do something drastic about the security system. Until she came here, all the men in her life were douchebags. She went from a crappy upbringing to a crappy relationship to a price on her head. All the men in her life let her down. I *know* you won't, but it's time to let this happen organically. She's safe now. I'll even be moving in with Brooke, though I do have an eye on a good guard dog for her. She'll still be a woman living alone." And he planned to train said dog himself.

Dropping his head back into the pillow, Eric looked up at the ceiling. "I hear you and will follow your instructions accordingly. I'm a protector, E. It's just who I am."

"You're good at it." Ethan pushed off the side of the mattress. "I'm going to let you rest now. I've got some packing to do."

"That's good news." Eric smiled lightly, but his happiness for Ethan didn't meet his eyes. Ethan also remembered that well from the time he was injured. "It would really set my mind at ease if you at least left Bravo there until another very large, very mean dog could be found."

Chuckling, Ethan shook his head. "No to Bravo, unless she asks for him."

Eric nodded. When they heard, *"Daddy!"* ring out on the stairs, Eric finally lit up. His daughter ruled his life. Though Ethan didn't know Eric before like Danny did, he could imagine the chaos she caused in the life of the eternal bachelor when she unexpectedly entered it.

Leaving the room, Ethan called out a greeting to Emma, who tore past him with a nurse hot on her heels. Intent on saying hello to his brother and sisters downstairs, Ethan made his way first to the office, but stopped just outside the door when he heard voices. Jackie and Danny were in there, and Jackie was in tears. They spoke in low volume.

"I'm so sorry I've been so mean," Jackie sobbed.

"It's okay. I wasn't very nice either. I was tired, and when you snapped, I snapped back." Danny said. "I handled it wrong."

"It's just the baby is making me emotional, and I'm having crazy mood swings."

Whoa!

"Come again?" Danny asked, and Ethan grinned at what he imagined was Danny's stunned face.

Ethan knew the conversation was meant to be private, but it still made him feel lighter now with Jackie's announcement of a second baby to Danny. He crept away as quietly as he could manage. He'd let them have their privacy and wait with the rest of their family for the big announcement.

Natalie came out of an exam room and stopped short when she saw him.

"I just saw him." Ethan said to her, pulling her out of the middle of the hallway to the wall.

"He's awake then?"

Ethan nodded. "Based on what you and I talked about, I talked to him. I told him to step back. He said he would."

Pressing a hand to her chest, Natalie leaned back against the wall. "I don't know what's going on inside of me now, E. One minute I'm angry with him for being smothering, and the next I'm terrified to lose him. What do I do with that?"

"Nothing at the moment." Ethan shrugged. "He's got recovery ahead of him. He's out of commission with work, and he's up there focusing on his daughter. You've got your breathing room. You have time to figure it all out—time to figure out who you are and who you want to be. Believe me, it's a bitch of a spot to be in. I know first-hand."

"So many people we know came to this little, bitty town for a second chance." Natalie said. "How many others are here like us? It's a nice town, you know? It fits like a hug."

Smiling, Ethan couldn't agree more. "I'll see you at home?" Natalie nodded then kissed him on the cheek. Rather than looking for Sebastian, Ethan just left. He had work to do—he had packing and a Christmas present to plan.

"FUCK!"

Brooke was just putting the final touches on a gingerbread house that would serve as one of the center pieces at the wedding when her cousin's outburst came. They were over in the café area where they were each working on a house. The wedding was days away, and now all the small details had to come together. Sophie slammed down her phone. Brooke looked over, still hunched over her house and applying white icing to the roof. They were trying to make each house a little different.

"Something wrong?" Brooke asked, turning the house on its cardboard plate for inspection.

"It's supposed to snow on Christmas Eve!" Dropping her head back, Sophie groaned at the ceiling.

Shrugging, Brooke picked up the house and walked into the kitchen to set it with the others. "It's New Hampshire in December." She called back to her cousin in the café. "That's sort of to be expected." Brooke picked up another house box and walked back out, setting it on the table where she was working. "Besides, fresh snow will make the pictures perfect. We won't have to fake it."

"People are coming from out of town." Sophie reminded her. "There's no close airport."

Brooke walked to the wood-burning stove and opened the door. Singeing heat met her face. The fire was roaring, but they would need it to start dying down in a few hours. Opting not to add any additional wood, she picked up the fire poker and shifted the wood around for optimal burning and oxygenation, then closed the door again, setting the poker back in its place.

"The important people will already be here," Brooke replied. "Both your parents and Ryan's dad are coming in tomorrow, and most others are coming on the twenty-third. The hotel and the bed and breakfasts in town are booked up. And people are staying up on top of the mountain in rentals up there. It's not that big of a deal. They just need to get to the resort."

"We're going to go up the mountain in a snow storm?" Sophie countered. She picked up her icing, squeezed some on her fingertip and licked it off.

"If I have to put you in a plow, I'll get you and the VIPs there," Brooke vowed. Hell, she'd put people on horseback. "The ski resort maintains the road up the mountain very well in snow storms. They want the Christmas customers. They have your event. They're going to stay on top of it."

"You're awfully calm about this." Sophie said, furrowing her brow and pointing an icing filled finger at Brooke.

"Because there's nothing to be done about the weather," Brooke replied. "I assumed when you picked Christmas Eve in New Hampshire you considered snow a factor. Hell, I assumed you *wanted* a white Christmas this year. Seriously, don't turn into a Bridezilla now, especially over something we can do nothing about."

Huffing again, Sophie picked up her house and disappeared into the kitchen, returning with another box to start a new one. The shop was slow today, which was odd given how close they were to Christmas. It worried Brooke a bit since they were closing on Christmas Eve so the part-time employees could attend the wedding. They would not be able to accommodate last-minute shoppers. She had put signs on the doors the week prior letting everyone know that they wouldn't be open, but it definitely made her want to beef up the website all the more for the online Christmas shoppers. After the New Years' ball, she would go full steam ahead with the website.

"Soph, the only things that matter that day is that you marry Ryan Willis and that you do it in a fabulous dress. If we get stuck half-way up the mountain, I'll have the priest brought down on a snowmobile, and we'll do it on the side of the road. Don't miss the forest for the trees—or the wedding for the snowflakes."

Nodding, Sophie blew out a long breath then rolled her head around to release the tension in her neck. "I know, I know." She went to work opening the box. "I don't know why I'm freaking out so much. I hired you so you'd freak instead of me, and you're not freaking, which is freaking me out even more."

Arranging her gingerbread planks for setup, Brooke cocked her head and studied what she had, trying to think up a new layout.

"Don't forget this was pretty much all I did married to Josh. I was constantly planning *something*, and if it wasn't something hosted by us, I was on a committee with my mother planning something else. Things go wrong. You deal with it. Weather is out of your control. Are the stocking favors stuffed?"

As favors for each guest, they had little plaid Christmas stockings that were stuffed with candy canes. They would make a nice touch on the table with the houses and poinsettias. Brooke could care less if people actually ate the candy canes. Anything left over, they could feed to the horses.

"Yes, they're stuffed," Sophie said. "And Brooke, you have, and have always had to me, more value than your ability to plan the perfect event."

Brooke's eyes watered, despite the fact that she had made peace with the way her life was in Boston versus what she made of it now in Grayson Falls. Looking up to her cousin, Brooke said, "I know that now. Thank you. It was something that took me a long time to understand and truly believe. The people here in this town, most of them have been so nice and welcoming to me. There were some that didn't like my 'city folk ways,' but I don't see them too much and I'd like to think I've proved them wrong anyway. I hated my parents for sending me away to boarding school, you remember? There were years I thought maybe Danny was onto something always trying to get kicked out. But for the most part, I liked it because I liked being *here*. I liked being with the horses. And when it was just us in our room, I liked that I truly got to be *me*, and not that person my parents wanted me to be and show the world. I think other than Grandma and Grandpa, you're the only person in the world that's always known the real me."

Sophie's eyes watered now too, and she fanned her face. "Sorry. I'm overly emotional right now. That's just the sweetest thing anyone's ever said to me."

Rolling her eyes at her cousin's dramatics, Brooke said, "I'm sure Ryan has said sweeter words to you than that."

"He's a different person. His words mean something different to me."

"Well, it's all true."

Rather than continue the emotional dive into all the feels, Brooke and Sophie concentrated on their houses. They could comfortably share silence. They had perfected that growing up—just taking comfort in each other's presence without having to talk a lot. It was especially handy when one of them was out of sorts for one reason or another and needed to work out what they were feeling on their own, but at the same time, didn't want to be alone. It was something Brooke missed greatly when they graduated from Trent Academy and went their separate ways to college.

Once the final house was finished and they were all safely set aside to cure and stay out of the way for the next few days, Brooke and Sophie began their closing routine. Typically, only one of them stayed until closing, but they doubled up in the hopes of getting the gingerbread houses done. According to Brooke's very detailed and intimidating master wedding list, there were very few details left to sort out, and most of them would be done the day of the wedding.

"So, are you and Ethan spending Christmas Day together?" As always, at the mention of Ethan's name, Brooke warmed inside, a slow smile spreading across her face.

"I believe we're all gathering at Jackie and Danny's at some point, but other than that, that's the plan." Brooke couldn't remember the last time she anticipated a Christmas as much as this one. Of course, they would gather with his family, and his parents would still be in town, but she did like the idea of a quiet Christmas together. Maybe next year.

"Did you get him a gift?"

"I did." Brooke replied. But she wasn't sure how he would feel about it. She was taking a very big risk. She *hoped* he saw that she was being thoughtful and getting him something he could use, but things were still so new between them, she honestly wasn't sure how he would react.

"And you're not going to tell me?" Her cousin coaxed.

"I'm keeping it to myself for now." She would be devastated if Ethan hated the gift, but at least if she kept it a secret no one else would know of her humiliation ... unless of course Ethan was so angry with her he told everyone. But he wouldn't do that.

Would he?

Eighteen

E THAN HAULED ANOTHER bag of trash out to the small garage attached to the house he shared with his twin sister. If his sister noticed that he was slowly purging his room, she didn't mention it. He was only saving the essential things. He wasn't a hoarder, but there were things he was holding onto that he didn't need to. He wanted to go into this next phase of his life with only what was most important to him and leave what didn't matter behind—or thrown away. A clean slate for both of them.

The doorbell rang, but Ethan paid it no mind as he eyed his military uniforms. He really only needed to keep his dress uniform, right? He didn't need the rest, did he? It wasn't like he was still active or even in the reserves. He just needed something for funerals and random other events. Maybe he should keep the dress blues and the greens.

"Ethan!" Natalie's voice called from the living room. She sounded concerned, so he quickly left his room and joined her at the front door. A tired-looking, balding man stood there dressed in a suit, holding up a badge from the Marshalls Service. Bravo sat quietly, staring the man down and intermittently showing his teeth. The Marshall eyed the dog warily in return. Ethan had been expecting someone from the agency but Natalie had not. Technically, Natalie shouldn't have involved him in this conversation as her identity was supposed to be kept secret, but she was scared. She didn't know what to make of their sudden appearance.

Ethan squeezed her shoulder. "It's all right. I've actually been expecting them." Ethan stepped back to allow the man into the house.

Since Bravo wouldn't budge, Ethan gave him the stand down command. The dog backed up, but only a few feet.

"You've been expecting them?" Natalie asked confused. "Did you call them? Why would you do that?"

"No, ma'am," the man said, stepping farther away from the dog. "I'm Deputy U.S. Marshall Steve Goodin. I'm here officially to deliver news." He looked over at Ethan with a raised eyebrow. "Perhaps we can have privacy."

Ethan shook his head. Not happening. This was an important day in his twin's life, and he would share it with her. "I know why you're here."

"You do?" Deputy Goodin and Natalie said at the same time.

Ethan turned to Natalie. "I do, and I'm sorry for not saying anything before now. I thought this best delivered from the Marshalls service." Ethan smiled, but Natalie shook her head not understanding why he would be happy to see a DUSM standing in their living room. To Natalie, this was bad news and likely meant a relocation and new identity. "Let's sit."

Natalie grabbed Ethan's hand as they sat down in the corner of the plush sectional couch and Deputy Goodin sat adjacent to them. "Ms. Shepherd," he began. "It's not often we get to make these visits. In fact, in my career, I never have. It's just something that so rarely happens in our line of work. I'm happy to report to you that the Espinoza cartel in Mexico was disbanded in a joint operation, and the Marshalls service has determined the threat to you and your safety to be over. Thus, as of the start of the New Year, our protection is no longer needed."

Despite already knowing this information, happiness spread through Ethan—for his sister, for his family. They couldn't ask for a better Christmas present than Natalie's freedom. Natalie sat silent by his side. When he looked over at her for her reaction, her face was blank. "I ... I don't understand." She whispered, her hand tightening around his.

"In a joint operation between the U.S. Military, the U.S. Marshall Service, and a private contractor, a raid was carried out on the Espinoza cartel in Mexico on December 19. Its members either killed in the raid or arrested. Very few escaped, and these are being hunted down. They would not be strong enough to rise up and certainly are too low in the organization to have known anything about you. The cartel has been completely disbanded. You're a free woman, Ms. Currie. A full report will be issued to you."

Ethan snapped his eyes up to the Deputy's the same time Natalie did. *Ms. Currie.* Natalie's birth name. He looked over at his twin, and she turned her eyes on him—a silent conversation passing between them in which he tried to reassure her that this was real. Something Natalie saw in Ethan's eyes encouraged her, and she nodded her head twice, turning back to Deputy Goodin.

"What happens now?" She asked, clearing her throat of the emotion he knew was bubbling up inside her. "Do I lose this identity?"

"As Sarah Currie has been wiped out of existence, it would be our recommendation that you do not resume your original identity. As I said, a few members of the cartel did escape, and while the Marshalls service does not perceive any of those men as a threat. Keeping your current identity will add an extra layer of protection."

Nodding, Natalie looked back to Ethan. "You knew this already." Ethan nodded back. "The private contractor was Delta Security. Eric was injured on *this* mission."

"I'm sorry, that's classified information," Deputy Goodin said.

But Ethan never signed anything that kept *him* from talking. He merely held his sister's eyes and bobbed his head in confirmation. "I didn't want to say anything to you until I knew what the Marshalls service was going to do. Danny and I were in Eric's command center that night. They've had a Deputy US Marshall embedded with that cartel for a while."

"Which is *also* classified information," Goodin said between his teeth.

"It wasn't classified to me." Ethan shot back. *That guy can go right to hell.* "And this is *her* life. She has a right to know how and why it changed."

Natalie put a calming hand on Ethan's and turned her attention back to the Deputy Marshall. "You'll have paperwork and some kind of exit procedure, I assume?"

Goodin glared at Ethan a moment longer before turning to Natalie and softening his gaze. "Yes, ma'am. We'll be in touch again to go over all that. And, of course, should you feel threatened in any way or have any reason to think the danger to you is *not* over, the U.S. Marshall Service will reevaluate our decision to close your case."

"That's very comforting, thank you." Natalie stood up, and Goodin quickly picked up on her cue. Ethan rose as well and put a supportive hand on her shoulder. Goodin walked to the door, giving Bravo a wide berth. The dog followed, shepherding their visitor out, who nodded his goodbye and left quickly.

Natalie and Ethan stood there in silence for a long moment—Natalie staring at the closed door, Ethan staring at his sister. He wanted to hug her. He wanted to call the others. He wanted to bust out at the seams. But he dared not make a move. It was what Natalie wanted that was important—her emotions ruled what they did. After some time, the first sob escaped his sister. Bringing her hands up to her face, she choked out another sob. When Ethan wrapped his arms around her, the ocean broke over the dunes. Her tears soaked his shirt, and his body absorbed the spasms of hers as she expelled the last few years from her system—fear, tension, stress, anxiety flowing from her body like a purged poison.

Rubbing her back and stroking her hair, he crooned in her ear. "I love you so much, Nat. You're my other half. We can be a real family now. You're safe."

"I never wanted anything so badly in life." Her choppy words broke his heart.

Ethan pulled back and cupped her cheeks in his hands. "You can stand on your own two feet now—no one controlling your life but you. I'll make sure of it."

Nodding, Natalie sniffled, step back and wiped her tears. "I want that. I'm going to start by kicking you out, E."

Smiling, Ethan dug his hands in his pockets. "Sounds perfect. I'm moving in with Brooke."

Natalie laughed and wiped more tears, then laughed again before throwing her head back and giving in to hysterical laughter that turned into more tears. But this time, they were good tears.

BROOKE WAS JUST FINISHING wrapping presents when her doorbell rang. Looking up, she could see Ethan's truck in the driveway and wondered why he didn't just use his key. Butterflies erupted in her stomach at the thought of seeing him. She hoped that feeling never went away. Scurrying across the floor in her fuzzy slippers, she flung open the doors. He stood there grinning on her porch. Not only did his smile meet his eyes, but it seemed to illuminate his entire being. He had a large camouflage bag slung over his shoulder, another at his feet, and Bravo sitting next to him, wagging his tail.

"All my worldly possessions are in the back of my truck," he said by way of opener. "Do you mind if a poor farm boy and his dog crash with you for the foreseeable future?"

Brooke felt like her whole body smiled. Hopping forward, she threw her arms around his neck and caused the dog to bark and jump around them.

"Best Christmas present ever!" she exclaimed. His arms came around her, one hand diving into her hair and holding her firmly in place like he never wanted to let her go.

"That's a yes?" he asked into her shoulder, taking a deep inhale of her scent.

"How can you even ask?" she replied. Pulling back, she pressed a kiss to his lips before continuing. "I feel like I've been waiting my whole life. Come in. We'll get the rest later. Tell me everything!"

Holding the door open, she backed up so he could pass. Bravo darted in, and she heard him run through the house doing his security check, clearing all the rooms and ensuring there was no danger. After wiping his feet, Ethan dropped his bags just inside the door and pushed them to the side with his foot. He shrugged out of his coat and hung it on the decorative coat rack by the door.

Grabbing his hand, Brooke tugged him over to the couch, and they dropped down together. Bravo curled up on the pillow next to the wood stove that currently housed a warm fire. Ethan propped his foot up on the table. If it had been anybody else, Brooke would have demanded they remove their dirty shoe from her brand-new Pottery Barn table, but it was Ethan. It was his home now, and he put his foot up to rest, not to be rude. She would never deny him anything about brought him more comfort.

"There's something I have to tell you." Ethan said. *Obviously*, Brooke thought. If Ethan was finally moving in then something happened at home with Natalie. "I couldn't tell you this sooner. When you hear it, you'll know why and I really hope you understand. A few years ago, a woman by the name of Sarah Currie went on a relief mission trip to Mexico. While she was there, she was witness to a political assassination by a well-known drug cartel. She was the *only* witness. Sarah was the government's star witness in the trial and incarceration of Juan Espinoza. However, Espinoza put a significant price on her head and Sarah was taken into the Witness Protection Program by the U.S. Marshalls and given a new identity."

It didn't take long for Brooke to make the connection, given where her thoughts already were where Natalie was concerned.

"Natalie Shepherd."

"Right," Ethan said. "Natalie is our sister. She's *my* twin sister."

Brooke's jaw dropped—not in shock, but in that final "ah-ha!" moment that had been eluding her since Ethan confirmed some of her suspicions were true. They were siblings, not cousins. And twins!

"Oh, Ethan," Brooke said. "And growing up, you had no idea you had a twin?"

"I didn't know I had any siblings." Ethan shrugged. "I found out that Natalie was my twin last year when Zach, Jackie, and I went to see our mother, Daisy. A light breeze could have leveled me when she told us. Our birth mother isn't well, and her memory's been failing for years, but I knew—I *knew*—she was right. Since Nat and I met we were different than the others. We understood each other immediately, bonded faster than with our brothers and sister. I'm different now that she's in my life. She's the other half of me."

"I understand." Brooke said, reaching out and cupping his cheek, running her fingers gently along his beard. Ethan turned into her hand and kissed the inside of her wrist before covering her hand with his. "It's wonderful that you have someone like that in your life and that you found each other again."

Ethan tugged her over until she straddled his legs and his hands fell to her hips. Their physical reaction to the intimate position was immediate. Sitting up straight, he lifted his head and pressed his lips to hers. She sighed against him, and her arms wrapped around his neck. With the fire going and the soft glow of the Christmas lights on the tree, Brooke knew without a doubt that of all the years they had ahead of them, this Christmas would be one she would never forget.

"You're so strong," he said softly, trailing a finger down her cheek. "Other women would be jealous that a woman other than them held such a prominent place in my life, but not you. *You* know that having someone I'm so close to in no way diminishes how much I love you. You know that, right?"

Tipping her forehead against his, she said, "Of course I do. Ethan, she's your *twin sister*. If she were, say, a best friend, I might not be as strong as you seemed to think I am. But you've been together since conception. Maybe you were apart for a while, but the universe brought you back together. Ethan, that's amazing."

Leaning forward, Ethan pressed a soft kiss to Brooke's neck sending delicious tingles straight down her spine. She rolled her hips, looking for friction to help relieve the fire that was kindling deep inside. His arms banded tightly around her, and he groaned into her breast—the vibration gave her shivers. Rocking herself on his lap, she clenched her fingers into his shoulder.

"Okay." Ethan said abruptly, dropping his foot from the table. "It's time to move this somewhere more comfortable." He stood up with Brooke still wrapped around him. She marveled at his strength and knew by now not to comment on his leg. He had enough hovering from his siblings, and she had vowed to herself to let him be the judge of what he could handle—despite her inner guilt over the soft grunt when he started moving.

Entering the back bedroom, they moved quickly across the heated slate floor before tumbling down onto the bed. Ethan removed his leg while Brooke scrambled to pull the blankets down and toss most of the pillows aside. After she yanked off her slippers, she paused mid-movement as she was reaching to take off her shirt. It was lightly snowing outside, and the sun was setting over the lake. As Ethan undressed next to the bed, she realized her vision had come true.

This was what she saw—she and Ethan, together, and surrounded by the beautiful background of nature. And in that moment, she realized she had finally gotten everything she wanted.

Nineteen

IT WAS CHRISTMAS Eve. The day of the wedding had finally arrived. Ethan was impressed with how calm Brooke was in the early morning hours. He expected her to be frantic with stress and last-minute details, but she woke up that morning with steady nerves. After attaching his prosthetic, Ethan padded into the kitchen to start coffee in flannel pants and a sweatshirt. He found the pot already full and hot and poured himself a mug. Furrowing his brow, he moved to the living room where Ryan sat on the couch looking at the lit tree, the only light in the room other than the fire going in the wood stove.

Sophie and Ryan had, reluctantly, split up last night as tradition demanded. Ryan stayed with Brooke and Ethan, and Sophie stayed at her house with her parents, Jackie, Megan, and Piper. As maid of honor, Brooke *should* have stayed there, too, but she begged off to stay with Ethan. While Ethan encouraged her to go to Sophie's, Brooke simply told him that she wanted to spend every Christmas minute with him she could, and he really wasn't interested in arguing with that logic. Zach, Danny, Sebastian, and Ryan's father Toby would come to Ethan and Brooke's, and once she was satisfied they were running on time, she would leave to go get ready at Sophie's before heading up to the resort for the last-minute details and to ensure everything was running smoothly there.

His girl had it together.

Ethan sat down next to his brother. Ryan hadn't moved or acknowledged his presence. A full, and likely cold, cup of coffee sat clutched in his hand. Ethan sipped his coffee but didn't try to engage his brother in conversation. Ethan wasn't the talker in the family, and he was content to share silence with someone if that's what they needed. He himself would take all the time he could this morning to ready himself to spend the afternoon and evening with a lot of people.

Bravo entered the room, his nails clipping along the floor. Ethan didn't look at his dog until Bravo sat next to him and whimpered. It was the sound the pup made when he was out of sorts, so Ethan immediately looked over to him when he heard the distress signal.

But nothing was wrong with his faithful companion—at least not in the way Ethan had thought. Instead, the stoic and proud dog sat there in front of Ethan with a red and green plaid bow around his neck and a Santa hat on his head. Brook had even made holes for Bravo's ears to pop through.

Laughing, Ethan said, "Christ, buddy, what'd she do to you?"

Ryan finally moved, looking over at the dog and letting out a huffed laugh. "Damn, E, your dog is crazy disciplined."

"Yeah," Ethan agreed, leaning over and giving Bravo a good scratch. "He'll keep that shit on all day, too. He'll be miserable, but he'll do it because he was told to." Bravo gave another whimper. "Sorry, bud. She's the boss."

"I'll take it off him in a bit," Brooke said, wandering into the room in white satin pajamas with a coffee mug in her hand. "You can put it back on him before you leave. If he's going to be at the wedding, he needs to be dressed for it."

"Baby, I told you he could stay here."

Brooke waved her free hand in dismissal. "You're going to be in a crowd, dressed up, with a lot of pictures being taken, and stuck having to talk to a lot of people. It's an introvert's hell, and I won't always be able to be by your side. You'll need him today. He's getting a special dinner prepared by the resort just for him. It's his reward for wearing that all day."

She had literally thought of all the details. Perhaps this part of Brooke's past life saddened her, but Ethan saw it as a superpower. She had all her ducks in a row, kept everybody on track, and made special days beautiful and stress free for everyone.

His girl's game was on point.

Brooke stepped in front of Ryan, hooked her finger under his chin, and studied his face with a sharpened eye.

"You're up too early." She said critically. "Let's see how puffy you made your eyes." She turned Ryan's head one way then the other. "Wow. You look great."

"What's the tone of surprise?" Ryan asked her with a laugh.

"You're up really early, and I know you didn't go to sleep until late because you were on the phone with Sophie. She better not have puffy eyes this morning."

Ryan turned his head out of her grip. "I'm up early because I couldn't wait for this day to get started. I'm getting married today."

"You bet your ass you are," she grinned.

Brooke sat down next to Ethan and curled into his side, taking another sip of her coffee. Ethan put his arm around her and pulled her in close. He *did* want her by his side today and knew that was impossible. He'd just have to keep in contact with her when they were separated, and when they were all together, he would make sure to always keep her in his line of sight. Between that and Bravo, it would be enough to get him through. He refused to be a burden to anyone today—*especially* to her. She had too much to focus on and accomplish today to also worry about him.

"Who would have thought all those years growing up Dixie and I would be getting married?" Ryan said, almost in wonder and using to his childhood nickname for Sophie.

"Gotta' admit, I thought it was going to be me," Brooke quipped. She and Ryan shared a laugh. Ethan *knew* that they were joking and Brooke was trying to keep things light so Ryan didn't start to stress out. But he'd be lying to himself if he didn't admit that a part of him wondered if Brooke was sad today that her childhood crush was marrying someone else.

"You make her so happy, Ry," Brooke said.

"She makes me happy." A soft look came into his eyes as he looked back up at the tree, it's soft glow adding a sense of serenity to the room. "I was just sitting here this morning thinking that my life took a direction I never saw coming. Ever since Jacks came into my life it's been one curveball after another. If there's anything I learned along the way it's that life is definitely unpredictable."

"No kidding." Ethan raised his mug in cheers and took a long sip.

"I was never ready for anything thrown my way. Everything threw me for a loop and had me reeling. But today ... today I'm *ready*. Don't guys usually get cold feet or something on their wedding day?"

"*Guys* do," Brooke said. "But real *men* don't. You were smart to wait for Sophie. You didn't let anyone push you into something you didn't really want. That's what makes you ready. On my wedding day, *I* was the one with the cold feet. I knew I was making a huge mistake, but I couldn't stand the thought of my parents' disappointment and embarrassment if I called the whole thing off. I should have done that. I should have said, 'fuck this,' and bolted then—gone to Sophie then. She had just put the offer in on the store then, and all I could think about was how brave she was to go after what she wanted." Ethan stroked Brooke's hair while she spoke.

"You're brave, too," he said, pressing a kiss to her temple. "You did bolt. It doesn't matter when you did it, only that you did. The timing was good, and you were in the right frame of mind. What if you got here too soon and fell in love with one of Megan's brothers or Laurie's? Those Over the Hop guys are probably a catch."

Brooke placed a hand on one of his cheeks and kissed his other one. "Impossible," she whispered. He tipped his forehead to hers. The three of them put their feet up onto the coffee table and enjoyed the cozy morning—fire blazing, the soft, peaceful glow of the tree lights and no snow.

Bravo lay down on his pillow, dropped his snout to his paws, and whimpered again. Ethan, Ryan, and Brooke all laughed. Eventually, Brooke stood up to go put together breakfast, and Ethan rose to help her. Ryan stayed behind still lost in his thoughts.

Ethan wasn't ever ready for the universe threw at him either. He certainly wasn't ready for Brooke. But he knew what Ryan was feeling. Because that morning, Ethan was also ready to spend the rest of his life with an amazing woman.

BROOKE FLUTTERED AROUND the ballroom at the ski lodge, checking to make sure everything was in place. The wedding party arrived safely, and boys and girls were ensconced in their separate suites. They lucked out with the weather. The snow was still coming, but now it wasn't supposed to start until after the ceremony, which was set to begin in half an hour. The guests were able to get up the mountain. How everyone was going to get back down again was a problem for later.

Friends and family were being seated in a beautiful stone and wood room, which was designed and built just for occasions such as this. The reception would be in the ballroom, which Brooke was now closely scrutinizing—checking the gingerbread houses on the tables to make sure no one had taken a swipe of the icing, making sure every light in the poinsettia jars was lit, ensuring each little stocking at each seat at the same number of candy canes.

"Oh, honey!" Her aunt gushed entering the ballroom with Brooke's mother. "Everything looks just perfect!"

Before Brooke could offer her thanks and feel any sense of pride, her mother cut in. "*Nothing* is perfect." Lenore said matter-of-factly.

"So, let's split up and make sure everything is in order. We can't have anything marring our Sophie's big day." Lenore turned on her Louboutin heel and headed off to inspect Brooke's hard work and make a list of everything she disapproved of.

Brooke and her aunt rolled their eyes at each other as Brooke's muscles tightened with annoyance. Lenore was nothing if not completely predictable. Her aunt smiled brightly and opened her arms to Brooke. Gladly, Brooke fell into them. Lili Van Stewart had been more of a mother to her than Lenore ever had. In fact, in all her life, Brooke had spent *more* time with Lili than her own mother. The hug was genuine, warm, and full of love.

"You are a gorgeous mother-of-the-bride," Brooke smiled. Lili patted her graying hair and ran a hand down her trim figure, clad in a deep emerald satin dress that was much sexier than the typical mother-of-the-bride wear. Brooke's own mother, of course, looked absolutely stunning in a black Stella McCartney. Having already seen the bride, though, Brooke could say with confidence that though Lenore Larrabe looked exquisite, she did not outshine Sophie. Her mother would have to come to grips with that.

"Everything *is* perfect, sweetheart." Lili said. "This is how Lenore makes herself feel useful."

"I remember the feeling well." Brooke said. She paused for a second. It had never occurred to her that maybe her mother felt the same way Brooke had in her loveless marriage. But if that was true, Lenore had obviously found the money and prestige more important than independence and a sense of self-worth.

"I won't take up too much of your time, dear." Lili linked arms with Brooke and walked her farther away from where her mother was inspecting the gingerbread houses with something that looked a lot like disdain. Brooke felt her body begin to tense in annoyance, but took a deep breath instead and forced her muscles to relax. She refused to let her mother ruin the day or take away any of the pride

Brooke had for her hard work. They were charming, and she and So-phie did an amazing job with them. They were surrounded by a circle of tall thin vases with poinsettias and white lily stems. All the glass vases were lit up inside by fairy lights.

"I have some time now," Brooke assured her. "And of course, I'll find you again at the reception."

"Of course, dear." Lili patted her arm. "Now, tell me about this man of yours that has your parents wrapped up tighter than a Christ-mas present."

Glancing over at her mother, now picking up the small stocking favors, Brooke's stomach knotted. Her parents hadn't mentioned Ethan at all to her in any of their conversations leading up to the wedding. If they were "wrapped too tight," it was likely they got their intel from Josh. *Fantastic. How much fun was this not going to be?*

"Sophie's told me a lot about him, of course," Lili continued. "Him officially becoming her kin today and all. He sounds just won-derful."

"He is," Brooke couldn't help the joy that bubbled up whenever she talked about Ethan. "I love him so much. I can't wait for you to meet him."

"Neither can I, sweetie, neither can I," Lili said. They saw Lenore heading their way, and Brooke braced herself. Lili lowered her voice. "Everything looks beautiful, and you've done an amazing job. Sophie was beside herself telling me all about it. I don't care what she says, you should be very proud of what you did here." Lili gave Brooke's hand a supportive squeeze as Lenore approached.

"Well, it's not what I would do, but it's nice enough." Lenore said looking around again. "Lili, shall we check on Sophie one last time?" Lenore leaned forward, and air kissed Brooke's cheeks before she swept away.

"Oh, why can't she just admit that she loves it?" Lili huffed.

"Lenore Larrabe doesn't love anything or anyone, Aunt Lili. I don't think she's capable of it. I've come to terms with that long ago."

Picking up both Brooke's hands, Lili gave them a squeeze. "You've done well for yourself, and I'm proud of you. I love you so much." Lili hugged Brooke one last time, and Brooke savored the love that rolled over her.

When Lili walked away, Brooke gave the room one last long look. Wreaths were evenly spaced between the windows. Evergreen garland was draped over the fireplace, which would soon have a roaring fire inside. And the archways leading in and out of room were decked in evergreen, lights, and large, decorative Christmas ornaments. It *was* perfect. She had created something classy, festive, and fun. It all fit Sophie and Ryan to a T—traditional, cozy, and charming.

Clapping her hands twice in glee, she left the ballroom to take her place with her cousin and start the ceremony.

ETHAN SCANNED THE BALLROOM after the ceremony. He told himself he was looking for someone he knew, but in reality, he was looking for somewhere to hide. There were too many people. He was holding up just fine, but he just wanted a breather for a minute. With Bravo by his side, he headed to the corner where the cake sat in front of a window that overlooked the ski slopes. Nobody was over there, and he could breathe a bit better. Bravo sat and leaned against Ethan's leg.

"Will he bite?"

Ethan turned at the sound of the voice. After he finished talking with this person, he'd just leave the ballroom for a few minutes to get his head together. All he needed was five or ten minutes to himself. There were plenty of places to hide in the ski lodge. He would find one—even if he had to strap on a pair of skis and take a run down the mountain.

When Ethan looked up, he saw who he now knew was Lenore Larrabe, though they hadn't been formally introduced yet. *Lovely. Cornered by his girlfriend's mother.*

"No." Ethan assured. He didn't approve of the way she looked down her nose at his dog. Bravo had done more for his country than this lady had. How dare she judge him? He sniffed out bombs in a warzone for fuck's sake.

"He's getting hair all over you."

"Doesn't bother me," Ethan said, determined to be polite.

Lenore's disapproval was apparent. She held out her hand to Ethan, but with the way she offered it, Ethan wasn't sure if he was supposed to kiss it, bow over it, or shake it. He went for a quick squeeze before stepping back again.

"I just wanted to introduce myself. My daughter hasn't gotten around to it yet, it seems."

The hair on the back of Ethan's neck prickled. If Lenore Larrabe thought Ethan would stand by while she said snide things about her daughter, she was sorely mistaken. Up until now, Ethan was anxious about what the Larrabes would think of him—whether they would approve of him. But Danny was right. After having met one of them, he knew they never would. He realized he was okay with that. What Brooke thought of him was what mattered.

"She'll get around to it." Ethan said. "She's had a lot to do today. This wedding has kept her very busy."

Lenore raised her eyebrow and looked around. "Not busy enough. There's so much potential, but it doesn't quite get there."

What. A. Bitch.

"I think she's done incredible," Ethan said through gritted teeth. "And Sophie and Ryan love it. Who else's opinion matters?" Ethan

watched as the jibe hit its mark. It seemed Lenore wasn't used to being deemed unimportant. Well, that was *her* problem.

"Indeed."

Ethan scanned the crowd looking for anyone who might save
him or give him an excuse to get out of this corner and leave the ballroom.

"Well, it was nice—" Ethan began, intent on leaving the battle-
field.

"I have a proposition for you, Mr. Donahue." Lenore cut him off.
"A deal, if you will."

Ethan didn't like the sound of that, but he stayed in place, in-
tending on hearing the woman out. What kind of deal could she possibly want with someone like him? She had no use for any of his
skills.

He cocked his head to the side and looked at her with interest.
"Fire away."

Though they were the same height, somehow, Lenore was able to
look down her nose at him. "I will give you two million dollars to
walk away from my daughter."

Silence hung between them. People milled around the room,
gushing over the decorations and ordering drinks from the
bar—completely oblivious to the insult that was just hurled at Ethan.
A ringing started in Ethan's head. Furrowing his brow, he looked at
her in confusion. "I'm sorry. I'm not sure I understood what you
said." He had, of course, but he just couldn't believe it.

"Three million."

Ethan didn't bother to try to hide his astonishment. Never in
his life had he been more offended than he was then, staring at the
woman who created his beloved while she stared at him like he was
something to squish beneath her expensive shoe. While Ethan stayed
quiet, Lenore continued.

"You see there is a great deal of money at stake here. When Brooke married into the Mars family—yes, *those* Mars—it was a merger of two powerful families, businesses, and empires. I'm afraid that's all about to be destroyed if she divorces Joshua. We can't have that. A great many people could lose their jobs. Surely as a working man yourself you can understand how horrible that could be for families."

Taking deep breaths, the ringing in Ethan's ears grew slightly louder. Bravo whined and leaned his head harder against Ethan's leg. But Ethan wasn't anxious. He was enraged. All this woman cared about was her bottom line. He was willing to wager she didn't give one shit about those families she spoke of. She cared only that her association with one of America's most wealthy families was about to end.

"You've got a lot of nerve." Ethan seethed. Lenore's eyes widened slightly. "This is *your niece's* wedding. It's no place for you to create family drama. Where's your integrity? Brooke is your *daughter*. Was it really so horrible to treat her like one all her life instead of a business asset? I know where you come from, *Lenore*. Do your friends at the country club know that? Have you ever taken Sophie's mother there, or is she not welcome in Boston?"

"How dare you." Lenore hissed low.

"How dare *you*." Ethan shot back. "I love your daughter, and unfortunately for you, she loves me. We live together, and as soon as her divorce is final, I'm going to marry her. *In Vegas*. Maybe even in a *Star Wars* chapel. You throw your money at me again, and I'm going to piss all over it. You don't even deserve her. You can take your deal and shove it up your pretentious ass. I'm not interested."

Ethan began to step by Lenore who stood there in shock and anger. He stopped, turned back and lifted the hem of his pants. "Oh, and I don't even have my whole leg."

Horrified, Lenore looked down at Ethan's prosthetic foot. Satisfaction ran through him. Then he and Bravo made a beeline for the door. He needed to find someplace to be alone, fast. He wasn't a confrontational person by nature and the exchange took a lot of out him when he already needed to regroup.

As he broke through the doors, he immediately felt the difference in the air. It was cooler in the hall. Ethan pulled his bow tie out and unbuttoned the first two buttons of his shirt, giving him a festive Tony Bennett look. Bravo stood by his side looking up at him, tongue hanging out silly had and bow tie in place, and waiting for instructions. Since being reunited with his pup, Ethan had been trying to work with the dog and teach him that he doesn't always need instructions to do something, but it seemed Ethan trained him too well the first time. Ethan raised his flat hand and Bravo's butt hit the floor.

Pacing, Ethan took deep breaths. He was livid with Brooke's mother and needed to cool down. Now he was stuck with excess energy and no way to burn it off. Signaling Bravo, Ethan turned to walk down the corridor. He'd walk around the lodge a bit and maybe work off the adrenaline.

"There you are."

Spinning at the sound of her voice, Ethan drank in the vision that was Brooke gliding toward him. Her hair was sleek and pulled off her porcelain face, eyes sparkled in the soft light of the wall sconces. His heart filled just looking at her stunning beauty. His nerves eased. Reaching up, she cupped his cheeks, gently scratching her fingers in his beard. "I saw you talking to my mother. I'm so sorry. I wanted to be there when you met. I tried to get over to you but the events coordinator cornered me about the New Years' ball."

He knew she was talking to him, but he wasn't listening. He was so overcome by the way she simply glowed that he cupped the back of her head and pulled her to him for a hard kiss. Not caring who was around to see, Brooke immediately responded and brought her own heat.

"Come," Ethan grabbed her hand and tugged her down the hall. Bravo was hot on his heels.

"Ethan, we're going to be eating soon. They'll be looking for us." Her attempt to get him back into the ballroom was half-hearted as she didn't even try to tug him in the opposite direction.

Ethan watched the signs on the doors go by as he looked for somewhere they could disappear into. He had the key to the suite that the guys were gathered in earlier, but they didn't have the time to go all the way upstairs. He'd only want to get her into the bed, and he wasn't the only one with a key. No doubt one of his brothers was plotting to disappear from the reception for the same purpose. Finally zeroing in on a family bathroom, he yanked the door open, ordered Bravo to stay in the hall. Once inside he locked the door and pushed Brooke up against it. Her hands ran up his chest and she squeezed his shoulders under his jacket.

"You look so hot in a tux." She said between heavy breaths.

"You're my fucking Christmas angel." Ethan locked his lips on the smooth skin of her neck and fumbled with his pants. This was the best way to expend the anger and emotion that had built inside him.

"Hurry, Ethan." Her breaths came in heavy pants. Boosting her legs up and around his waist, he desperately hoped she didn't remember her ban on sex up against the wall. The tension inside him was nearing explosive levels.

Finally freeing himself, he pulled her panties to the side and plunged inside her. She gasped at the erotic invasion, matching his thrusts with the same blind need that spurred him on. Thoughts spiraled out of his head, leaving only the haze-filled frenzy that now consumed him. His rhythm grew faster—harder—as his hips pistoned and her moans turned into little cries of pleasure. The pressure built up. He felt it move through his life's blood, bring with it the mindless tingling that sparked at the end of all his nerves.

He caught her scream just in time as she detonated around him. Two more thrusts and he melted into her. Sensation shot from his core and burst behind his eyelids bringing tears with them. Boneless, he pinned her against the door and she feathered kisses all over his face.

"Fuck, I love you," he sighed and picked up his head.

Brooke ran her fingers through his hair, lightly scratching his scalp. Ethan slowly turned his head, following her fingers. "What did my mother want?"

"She offered me three million dollars to walk away from you." He lowered her feet to the ground and tucked himself back into his pants. "Obviously, I didn't accept." Brooke's head fell forward, and he hooked his finger under her chin, bringing her back up to look at him. Tears shimmered in her eyes. "Hey, they could offer me every penny they have, and I wouldn't take it. You're priceless to me. Having you is what makes me rich."

"I'm sorry she did that. It was rude and just plain mean."

"Don't you ever apologize to me for the actions of someone else." He scolded gently. "You're not responsible for them." She knew that, but a bit of shame still bubbled up as she thought of any part of Ethan's day being marred by her witch of a mother. This was a day of happiness for Ethan's family and Lenore had, once again, made someone else's spotlight about her.

"Dare I ask what you said in return?"

Smirking, Ethan stepped back, allowing her room to clean herself up before they returned to the ballroom. He answered as she checked her reflection in the mirror, smoothed her dress out. "I basically told her to shove her money up her ass and then showed her my fake foot. She was sufficiently horrified."

Brooke stopped what she was doing and stared at him in the mirror. For the smallest fraction of time, he thought maybe he messed up. Then she threw her head back and laughed—hell, she *cackled*. His most favorite sound in the world came right from her toes and reverberated on the tile walls around them. She threw her arms around his neck, and he picked her up again and spun her around before planting a long, devouring kiss on her. It wasn't until they heard the pounding on the wall and baby crying that they broke apart, looking at each other wide-eyed.

"For the love of Christmas, Ethan, get out of there already!" Jackie's irate voice came through the door. "Your dog has outed you, and I need to get in there and change Ally."

Ethan moved to the door and swung it open. Jackie took in both Ethan and Brooke and scowled. "Seriously, Ethan? You're such a dog. This is your brother's wedding."

"Speaking of dogs," Brooke said stepping forward to Bravo. She reached down and removed his hat and bow tie. Bravo shook himself out and executed three hopping turns in approval of his mistress' actions. "You were a very handsome and good boy." Brooke said to him.

"And you two are ridiculous." Jackie said, trying to sooth her daughter. "Get out of here. And this bathroom better not smell like sex."

Jackie walked by them and kicked the door shut. Ethan and Brooke looked at each other and laughed. Brooke stepped forward and smoothed his hair down. He held out his hand, and she took it as they began to make the walk back to the wedding reception, Bravo walked between their outstretched hands. Just before the ballroom, Ethan stopped. Brooke turned and looked at him expectantly.

"Baby, before we go back in there, I just wanted to ask you something." Brooke cocked her head and waited for him to continue. "Just tell me whether or not there was any point during the day that you wished it was *you* marrying Ryan and not Sophie."

Brooke's expression never changed. She simply stepped forward, swung up her arm, and smacked Ethan in the head. Ethan's hand immediately came up and rubbed the sore spot she left. Then she spun on her heel without a word and marched back into the ballroom.

Ethan looked down at Bravo, who was hanging his head in what Ethan assumed was embarrassment for his owner. Ethan looked up to the doors of the ballroom and back down to his loyal pet.

"I guess that's a no."

Twenty

BROOKE AWOKE CHRISTMAS morning wrapped up in Ethan, ensconced in warm blankets and pillows, and huddled in front of their Christmas tree. The fire had died down, but the lights on the tree were still on. The house smelled of pine needles and wood burning. Craning her head, everything outside the window was snow covered. Weren't white Christmases the best? She couldn't ask for a better morning.

The wedding ran late into the night, but was a success. Getting down the mountain in the snow was not even as treacherous as predicted, given how well the resort maintained the road. Brooke had managed to avoid any further conversations with her parents after Ethan told her about what Lenore said to him. Of course, that meant it was left to simmer inside Brooke, but she was far too angry and insulted on Ethan's behalf to risk a confrontation on Sophie's special day. Everything had gone off without a hitch, and despite what Lenore had said about Brooke's choices, many people had taken the time to compliment her on a job beautifully done and to inquire if she was interested in planning various events. That would take some thinking about.

Brooke couldn't wait any longer to answer nature's call, but when she began to ease herself out of Ethan's arms, he tightened them.

"Not yet," he murmured without opening his eyes, his voice husky and sexy.

"I just want to throw more wood on the fire, start coffee, and go to the bathroom," she said. "I'll be right back."

Opening his eyes, Ethan ran a hand down his face. "Okay. I'll take care of the fire and let the dog out." Sitting up, Ethan looked around him.

"What's the matter?" she asked.

"I'm not sure how I'm going to get up. I can't find my foot or my crutches."

Scurrying out of the living room, Brooke moved back into the bedroom and grabbed the crutches from what had become Ethan's side of the bed. When she returned and handed them down to him, he took them and got up to his knees.

"I can use the foot," he said, scooting up to the couch and then onto the crutches to stand before her.

Crossing her arms, Brooke arched a brow. "Oh, really?"

"Yes?"

"You're asking me a question?"

"I don't understand what's going on here."

Brooke dropped her hands on her hips and leaned toward him. "Two words, Ethan. Wall. Sex."

Ethan smirked. "But it was really good wall sex."

Brooke's whole body warmed at the memory. It *was* really good. "Yes, but I also recall how sore you were for a few days last time. Maybe you can take it easy today and only use the foot when we go to the barn."

Ethan looked around the living room. "Where *is* my foot?"

Brooke smiled knowingly and ran to the bathroom before heading to the kitchen to start the coffee. She heard Ethan moving around as he let the dog out and then moved back to the living room to stoke the fire. She was so happy things worked out for Natalie. She wasn't sure when Ethan would ever be able to move in, and she had resigned herself to that fact of "someday." But he was here now, moving around *their* house. He brought very little with him, which Brooke thought was a little odd, but then again, when she left Josh, she came to Grayson Falls with just a couple of suitcases. Over time, Ethan would leave his mark on the house.

She pulled down two large Christmas mugs she had brought home from the store as Ethan came back in from the living room, pulling open the door to let Bravo back in. "Wow. There must be a foot of snow out there," he said. "Glad I hassled my brothers into helping me fill up the indoor hoop with wood yesterday."

Going up on her toes, Brooke pressed a kiss to his cheek. "You think of everything, Ethan. I like being taken care of by you."

Pressing his lips to her forehead, he said, "I like being taken care of by you, too."

"Presents?" she asked gleefully, pouring coffee into her mug.

"Okay," he said, pushing his toward her to fill next. "I hid yours at the barn though."

"That's okay." She returned the coffee pot to the burner. "We can get it when we go take care of the animals. Maybe we can see your parents, too. It was so nice of Jackie to let them stay with her and Danny."

Picking up the mugs, Brooke led the way back to the living room. This time they took the couch. Brooke set the mugs on coasters on the table and handed Ethan a large blanket. Once he looked settled in, Brooke retrieved his presents from under the tree. His eyes widened when he realized the three boxes were for him.

"I know we didn't talk about gifts or what we wanted or how much we should spend or anything like that. I confess that I did spend a bit, and I promise not to make it a habit, but I went a little overboard this year, and I'm not sorry."

She set the boxes in front of them. They were wrapped in shiny gold paper with fat red ribbon tied around them. Reaching over, Ethan took the smallest box off the top then tore into it. When he took the lid off the box, he paused. Inside was a smart watch. Picking it up, he moved it around to look at it.

"It's a smart watch." She said. "You can pair it to your phone."

"Brooke, baby, this is too much."

"I know." She rushed on. "But it has an app on it specifically designed for veterans with post-traumatic stress disorder. You wear it when you sleep. It can sense when you're having an attack and uses vibrations and sound to make the attacks stop without waking you up."

Ethan looked up at her, and Brooke nibbled on her bottom lip nervously.

Cupping the back of her neck, Ethan pulled Brooke to him and kissed her. "I can't believe you thought of something like that for me, baby. I'm touched."

Bolstered by his words, she bounced a bit in her spot next to him. "Since I'm on a roll then, open the big one next."

As Ethan slid the rectangular box to his lap, Brooke drew in a breath. This was one she *really* wasn't sure about. She was definitely going out on a limb with this gift and prayed it didn't blow up in her face.

Ethan pulled the lid off the box and froze. Brooke kept holding her breath, her whole body began to tremble with nerves. "Now I know you spent too much," he whispered.

Slowly, he pulled out a new demand response foot. They were expensive. She knew he only had two, but she couldn't stand the thought that he might go without something he needed. The one he wore to the farm already broke a time or two, and she knew he fixed it himself.

"I had it personalized." She whispered.

He turned the foot over and looked at the suction cup. The words, *I do all my own stunts,* were displayed in happy black font. Brooke thought she was going to explode waiting to find out what he thought, but when he threw back his head and laughed, she finally expelled her breath.

"You really like it?"

Ethan laughed so hard tears ran down his face, and he brushed them aside. He nodded his head. When he could get himself under control, he looked over at her. "I fucking love you," he said. "You spent way too much money, but you were thoughtful. I'm touched, really. I may even wear shorts in the summer now."

"That was the intention." She said. "Last box."

"Okay." He took a sip of her coffee before he reached for the final flat box. Opening it, he pulled out two handmade, personalized Christmas stockings to hang on the mantle next to hers. Reverently, he ran his hands over them—one for him and one for Bravo. Clearing his throat, he looked back up. Her breath caught when she saw the emotion in his eyes. "I can't believe you're mine," he said in wonder. "You're just so amazing." He looked back down at his gifts. "Everything about you is amazing."

Pushing the gifts back onto the table, Ethan slid Brooke across his lap, wrapped his arms around her, and buried his face in her neck, taking a deep breath and letting it back out. This moment and his appreciation of her meant more than anything anyone else had ever given to her. Pleasing him made her blissfully happy. That he knew the real her and loved that person made her heart skip a beat every time she thought about it.

The doorbell ringing broke the moment, and she wanted to smack whoever was intruding on her perfect Christmas morning. She pushed herself up and looked out the picture window. Her good mood instantly deflated. "It's my father," she said. "My mother seems to be waiting in the car."

"Maybe this is the Christmas miracle we're looking for," Ethan quipped, pushing himself off the couch and propping the crutches under his arms.

"I don't think so," she said.

"I'll go back and get dressed." Ethan called Bravo, and the two of them went back into the bedroom and closed the door.

She appreciated him giving her privacy. The thought of him hanging out in there waiting for her father to leave saddened her a bit, but only because there was only so much he could do to entertain himself back there. In nicer weather, he could go out the door in there onto the patio, but today wasn't a good day for that.

Not bothering to fix her appearance at all, Brooke swung the door open and shivered with the blast of arctic cold that blew in. She opened the storm door and her father quickly shuffled inside. After closing the door, she ran her hands quickly over her forearms to warm them back up again. Needing the armor, she kept her arms crossed over her chest.

Preston Larrabe was a man with power. You knew it by the way he commanded a room. His dark hair was graying. His expensive overcoat, hat, and gloves subtly depicted wealth and importance. Once upon a time, she would think he looked good. Now, she looked at the expensive attire, and it saddened her. This is what mattered most to her parents—appearances.

Preston leaned in and kissed his daughter on the check. It wasn't the warm embrace she received from her aunt and uncle yesterday—far from it—but she supposed it was something.

"Merry Christmas, princess." He stomped the snow off his boots then walked around the small living room looking around. "It's quaint," he said. "New England charm and comfort." It was the best she would get, she knew. Her mother couldn't even lower herself to come inside.

Preston turned and looked at her, hands in gray mohair coat pockets. "Lenore told me about what happened with your friend."

Brooke sighed. "He's not my *friend*, Dad. He's the man I love, and he lives with me. I want to spend my life with him. He fought for his country—for *her* right to be an absolute bitch to him. He has more integrity and loyalty in his little finger than anyone I socialized with in Boston. He's ten times the man Joshua Mars is."

"Yes, I'm to understand there's no hope there. He must be something else if he caught my little girl's eye. She only goes after the best." Brooke blinked her eyes in surprise, not really sure she heard her father correctly. "Lenore wants to cut you off. She wants to teach you a lesson about not toeing the line and meeting your responsibilities. She thinks you need to be punished."

"Is my divorce *really* going to be that disastrous for the company?" Not that it would change her mind one way or the other, but she was curious about how much power she did have.

Preston waved his hand. "Of course not. Lenore was guilting you to get her way."

Brooke shrugged. "She's welcome to cut me off. I have my own way to make money now. Maybe this is the biggest house I'll ever have. I'll probably never see a luxury car again. But my life is fulfilling. My soul is fed, and that's more important to me."

"When did we lose you?" her father asked quietly.

"Pretty early on when the decision was made not to spend any time with me. I was raised by the teachers and counselors at Trent—my nanny, and grandma and grandpa. You rarely took me on trips with you. I learned avoidance in relationships from you, and my mother taught me that I couldn't—or didn't have to—stand on my own two feet. I was rich, spoiled, and uncaring of anyone but myself. I married a man for a business deal. Despite all that, I still love you both, but I need more from you. And it's something you can't cover by writing a check."

"Harsh." Preston nodded. "But accurate. I'd like to the chance to improve our relationship, honey."

Anything would be an improvement, Brooke wanted to say, but she kept her opinion to herself.

"I thought I was being cut off," she countered.

"No. I said Lenore *wanted* to cut you off. I won't allow that, princess. I'm afraid I've sort of let your mother do as she pleased all these years and trusted her decisions where you were concerned. I'm sorry I've done that. I'm sorry I've let you down. I'd like to make it up to you. Can I meet this wonderful man?"

Brooke wanted to believe his words, but she would need more time before she started to trust him again—if that time ever came. "Not today." She said. Genuine disappointment seemed to cover her father's features. "But maybe in a month or two, we'll come to Boston, and we can have dinner."

"I went down to that Over the Hop when we got into town. I snuck out and went by myself. Why don't I come back, and you can show me what you love so much about this place?"

It was more than Brooke would have hoped for. Of course, he still had to follow through. "I'd like that." She said.

"Merry Christmas, honey." Preston stepped forward and pressed another kiss to her cheek.

"Merry Christmas, Daddy," Brooke whispered. With no more words said between them, Preston let himself out. Brooke closed the door behind him without acknowledging her mother in the car. As she stepped away, Ethan walked out of the bedroom wearing a pair of sweatpants and a hooded sweatshirt. If they didn't have to go take care of the animals, they could have stayed in their pajamas all day. But that was the life of a farmer, and she loved it.

"Do you believe what he said?" Ethan asked.

Brooke shrugged. "To his credit, he's never lied to me." She replied. "But he's promised things, and then other things happened, and he couldn't follow through. We'll see how much of an effort he makes."

"Well," Ethan said. "What do you say we go the barn and get your present?"

Happiness filled her soul. Squealing, Brooke ran by him to get dressed. She couldn't wait to see what he had gotten her, and she was so relieved that he liked her gifts. She vowed to spend less money in the future—as long as he always had what he needed.

Once she was dressed, and she was pulling her fuzzy boots on, her cell phone pinged with a text message. She leaned over to read it where it lay on the bed while yanking up a boot. What she saw made her entire body freeze up and her jaw drop.

That message changed everything.

Twenty-One

BROOKE WAS QUIET as they drove to the farm. She seemed pensive as she looked out the window. Ethan didn't understand what was going on. She was excited when she went back to the bedroom, but when she came out, she was less so. She assured Ethan that nothing was wrong, but something was definitely off. He'd get it out of her eventually, but for now, his own nerves were sparking. Her present took very little effort, and when he thought of it, it seemed so obvious. He almost felt guilty. It was clear she went through some trouble with his, whereas as his gift to her just presented itself to him. His foot took very precise measurements. She'd done a remarkable job. It was a perfect fit when he put it on to get dressed.

He loved that she personalized it like that. Even thinking about what she had put on it made him smiled. He would definitely wear shorts in the summer with it and enjoy watching people's reactions when they realized what it said. It wasn't that he was self-conscious about his leg and didn't want people to see it. It was just that wearing shorts on the farm wasn't very practical. The foot could get caught on things, so he was just used to wearing pants. But with her gift, he would make an effort to wear them when he wasn't on the farm.

Bravo barked as they passed Jackie and Danny's house, and Ethan saw the barn doors already opened. It was late when they came through last night, but he could swear he closed the doors again. It would have been a cold night inside if he left them open, and the electric bill would be somewhere up in the stratosphere.

As he parked the truck, he filled up with delight as the pigs came running out, followed by his mother carrying a bucket, bundled up against the cold. He father walked out after her leading Kodak. Ethan imagined they were headed to the paddock so the horse could stretch his legs a bit.

Sitting back in his seat, Ethan leaned his elbow on the door of the car and ran a hand along his jaw before laughing. "I should have known."

Brooked looked over to him, smile bright. "They couldn't keep away."

"No," Ethan said. "They'd never be able to just stay inside Jackie's when they knew there were animals right next to them that needed care. Sorry, baby, but it turns out we could have stayed in our pajamas longer."

"Wouldn't have mattered." Brooke shook her head. "You said my Christmas present was here, and I'm ready to see it."

Ethan leaned forward and gave her a peck on the cheek. Then opened his door. By the time she was opening her door, he was there to give her a hand out. She was right. His stump was sore today, but just like last time, it was well worth a little pain. They brought his crutches with him, so he'd take it off when they went inside his sister's house for Christmas brunch.

"Well, Merry Christmas, sleepy head!" his mother greeted him. Leaning down, he kissed her cheek and hugged her, pulling her up onto her toes.

"I'd have slept longer if I knew I had two extra pair of hands today." Ethan gave Bravo the command to sit. This was the first time his parents were meeting his dog—as Bravo stuck close to Ethan's side during the wedding and at the reception —and he didn't want them to feel intimidated by him. Bravo had been such a big part of his life and recovery in the military, it was hard for Ethan to remember that Bravo wasn't with him his whole life.

"These animals here were hungry!" His father boomed, coming over to clap Ethan on the back. "Just because there's snow doesn't make farm work start later." Ethan rolled his eyes at his father's good-natured ribbing.

"Merry Christmas, Mr. and Mrs. Donahue." Brooke said. "I'm sorry I didn't get to visit with you very long last night."

"Oh, poo," Penny Donahue dismissed. "We knew we'd have you longer today. And you did such a pretty job. Everything was just wonderful."

"Come here, give us a hug." Jake Donahue waved his hands indicating to Brooke to bring it in. "We're so happy to finally meet you. Everyone says such good things about you."

"All right, Dad, let her go." Ethan said. "She wants to see her present inside."

Ethan gave Bravo the release command, and Bravo tore off inside the barn. "Something interesting in there?" Jake asked.

"He's checking it for safety." Ethan said.

"Good gravy," Penny said, putting her hand up in front of her mouth. "He thinks there's terrorists in the barn?"

"He thinks there's terrorists everywhere." Ethan said. "It's what he was trained to do, and it seems it's an impossible habit to break."

"We'll just wait out here a minute." Ethan said. "He gets pissed when you go in before he's cleared it."

"But we were already in there." Jake said.

"*I* wasn't." Ethan said. "And neither was Brooke. We're the ones he's protecting." Bravo gave a bark when he came back out and sat down in the snow. "All clear."

"Well, I should hope so!" Penny said, waving her hand at the barn and then landing it on her plump hip. "I'd hate to think we were in there for the last hour and someone was hiding behind the hay bales!"

Ethan released Bravo from his spot and Bravo ran off to check around the farm and keep the pigs from wandering too far. He may have been trained to sniff out drugs, bombs, and insurgents, but he was still a German Shepherd. He liked to keep everyone together.

Ethan grabbed Brooke's hand in his and led her into the barn, smiling while she looked all over for a wrapped box. His parents followed but hung back a bit to let the young couple have their moment.

Normally, Brooke was naturally drawn to Christmas Morning's stall, but today she was like a magnet being pulled by force. The horse's stall was decorated with white Christmas lights, evergreen bunting and bows. Christmas Morning herself had little red bows on her bridle.

"Look how festive." Brooke side, bringing her hand up to stroke the horse's neck. "She's so pretty today. Aren't you so pretty, girl? We should do your hair more often. Should I braid your mane?

"Well, she wanted to look her best when she met her new owner." Ethan said. He stuck his hands in his pockets and slid a glance over to Brooke. What he found there though was unexpected. Brooke looked devastated and like she was trying to hide it. She wrapped her arms around the horse's neck, and when Ethan saw her shoulders hitch, he grew concerned.

"Brooke?" He asked. This wasn't the reaction he was expecting.

"I'm sorry." She said into the horse's mane. "I'm just going to miss her so much. I got attached to her."

"She's not going anywhere." Ethan said.

Brooke pulled back and looked at him. Tears were in her eyes but they hadn't fallen down her face. "I don't understand. You said she had a new owner."

It was then Ethan realized his error and he felt terrible for having unintentionally broken her heart. Luckily, it was an easy fix.

"Baby, *you're* her new owner. She's your gift."

"What?" Brooke asked through a sniffle.

"She's your horse. I'm signing her over to you. You can call all the shots for her. You can show her, let her give riding lessons or trail rides or not. You can share her with everyone or keep her to yourself. You make all the decisions with her, and I'll stand by whatever you do. She was never *really* mine anyway. The second you two met she became yours."

"I don't understand. You're giving me Christmas Morning? She's mine?"

"Yes." Now Ethan was unsure of himself. He thought she'd be happy with the gift, but was she disappointed he was giving her a gift he already had?

He watched as true understanding dawned on her, and her entire body lit up like her horse's stall. He had to admit he was a little surprised when she threw her arms around the horse's neck instead of his. "Merry Christmas, girl! Let's get your bells on! We're going for a ride!"

Ethan looked over at his parents, who were enjoying his obvious indignation over playing second fiddle to a horse. He was just turning around when Brooke threw herself into his arms. "I love you! It couldn't be a more perfect present. I'm amazed at how well you know me. I'll take good care of her."

"I know you will, baby." Ethan said, hugging her tightly in return.

"Look up, sweetie." At his mother's words, Ethan and Brooke looked up. Hanging above Christmas Morning's stall was mistletoe. Grinning like loons, they leaned in to one another. When their lips met, the most amazing feeling of home overcame Ethan. Everything he wanted and loved surrounded him right now. His beloved in his arms, in his barn, with his family watching on, and somewhere around was his dog.

Ethan leaned back and picked Brooke up. "I'm going to marry you as soon as the ink is dry on those divorce papers."

She cocked her head to the side. "How about next week? After the New Years' ball, we can fly to Vegas."

"Except your mother and asshole husband are holding the metaphorical gun to you head."

Brooke shook her head. "When I was getting dressed, my lawyer sent me a text. Josh signed the papers, and they were filed yesterday. It's done. I'm a free woman."

With Brooke still in his arms, he turned to his parents. "What do you think, Mom and Dad? Feel like flying to Vegas for your son's wedding?"

"Are you kidding?" Penny ran forward and nearly knocked Ethan off balance when she wrapped her arms around them both. "My boy," she said through her tears. "You've given me nothing but joy since the day you got home."

"Not true, Penelope. He nearly got himself killed in a war. There was no joy in that." Ethan laughed at his father's scowl.

Penny waved Jake off. "Except that one time, maybe. You've given us more than you could ever know, and now you're giving me a daughter, too. Oh, Ethan."

Jake walked over and clapped Ethan on the shoulder. "Congratulations, son."

Lowering Brooke to the floor, Ethan lifted his pant leg to expose his new foot. "Look what she got me for Christmas." When his father read the words on Ethan's prosthetic, he threw back his head and let out a big, belly laugh.

"Oh, this one is definitely a keeper!"

Ethan looked back at Brooke. "I think so, too. All right. Let's take the horse out before we go inside and announce our news to the rest of my family."

"Well, there is one more thing." Jake said. Something about his voice made Ethan wary. His father was up to something. "If you're getting out the bells, maybe you want to decorate this instead of the horse."

He turned and walked out of the barn. Ethan followed curiously leading Brooke and his mother. Outside in the snow, coming just around the barn was Danny, leading Kodak, who was pulling a small two-seater sleigh behind him. Brooke gasped, threw her hands up to her cheeks in astonishment, and ran over.

Ethan merely gaped. "Where did you find that?" The sleigh was by no means in mint condition, but it looked to be in good enough condition. It would just take a little work to restore it to its former glory.

"It found us." Jake shrugged. "The day before Christmas Eve we were driving around the area, and there it was for sale on the side of the road. I couldn't believe someone was getting rid of it. It's not the prettiest carriage, yet, but it's sound. Some fresh paint and new interior and people will be clamoring to take a ride in her. It got me thinking. We could put wheels on her in the nicer weather and give rides around town. Romantic rides, kids rides, winter rides. It could be a nice little business."

Tipping his head to the side, Ethan studied his father. "What do you mean *we*?"

Jake kicked at the dirt and looked over at his wife. Penny stepped forward, her hands clutched together.

"The thing is, honey, we really did think you would move to Florida after you got out of the military. It never occurred to us that you wouldn't like it. Don't get us wrong, we understand why you don't like to spend time there, and there's no blame to put on you. We did, after all, sell the farm you thought you were going to spend your future on. But when you found out about your brothers and sisters and settled in up here, well, we realized we'd miss out on big things in your life. When we stumbled across this sleigh, it kind of got us thinking. Maybe we could sell our house in Florida and move up here to be closer to you. A lot of people down there live up north and tow campers down in the cold months. We could do that after Christmas and come back up in March or something like that. Look, now you're getting married. You'll have children, and we'll be so far away from them."

Ethan looked at the two people who took him in and gave him a life. It was a hell of a life, too. It wasn't always easy, but it was always satisfying. Since finding out he was adopted, never once did Ethan feel like he didn't belong to them. It was odd reconciling that feeling when he had a twin sister who didn't know her parents.

Ethan looked over at Brooke. She looked ecstatic. Her eyes danced. Her face glowed, and she looked like she was going to burst with light. He looked back to his parents. His past and future standing with him. "I think that's a great idea." Ethan said.

"We can help with the farm." Jake said. "It would free you up to work with the dogs. The money we got from the sale of the farm is more than enough to sustain us, so we don't need any more." Jake looked around them at the farm and the surrounding woods. "But boy, I do like the potential here."

Brooke squeezed Ethan's hand and looked up at him. "Me too."

"Are you guys getting into this thing or not?" Danny called out gruffly.

"*I'm* taking *my* horse." Brooke announced. "Ethan, maybe you'd like to drive the sleigh for your parents?"

Looking at Brooke with a furrowed brow, Ethan turned and strode back into the barn for blankets for the sleigh. He turned back out just as Bravo dropped something at Brooke's feet. Ethan groaned and quickened his step. Please let Bravo not have dropped something dead in front of her. But when he heard Brooke's laughter, he slowed down.

There at his fiancé's fuzzy booted feet was what remained of a Santa hat. It had been shredded nearly beyond recognition. "Okay, buddy." Brooke bent down to love him up. "Point made. I will never make you wear that again."

Ethan stopped as he watched Brooke bend down and hug his dog as his parents watched on with apparent love for the two most important beings in his world. Right then, he felt richer than Midas. A neigh came from Christmas Morning's stall, and he looked over his shoulder back at her. And if he didn't know better, he could swear she winked.

THE END

Additional Books by A.M. Mahler
Guardians of Eternal Life Series
The Guardian
The Scholar
Grayson Falls Series
The Good Race
The Slow Lane
The Perfect Game
Breaking Free
Second Chances

ABOUT THE AUTHOR

ANNE MARIE RECEIVED a Bachelor's of Fine Arts in Creative Writing from Southern New Hampshire University. She writes in the contemporary romance and fantasy genres. She lives in the Richmond, Virginia, area with her husband, son, two dogs and cat.

To keep up to date on the Grayson Falls and Guardian series, follow Anne Marie at:

Website: https://www.ammahlerauthor.com/

Facebook: https://www.facebook.com/AMMahler3206/

Twitter: https://twitter.com/AMMahler3206

Made in the USA
San Bernardino, CA
26 December 2019